**CANDLELIGHT Ecstasy Supreme**

### "YOU JUST DON'T *WANT* TO BELIEVE LOVE'S REAL!"

Her eyes blazing, Debbie stared at Ben, the man she had just made love to. "You look for the worst in a relationship! You try to find holes to support your belief that love doesn't exist."

"That's because it doesn't," Ben said calmly. "You just want to believe in it. You're not willing to look at reality."

Debbie recoiled as though she had been slapped. This was the man she had given her heart to. "I've loved you for a long time, Ben, but I can't continue as your lover. I can't stay in a one-sided relationship, giving love but receiving none in return. It's going to destroy me."

"What do you want me to do, Debbie? Lie to you?"

"No, Ben, I want you to love me."

## CANDLELIGHT ECSTASY SUPREMES

# SEASON OF ENCHANTMENT

*Emily Elliott*

A CANDLELIGHT ECSTASY SUPREME

Published by
Dell Publishing Co., Inc.
1 Dag Hammarskjold Plaza
New York, New York 10017

ISBN: 0-440-17662-X

Printed in the United States of America

First printing—April 1985

To Our Readers:

Candlelight Ecstasy is delighted to announce the start of a brand-new series—Ecstasy Supremes! Now you can enjoy a romance series unlike all the others—longer and more exciting, filled with more passion, adventure, and intrigue—the stories you've been waiting for.

In months to come we look forward to presenting books by many of your favorite authors and the very finest work from new authors of romantic fiction as well. As always, we are striving to present the unique, absorbing love stories that you enjoy most—the very best love has to offer.

Breathtaking and unforgettable, Ecstasy Supremes will follow in the great romantic tradition you've come to expect *only* from Candlelight Ecstasy.

Your suggestions and comments are always welcome. Please let us hear from you.

Sincerely,

The Editors
Candlelight Romances
1 Dag Hammarskjold Plaza
New York, New York 10017

*PROLOGUE*

Saigon
April 1975

Nguyen Li Ha stared out her living room window and listened to the sounds of the gunfire that echoed across the city. The early morning was gray, quiet, a time when the people of Saigon should have been sleeping, but Li suspected that very few of them were. The lights were on in the house across the street and in the one next to theirs, and Li wondered if their neighbors—the doctor just across the street and the government official next door—were also listening to the sounds of Saigon falling. Probably so. It would be hard to sleep tonight, with the city under fire and everything her father had spent a lifetime trying to achieve about to disappear before their very eyes. As her eyes filled with tears, she turned to the thirty-one-year-old man who sat on the sofa, speaking quietly with her father. "Saigon's going to fall today, isn't it?" she asked.

General Nguyen Ty Loc frowned and shook his head slightly. "We don't know that, Li," he said. "It might be several days."

"Come on, Li," the blond newspaper reporter who sat beside her father admonished her. "It may be a week or more. We still have a good chance of getting out of here. Besides, the paper would have pulled me out before now if the takeover was imminent."

"But those guns sounded so close!" Li protested. "Jim, come over here and see if they don't sound awfully near to you."

Jim Anderson got up from the sofa, where he had been sitting for most of the night and walked over to the window. He smiled down tenderly at his fiancée, and put a comforting hand on her arm. "They don't sound all that close to me," he lied valiantly.

"You're just trying to comfort me," Li said quietly, clasping her hand over Jim's. "And for that I thank you." She smiled up at him through tear-filled eyes.

"I should have known better than to try to tell you a lie," Jim said as he reached out with a tender finger and wiped away the lone tear that was running down Li's cheek. "But I am not lying to you when I tell you that we can get out of here. The paper's sending a plane for us this afternoon. We'll be in Guam by nightfall." Jim turned around to General Nguyen. "You are coming, aren't you, sir?"

General Nguyen had expressed his doubts about the wisdom of fleeing several times during the long night. He looked shrunken and bitter when he spoke. "What do you think would be better—to start over at my age in a new country, with a new language and a new home, or to rot in a prison in my homeland? Yes, yes, I'll come with you, Jim." He glanced down at the three small bundles on the floor. "What time is the plane coming?"

Jim pulled Li away from the window and sat her down beside him. "The pilot's supposed to fly in sometime this afternoon," he said. "Just when, he wasn't sure. He said to meet him at the airport."

"But the airport's a madhouse!" Li objected. "Everybody's trying to get out while they still can."

"I know that, Li," Jim said, flinching as the sound of a machine gun tore through the air. A woman started screaming, and Li stood up to go to the window. Jim grabbed her hand to hold her back. "Go get your father and me something to eat," he told her, more to give her something to do than because he was hungry.

"I guess I'll be waiting on you for the next fifty years," Li grumbled as she walked into the kitchen.

*I hope so, Li,* Jim thought as he turned to her father. "What do you think, sir?" he asked softly. "Will we get out of here today?"

"I think that if we don't leave today, it will be too late," he said softly. "This nation of mine is falling and it is falling fast. We will be a Communist country within the week."

Jim winced. Li's beautiful nation was going to become a Communist country. He hated to see it happen, and he knew how awful it would be for Li and her father. They'd miss their homeland, but the paper's small plane was the only chance that Li and General Nguyen had. Since her father had been a strong supporter of democracy, he would be one of the first to be imprisoned, and Jim shuddered to think of what would happen to Li. Beautiful Li, just twenty-one years old, college-educated, with close friends in America and an American fiancé. No, they wouldn't let Li go. There would be plans for her too.

Li brought Jim and her father a light meal, and as the sun came up the three of them resumed their vigil. Li tried to tell herself that the machine guns were not getting any closer, but as the morning passed and she watched her father's and Jim's faces tighten, she knew that it was getting closer and closer. "Will we be able to get to the airport?" she asked.

"We'll have to," Jim said grimly. He turned to the general and asked, "Do you think we had better start on over there?"

The general nodded. "Do what you have to do—we'll leave in ten minutes."

Jim and Li waited impatiently while the general went into the back room. "Just think," Jim said as he put his arm around Li, "by this time tomorrow we'll be on our way to a new life."

"I know," Li said. "It's sad, but I keep trying to think of all the positive things. It will be good to live in a place that isn't constantly at war. To walk the streets without fear of bombs or guns. And I can hardly wait to see Debbie Cheong again. And you must be eager to get home. You will take that job on the San Francisco paper, won't you?"

"Probably," Jim said. "You're ready to go?"

"Yes, I'm ready to live in peace," she said bitterly. "I'm tired of bullets and land mines." As if to underscore her words, the sound of a machine gun ripped through the air. They both flinched as a bullet struck the glass in the window and shattered it.

"Get down, Li!" Jim shouted as he pushed her away from the window.

"Where's my father?" Li screamed.

"He's still in the back. He's safer than you are," Jim said as he and Li fell to the floor. They lay face down on the floor as the bullets whizzed over their heads, Jim trying to plan an alternate route to the airport in case the major thoroughfares were already in Communist hands. When the bullets finally stopped whining, Jim took Li's hand and together they crawled across the floor into the back of the house. "Now get up!" Jim said harshly. "Get up and run, Li!"

"But Father!" she protested.

Jim shook his head, pulling her across the small courtyard to the wrought-iron gate. He pushed it open and ran through, then backed up in horror when he hit the end of a Chinese rifle aimed at his chest. "Going somewhere?" the Communist soldier asked mockingly. A second soldier grabbed Li from behind and tore her away from Jim.

Jim grabbed for the rifle and felt a searing pain in his shoulder. He heard Li's terrified scream as he crumpled on the sidewalk. "Oh, no, you've killed him!" she cried, hoping the young soldier didn't realize that a shot in the shoulder would not kill a man instantly. "Let me go to him."

Maybe the soldier was tired, or maybe he had a shred of mercy, for his grip loosened just a fraction, and Li tore herself away from his grip. "Oh, Jim, I love you," she said as she knelt beside his torn, bleeding body. "Oh, you've killed him," she cried over and over, her anguished wail convincing the ignorant soldiers that Jim was indeed dead. As Jim fought to stay conscious, she put her head on his chest. He struggled to open his eyes, but a warning squeeze of her fingers stopped him. "Go to Debbie," she whispered. "In San Francisco. She will help." She raised her head, her face streaked with tears. *Em yeu anh,* Jim," she said. "I love you."

The soldier pulled Li to her feet. "That's enough mourning over the imperialist dog," he said as he marched Li toward the waiting truck. "You won't be seeing yellow-haired men in this country anymore!" he said and laughed as Li's stomach turned. He pushed her onto the truck and shoved another prisoner in behind her as the truck started to roll down the street.

13

Two tears trickled down Li's face as she sat down on the hard, wooden bench beside another hapless prisoner. Would Jim be able to get out of the country, or would they kill him when they found out he was still alive? And what happened to her father? Jim had pushed her out of the door so fast that she hadn't even caught a glimpse of the general. What did the future hold for her now? If Jim survived, would he ever be able to get her out, or was she condemned to spending the rest of her life on a work farm, alone, without Jim? Terror and despair gripped her heart, but she refused to cry anymore in front of the soldier guarding the prisoners. If Jim did survive, if he did get back to America, he *would* find a way to get her out. She had to cling to that. She had to believe in him. . . .

# CHAPTER ONE

Debbie Cheong looked up from the Chinese newspaper she was reading and sighed. Honestly, these People's Republic doctrine rags had to be the most boring literature on the face of the earth. Sticking her tongue out at the offending paper, she put her thumb back down on the line she was translating and went on with the dull tribute to the current Chinese leader, translating the article symbol by symbol into English. Occasionally, she would scratch her head and reach for the thick English–Chinese dictionary that was her constant companion, but most of the time she knew not only the literal meaning of the Chinese word but the subtle nuance of the word also. After all, she had grown up speaking both English and Chinese, and she honestly couldn't remember which one she had learned to speak first.

She finished the article, and tossing the paper aside, typed up her translation on her IBM Selectric. Now let the analysts in Washington make what they like of it, she thought as she covered the typewriter and picked up a Vietnamese newspaper. She scanned the front page and predicted another dull Communist diatribe before she got out her pencil and started to translate the article into English. It was slower going than the Chinese newspaper because Debbie had only been reading Vietnamese for the last ten years or so, since she had studied it in college, but she was still the best Vietnamese translator in the office, except for Jim. After spending ten years in Vietnam as a foreign correspondent and nearly marrying a Vietnamese woman, Jim was as fluent as a native, even though his spoken Vietnamese had a stronger English accent than hers did. Debbie waded through about half the article before she came across a symbol that made absolutely no sense to her. She looked it up in her Vietnamese dictionary but couldn't find it. Oh, well, Jim had said he wanted to talk to her anyway. She picked up the paper and walked from her miniscule office to his, knocking on his door before she pushed it open. Jim was bent over another issue of the same paper, his pen moving quickly over the surface of the notepad.

"Jim, I've come across one I can't make heads or tails of," Debbie said as she stepped into Jim's office and handed him the paper. She pointed to a symbol about halfway down the article. "What's this?"

Jim looked at the symbol at the end of her well-manicured fingernail. "It's another word for leader or director," he said. "But it isn't a very favorable term. It's really rather derogatory."

"Well, it's about our President," Debbie said, laughing. "I should have known."

Jim nodded and handed the newspaper back to Debbie. She made a note to indicate in her translation that the word was not complimentary and turned to leave the room, but hesitated and faced Jim instead. "How's it going?" she asked softly.

Jim turned tired, unsmiling eyes on her. His face was becoming lined, and his blond hair was rapidly turning gray, probably in part from the last ten years of disappointment and sadness. "Why don't I take you out for a

16

drink after work and we can talk about it? I'll meet you at your office in about an hour."

"Sounds good," Debbie said as she left his office and returned to her own. She continued with the article, only half her mind on her translating. Jim was as glum as he had been when he had first come home to San Francisco ten years ago. After the underground had finally found Li, and she had written and indicated that she wanted to join him here, he had seemed happier as he had scrimped and saved to raise enough money for Li to bribe her way out. But today he was back to the quiet, sad man who had come home from Vietnam without the woman he loved. It had been almost a year since he sent the money and Li still wasn't out.

Debbie finished the article and turned the page to start another when Jim knocked on her door. She motioned for him to enter as she put her newspaper and notepad aside. "Let me run a brush through my hair and I'll be ready," she said as she took a brush out of her desk drawer and pulled it through her waist-length black hair. She put away the brush and stood up. "All right, where to?" she asked Jim.

"How about that little place down on the wharf?" he asked as they waved good-bye to the receptionist and left the government offices in the Bank of America building. Debbie was grateful she was wearing a wool jacket as she stepped out into the cool breeze that blew in off the bay.

They set out to walk the several blocks to the bar on Fisherman's Wharf, the wind blowing their hair and reddening their cheeks as they walked from downtown to the wharf. The traffic was noisy and they made no attempt to talk as they walked toward the tiny bar that they had enjoyed before.

Jim glanced over at the woman on his arm, the wind

whipping her hair off her face. He thought, not for the first time, that she was a beautiful woman. She was thin and had the delicate bones of a bird, and it was only when she was standing close to him that he realized that she was tall, nearly as tall in her heels as his own five foot nine. Her face had the classic bones of an Oriental beauty, with lovely high cheekbones, slanting dark eyes, and a soft, sensitive mouth. Her hair was almost to her waist, and she often let it flow down her back like a silken waterfall. To Jim she looked out of place in her Western clothing, and she would have seemed more appropriately dressed in an *oau dai,* the Oriental costume that Li had worn often. But when he had said something to that effect, Debbie had laughed in his face, telling him that she might be Chinese on the outside, but that she was as American as he was on the inside!

And that she was, Jim had to admit. Although she had been brought up in a home where Chinese was spoken, her attitudes and her outlook on life were completely American. In spite of her gentle demeanor, she was outspoken and would tackle the devil himself, if that was what it took to get the job done. Yet, Jim was aware of her vulnerability and her loneliness, of the lurking sadness in her eyes even now, two years after her divorce from Kevin. Jim had to admit to himself that Debbie Cheong was very attractive, and that if he hadn't loved Li so very much, he might have been interested in Debbie. But although it had been ten years since he had seen Li's face, and nearly a year since he had even gotten a letter from her, he still loved her. His heart belonged to Li—and it always would.

Debbie and Jim walked along the wharf, dodging the fishermen trying to trap the tourists into making a purchase, and stepped inside a little bar. There was no one to seat them, so they slid into a vacant booth in the corner, away from the sound of the juke box. Debbie sat forward and leaned across the table. "So tell me about it," she said.

Jim shook his head slightly. "You tell me about it," he said. "It was through those mysterious contacts of yours that we got the last letter from her."

"They've heard nothing," Debbie admitted. "Just exactly where was she when she wrote you that last letter?"

Jim ran his hand through his rapidly graying hair and twisted the small dragon ring he wore on his little finger, a ring of Li's that he had been wearing the day Saigon was taken over. "She said she was on a work farm outside Hai Thong. I've heard nothing since."

"Where's Hai Thong?" Debbie asked.

"It's in what used to be North Vietnam," Jim explained. "Close to Hanoi."

"Could you tell from the letter whether or not Li had gotten the money you had sent her?" Debbie asked. Through the Vietnamese underground, Jim had sent Li fifteen thousand dollars worth of small gold coins that she could use to bribe her way out of the country.

"At the time I thought she had, but maybe she hadn't," Jim said as the waitress came to take their order.

"Well, you know she has to be careful what she writes in case her letters ever get into the hands of the Communists," Debbie reminded him after they ordered.

"I sent the gold coins two months before I got her letter," Jim said. "She might or might not have gotten them."

Debbie nodded. From what little she knew from her Vietnamese friends about the Vietnamese underground, it could take as long as three or four months for a letter or a message or a parcel to reach the addressee. But the fact that letters and messages and parcels came and went at all was amazing to Debbie. She had always thought that once the Communists had taken over a country that was it, but from her friends she had learned that there were many holes in the bamboo curtain, and that it was difficult, but not impossible to get people out of the country. Her friends had always been very reticent about the details of how this was done, and Debbie had never pressed them, not really wanting to know as long as they were willing to help Jim and Li. "I'm sure the money got to her eventually," she assured Jim.

"Well, I hope so," Jim said heavily. "But Li's smart enough to know who she can bribe and who she can't. She should have been out of there by now."

The waitress brought their drinks and Debbie picked hers up and sipped it thoughtfully. "Yes, she should have." She stared down into the ice cubes and licked her lips. "What do you think could have gone wrong?"

Jim shrugged. "Maybe someone stole the gold coins from her."

"That's always possible," Debbie said. "If they knew she had it. But again, Li is a smart lady. I think she could conceal the coins."

"Maybe the government got onto her trying to escape," Jim said. "After all, her father was one of the South's most anti-Communist generals, and they know I'm still alive. They caught her trying to leave that one time in 1979 and put her into prison for a while. They're bound to be watching her."

"Do you really think so?" Debbie asked. "After all this time? Her father's been dead nearly five years now, and Li was never involved with politics much."

"But they know she studied over here and that she has

American friends. They probably know I'm trying to get her out. Debbie, I just don't like it."

Debbie sipped her drink and stared across the table at Jim. "I don't like it either, Jim," she said. "It's been too long, and I know that Li would want to be with you. She used to talk about you all the time, and that was before you and she had definitely decided to get married. She was in love with you when she came over here to go to school."

"At the time I thought it was going to be the longest year of my life," Jim said. "It was ironic. I was working in her country and her father insisted that she go to school here, to grow up and to be sure that she really wanted to marry a foreigner who was ten years older than she was. She was going to be gone a whole year." He sipped his wine and grimaced. "The last ten years have been a whole lot longer." He sipped his drink and stared thoughtfully into space. "The first six years were the longest. I didn't know whether she was dead or alive, and she didn't know whether or not I had escaped, or whether they had killed me on the way to the airport. But I guess I don't know now whether she's dead or alive, do I?"

"No, Jim, she isn't dead," Debbie said quickly. "She can't be, not after all you two have been through. I won't believe that."

Jim reached out and patted Debbie's hand. "You love her too, don't you?" he asked.

"Of course," Debbie said softly. "She's one of the best friends I've ever had." Debbie brushed a tear from her eye and took a deep breath. "We have to think about the next step."

"I've already thought of it," Jim said. "I'm going back to her."

Startled, Debbie almost knocked over her drink. "Jim, you can't go back to Nam! You've escaped once! They take one look at that American face of yours and they'll shoot."

"No, not me personally," Jim said. "I know I can't go back in there. That's part of why I wanted to take you out tonight," he said quietly. "You might be able to find me someone I need."

"Who?" Debbie asked.

"An Oriental man, maybe a former soldier, who would be willing to go back in and find her for me."

*A mercenary. An Oriental mercenary.* The wheels in Debbie's brain began to turn. *A mercenary soldier.* "I do know a man like that," Debbie said slowly.

Jim's head shot up. "You do? Who?" he demanded.

"Let me think," Debbie said. "Ben—Ben something. Japanese name. Oh, yes. Ben Sako. He was one of my father's Green Berets during the war."

"How do you know about him?" Jim asked.

"Father mentioned him several years ago, back when you and I were still at the newspaper. He said that one of his men had turned mercenary and was going back to the Orient on paid missions. All very hush-hush. I did a little checking and found out that it was true. I thought it would make a great feature article, and I went by his house and talked to him about it."

"That's great!" Jim said, a genuine smile lighting his face for the first time in weeks. "You'll talk to him for me, won't you? You'll tell him we want him to go after Li."

Debbie shook her head. "Uh, I don't think so, Jim," she said. "I didn't make much of an impression on him." She grimaced when she remembered how in no uncertain terms he had not only refused to be interviewed but had

22

threatened to sue the paper if one word was printed about him.

Jim's face took on that determined expression that Debbie knew so well. "But, Debbie, if he knows you he'll talk to you. He doesn't even know me. For all he knows I could be a government agent who's trying to make trouble for him."

"He doesn't know me either," Debbie protested.

"But he does know your father, and he knows that Gordon Cheong's daughter isn't a federal agent," Jim argued. "Please, Debbie! This may be the only chance for Li and me."

Debbie wanted to say no, that she would never look the obnoxious Ben Sako in the face again. But Jim was right. No mercenary in his right mind would work for a man whom he had never seen before. Jim would need a go-between. "Well, all right," she said softly. "I'll find him and I'll talk to him. How much should I say you're offering?"

"Ten thousand," Jim said quietly.

Debbie turned concerned eyes on Jim. "I hate to say this, Jim, but even I know that isn't enough."

'It's all I have," Jim said, his voice shaking. "I sent her fifteen thousand last year. That's all I've been able to save since then."

"Let me find out what it costs, and I can make up the difference," Debbie said. "That CD Kevin gave me after the divorce is about to come due."

"Debbie, I can't take your money!" Jim protested.

"Yes, you can, if it's for Li," Debbie said firmly.

Jim reached out and squeezed her hand. "You're a wonderful person, you know that," he said softly. "You have been a true friend to Li and me."

Debbie nodded and swallowed the lump in her throat.

"As you have been to me," she said softly. "I'll have our friends at the newspaper locate Ben Sako, and I'll pay him a visit if he's in the country. Then it will be up to you."

Jim nodded. "Thank you," he said as he reached into his pocket and left some money on the table. "Can you get home from here all right?" he asked.

Debbie nodded. It was only a short walk to the ferry that would take her across the bay to her home in Sausalito. "I'll let you know how much he wants after I've talked to him," she said.

Jim nodded and made his way through the small bar and out the door. He had left enough to cover their drinks and a tip, so Debbie left the bar and walked the short block to the ferry that took her across the bay every day. Usually Debbie loved the feel of the cool salt spray in her face as the ferry skimmed the water, but tonight her mind was on Li and Jim and the request Jim had made of her. She dreaded facing the rude and boorish Ben Sako again, but she could hardly refuse to see him if it meant a possible reunion for Jim and Li. After all, wasn't that what she and Jim had spent the last ten years trying to accomplish?

Debbie sighed as the ferry carried her closer and closer to Sausalito. She remembered the day nearly ten years ago when she had gotten the letter in the mail addressed to her from a hospital in Guam. Jim's letter had described in heartbreaking detail what had happened to Li and himself in Saigon, and asked if Debbie would be willing to help him try to get Li out of Vietnam. Of course Debbie would. Debbie's father, a colonel in the U.S. army, and General Nguyen had become close friends during the colonel's two tours in Vietnam, and Li had lived with Debbie's family for a year when she was at

Stanford. Debbie had come to love her like an older sister, and she had been sick with fear and worry when Li went back to Saigon. So Debbie, a freshman in college when Jim returned after the fall of Saigon, had become a good friend to him, earning his undying gratitude when she and her Vietnamese friends started the search for Li through the complicated, secretive Vietnamese underground. And Jim in turn had befriended her. He had persuaded his newspaper editor to hire her straight out of college as a cub reporter, and later, after her divorce, he had persuaded her to leave the newspaper where her former husband still worked and apply for work as a translator, as he had done a year earlier. She and Jim had shared both their joys and their sorrows for the last ten years, and today she shared his disappointment.

Debbie squinted her eyes at the bright afternoon sun and peered up the winding gravel road that seemed to lead straight up the side of the mountain. She hoped Dave had his facts straight. It would be a crime against her old Corvette if she had put it through this for nothing. When she had questioned Dave, he had assured her that Ben Sako did indeed live on a small, rundown vineyard halfway up the side of a mountain and not in the Japanese section of town as he used to. The mercenary business must be pretty good, if he could buy a vineyard, she thought.

Crossing her fingers that the old engine would make it up this mountain without breaking down, she drove the wheezing car harder. She supposed she ought to trade the Corvette and get something newer and more reliable, but it was a relic from her marriage to Kevin—all she had left of the boy who had once loved her. She was reluctant to part with it. So she fixed it up and spent more on it than she should have, grateful that she did not rely on it to get her to and from work. She rounded the curve and groaned when she spotted another sharp incline. "Come on, car," she said out loud as she lowered her foot on the accelerator. The Corvette wheezed a little but made its way up the steep incline and around another corner. Just as Debbie rounded the corner, the road forked, the main road continuing up the mountain and a side road leading up through the trees. There was a rickety gate across the road that was closed but not locked and a mailbox that read "Sako." *I made it,* Debbie congratulated herself. She had to stop and open the gate, and butterflies fluttered in her stomach as she drove up the winding path that she hoped would lead her to Ben Sako.

She drove for about a quarter of a mile, her eyes admiring the cedar and redwood trees that lined Sako's property. It must be nice to live up here, she thought as she drove past rows of wildly growing vines. He needed a refuge like this, considering the danger he put himself in on every job. And if he took it, he would be in danger on this job. He would be entering Vietnam illegally and escaping with one of their citizens. But that didn't matter to Debbie. Ben Sako could put himself in danger if he wanted to. All that mattered was getting Li out of Vietnam.

Debbie drove past a small tractor and up to what looked like the main house, if you could call the small cabin a house. There was a wisp of smoke coming out of the chimney, but otherwise the house looked deserted. Debbie parked her car in front of the cabin and got out. Looking considerably more confident than she felt, she strode up to the front door and knocked sharply. After a moment she knocked again, then when there was no reply, she peered through the window at the simple interior of the cabin. There appeared to be two rooms, but the inside was so dark that Debbie could not see much more. She could see no one moving around inside, but if the wisp of smoke coming from the chimney could be trusted, Ben was close by.

She would just have to find him. Debbie stepped off the front porch and walked across the yard to the storage shed. She intended to look there first and then poke around a little in the forest of overgrown vines and trees behind the house. She had to find Ben Sako and talk to him soon so she could get down the mountain and back to Sausalito before dark. She stepped into the shed and peered around the deserted square. The shed was full of hay, but there was no evidence of any animals that might eat it or sleep in it.

"I'm sorry you didn't find what you were after," a rough voice grated across the barn. "Now, if you aren't out of here in fifteen seconds flat, I'll blow a hole in your head. Got that?"

Debbie jumped and, whirling around, she faced Ben Sako in the dim gloominess of the barn. Sure enough, he had a rifle trained on her head, and she had no doubt that he would put a bullet through it if she didn't do what he said. She swallowed and started to run out the back door, then remembered why she had come to Ben Sako's home today. Lifting her chin, she stared across the barn at the figure standing in the door opening, the light behind him making him a dark silhouette. "Hello, Mr. Sako. I've come to talk to you."

The figure in the door did not move. "By snooping around my barn? Sure," the voice grated. "You're wasting my time and yours. Get out!"

Debbie shrugged her shoulders. "Of course," she said sweetly, hoping he could not hear the trembling in her voice. "I'll tell Father you said hello." She started toward the door where he stood, forcing herself to walk closer to the loaded gun and the strange man who held it. When she had almost reached the door, he moved back only a step or two, just enough to let her pass. She walked out the barn door and past him, tossing her head a little as she passed him.

The man dropped his rifle as he reached out and grabbed Debbie's arm, whirling her around to face him. He stared at her for a moment, his black eyes squinting as they surveyed her face, and let her go when he recognized her. Paralyzed with fright, Debbie stumbled backward before she caught herself and forced herself to stare bravely into the face that was now just a foot away from hers.

He looked tougher than ever. She stared into the dark, lined face that was just a few inches above hers. The years since her only meeting with him had cut harsh lines in his forehead and around his mouth, aging him past the thirty-eight years she knew him to be. The slanting eyes that looked more Chinese than Japanese were cold and unfeeling, and his firm mouth with its thin lips looked as though it had never cracked a smile. His face, far from handsome to begin with, was further marred by a long thin scar that ran the length of the left side of his face, from his forehead down his temple and almost to his chin. He hadn't had the scar the last time she had seen him. She shivered a little and stepped back, but that only afforded her the opportunity to see his arms and chest, since he wore no shirt and was bare to the waist. He was hard and sinewy like a wild animal. Yet his face and his body were appealing in an unusual way, and Debbie was all too aware of the masculine appeal he radiated.

Hurriedly, she jerked her gaze upward but not before

Ben had noticed her observing his naked chest, and she was mortified when his mouth curved into a mocking grin. Debbie blushed furiously as she squared her chin and looked him in the eye, disturbed to find that she was far from repulsed by the man standing in front of her. "We've met before," she said.

"And how are you, Debbie Delaney?" he said gravely. "Out to do another story?"

Debbie shook her head. "It's Debbie Cheong now," she said.

"What happened? That rich boy get tired of his Oriental beauty?" he asked.

Debbie's temper flared, but she didn't want to argue with this man. "Something like that," she said, her cheeks red.

"Sorry, that was out of line," Ben said. "Well, no matter," he added, making a dismissing motion with his hand. "Debbie Delaney, Debbie Cheong, what's the difference? I'm still not letting you write about me. Now go on home and tell Gordon hello for me."

Debbie shook her head and stood her ground. "I'm not a reporter anymore," she said. "I haven't been since my divorce. I came to offer you a job."

Ben's mocking smile faded and his eyes narrowed. "Just what sort of job did you think of offering me?" he asked suspiciously. "Just what do you think I do?"

"I'm not trying to trap you into saying something that I can publish, if that's what you think. I said I wasn't a reporter anymore and I meant it." She whipped out her wallet and showed him her security clearance from her office. "I'm working as a translator these days for the government, and I have a job to offer you."

"I don't do work for the government."

"Nobody said you did," Debbie replied. "This is private. Look, I didn't want to come out here. I'm only the go-between. Jim was afraid you wouldn't talk to him."

"Smart Jim," Ben muttered. "So what does this Jim want me to do, and how much does he intend to pay me to do it?"

Debbie took a deep breath. "We—Jim wants you to go with him into Vietnam and rescue Li, his fiancée. They were separated ten years ago when Saigon fell, and he hasn't seen her since. He sent her fifteen thousand in gold a year ago to bribe her way out, but she isn't out yet." Debbie stopped and took a breath and stared into Ben's impassive face. "He's willing to offer you twenty thousand, plus expenses, to go in with him and get her out."

"No way in hell would I touch a job like that," Ben replied. He turned and walked into the house, shutting the door behind him.

# CHAPTER TWO

"What on earth?" Debbie sputtered as she watched the front door close. "How dare he walk away from me like that!" Her fear of him forgotten in her anger, she marched over to his front door and pounded on it with her fist. "You come out here!" she demanded. "You can't just say no!"

She banged on the door for a few more minutes, until her knuckles were sore, but Ben did not come to his door. Debbie peered through the cabin window but could not see him in the front room. What kind of nerve did he have to announce "no way in hell" and walk away from her when she needed his help! No way was Debbie Cheong going to put up with that! She pounded on the door for a few more minutes before she decided that stronger measures were in order. She looked for a rock to toss through his window but reconsidered when she could not find a rock. Gritting her teeth in frustration, she took off her high-heeled shoe and started pounding on his door. "I'll keep him awake all night if I have to," she muttered angrily as she banged the door with her shoe. But damn him, he wasn't going to tell her no like that!

Ben stuck his head under the pump in the kitchen and rinsed his sweaty head under the cool stream of water. How long had she been banging now? Fifteen minutes?

Twenty? She must be determined to talk to him about her cockamamie mission. Ben took a towel off the peg on the wall and dried his hair and his face and mopped up the rivulets that ran down his chest. He should have known she would have a lot of her old man in her. Gordon Cheong wouldn't have been put off like that either. He guessed she would bang on his door for the rest of the night if he didn't answer it. Grim amusement curved his lips. So why not talk to her again? It might be interesting to hear why she was so determined to reunite her friends.

Debbie cursed and swung her shoe at the door for what must have been the three hundredth time. "Answer the door," she muttered under her breath. She leaned back, intending to give the door an extra hard bang, when it flew open and Ben stood in front of her, his arms folded across his chest. "Three hundred and two," he said as Debbie lowered the shoe.

Debbie's lips curved into an unwilling smile of amusement before she schooled them to a businesslike twist. Swallowing back a knot of tension that arose suddenly, she took a deep breath. "Thank you for opening the door," she said with dignity.

"Didn't have much choice, did I?" Ben asked, a grim smile on his face. "I left Frisco to get away from the noise pollution."

Debbie bit back a sarcastic reply and walked inside. She sat down on a chair near the door. It was up to her to convince him to go in and rescue Li, and she didn't want to spoil everything by arguing with him. Ben shut the door and sat down on the couch in the middle of the room. Debbie waited for him to speak, but when several minutes passed in silence, she decided that it was up to her to begin. "Why did you refuse outright to help Jim find Li?" she asked.

32

"It isn't the kind of job I usually do," Ben replied steadily. "I usually go in for political prisoners or endangered Americans. Not people's girl friends."

"What difference does it make that Li's his girl friend?" Debbie asked. "She's still over there and can't get out. She needs help."

Ben shook his head. "Let me see if I got your story right. Your friend and his girl were separated when Nam fell. He got out and he sent her money to join him. And she didn't come, right?" Debbie nodded. "It's simple," Ben continued. "She didn't want to get out."

"WHAT?" Debbie yelled. "What are you thinking?"

"Look, Debbie, your friend Tim—"

"Jim," Debbie corrected him.

"All right, Jim. Anyway, he hasn't seen her for ten years and he sends her money and she doesn't come? I'm sorry, but it's obvious what happened. The woman kept the money and stayed in Nam. She could use the gold coins over there to live well for the rest of her life." He nodded knowingly as Debbie shook her head. "I've heard of several cases like this."

"No," Debbie protested. "Li wouldn't do that! She and Jim love each other!"

Ben shook his head. "Don't be ridiculous," he said impatiently. "You wouldn't know, you've never met the woman. And—"

"Li lived with my family for a year when she was at Stanford," Debbie protested. "I knew her quite well, and I know that she wouldn't do a thing like that."

Ben shook his head again impatiently. "Knew is the operative word, Debbie. You knew her what—ten, twelve years ago? And how long has it been since Jim has seen her?"

"Jim saw her in 1975," Debbie said.

Ben arched an eyebrow at her. "And why is your friend Jim just now getting around to going after her?" he asked. "Why wait ten years?"

Debbie started to tell Ben it was none of his business, but realized that the facts might very well persuade him to do the job. "It took the underground over six years to find her," she said. "Jim was able to contact her at that point, and a year later she was able to get a letter smuggled out to him. He contacted her for a second time and asked if she wanted to come out, and she wrote back yes. About this time last year he sent her the money, and we've been waiting to hear from her since."

"So you're saying that he hasn't even seen her in ten years or heard from her in one. Hell, she may be a totally different person than she used to be. She might not really want to leave, and I'll be damned if I'm going in and carry her out kicking and screaming."

Debbie shook her head stubbornly. "No, she wouldn't change like that. Look, Ben, she *loves* Jim. They were supposed to be married. She wouldn't do that to the man she loves."

Ben made an impatient motion with his hand and picked up a pack of cigarettes. "Love. That's irrelevant at this point. So what if she 'loved' him ten years ago? Even if she did, or she thought she did, ten years is a long time to hold onto a meaningless emotion."

"Love's not meaningless!" Debbie protested. "Love's the most powerful motivation on the face of the earth."

Ben's face erupted into cynical laughter as he lit his cigarette. "Love? Powerful? Good grief, woman, surely you don't really believe that."

"But I do," Debbie argued. "It would be the only thing that would last all this time between them."

Ben shook his head. "No. Love, whatever that is,

would be the *last* thing that would still be around after all this time. Bitterness, maybe, or a good healthy dose of good old greed. Or ambition or maybe lust. But love? No way."

"Ben, how can you sit there and say that there's no such thing as love?" Debbie sputtered as her fingers clenched and unclenched. "Of course there's such a thing as love. People fall in love every day. Haven't you ever been in love?"

Ben's humorless smile reappeared as he stubbed out his cigarette. "Me? Fall in love? If love does exist, which I certainly doubt, I would be the last man to experience it. No, Debbie, I don't believe in love. In a little bit of lust maybe, but not love. It doesn't exist."

"Of course it does," Debbie replied hotly. "I've been in love. I was in love with my husband."

"See what I mean?" Ben argued back calmly. "You're not together anymore, are you? The physical attraction wore off and away he went. It's just sex, Debbie. Nothing more than that."

"The hell it is," Debbie challenged him.

"Want me to prove it?" Ben asked as he slid off the couch, and before Debbie even realized what he intended to do, he pulled her up from the chair and clamped his arms around her. "You say it's love. I say it's sex. Let's see who's right."

Debbie shook her head, her eyes wide with fright. Yes, she had felt an attraction for Ben, she had felt it the moment he had confronted her in the barn, and a part of her wanted him to kiss her and to explore that feeling. "No, Ben, let's not see who's right," she cried as she tried to pull away from him. "Please don't do this."

"I have to," Ben said as he lowered his lips and parted her lips with his own. Debbie choked a little at the unexpected intimacy and strained her arms and shoulders as hard as she could, trying to pull away from him. *No,* she screamed inwardly at the sensual inroads his questing lips and tongue were making on her defenses. *I don't want to want you. I don't want to desire you. Don't touch me, please, oh . . .*

Not wanting to respond, Debbie nevertheless felt her arms slacken, then her fingers crept up his arms to his shoulders, smooth and hard and sleek. She couldn't be doing this, she protested to herself as she felt her lips soften and her face strain closer to his. Sensing that she was no longer fighting him, Ben let go of her arms and slid his hands around to her back, pressing her closer to his hard muscular body. She couldn't be liking this, she really couldn't, but even as her mind protested her eager fingers roamed downward to touch his naked chest, warm and hard and completely bare of hair. One of her fingers grazed a hard male nipple, and she jerked her hand back from the intimacy of her touch.

Ben let one of his hands roam to her chest and leisurely explore one of her small nipples, puckered with desire from his sensual caress. All rational thought gone, she gave him kiss for kiss, stroke for stroke, until the fire between them was about to blaze out of control and they both knew it.

If she didn't stop this now, she wasn't going to stop. As Ben's fingers crept past her waist and down onto her hip, she gathered all the strength she had and wrenched her lips from Ben's and pushed herself from him, backing off several feet and cringing at his muffled curse. She glared up at him, anger warring with desire in her tense body. "Well, did I prove my point?" he asked gravely.

It took a superhuman effort, but Debbie pulled herself together and faced his question with cool disdain. "I never said I was immune to physical desire," she said coolly. "And I must admit you have the technique perfected. Learned more on your travels than geography, I would guess."

The slightest flicker of admiration lighted Ben's eyes as he took in the disheveled, totally appealing woman across from him. "Yes, I guess you could say that," he drawled.

"And, no, you did not prove your point," Debbie went on, willing her voice to remain calm. "But I have no intention of standing here and debating the merits of love versus sex with you this afternoon. Let's see. You said the most powerful motivators of people were bitterness, greed, and ambition. Obviously, I can't appeal to your bitterness, nor your ambition, so how about your greed? If Jim doubles the amount of money he's offering you, will you do the job?"

"And where does your friend intend to get that kind of money?" Ben asked. "Forty grand is a lot of money, and he's going to have to pay for a second mercenary who speaks Vietnamese. The total will run over fifty thousand."

Debbie's head reeled as she did some quick mental arithmetic. It would take every penny of both her CD and Jim's savings, but together they could just do it. She stuck her chin in the air. "I was already footing part of the bill," she said quietly. "I'll just foot that much more. I have the money."

Ben whistled under his breath. "Forty grand for me and Jerry's usual ten. For that, it might be worth carrying her out kicking and screaming." He folded his arms over his chest and stared at Debbie impassively. "Forty grand. I'll think about it and let you know in a few days. And, Debbie—" he began.

"Yes?" Debbie asked warily.

37

"If I do take on the job, I'll stay over there until I get her out or hear it from her that she doesn't want to come. I don't care if it takes four weeks or a year to find her. I'll stay until I do the job."

Debbie nodded. "That's good to know. I'll be waiting for your call," she said as she tried to smooth her rumpled blouse. She picked up her purse and handed him a piece of paper with her telephone number on it. "Good afternoon," she said as she fled out the door and banged it shut behind her. She held her head high, and only when she had collapsed behind the steering wheel of her car did she allow herself to start shaking. Good heavens, what had got in to her? To argue with him as she had, and then to let him kiss her like that! She had let a man she didn't even like, a man who was hard, cold, and believed only in lust and greed, kiss the daylights out of her.

Debbie set the blow dryer down and ran a brush through her hair, wondering for the hundredth time if she should take the plunge and have it cut. From the time she was a little girl, she had always worn it long, but now that she was twenty-eight maybe it was time to try a more sophisticated style. She piled her hair on top of her head, trying to visualize what she would look like with it short and curled. She shook her head and held it at her shoulders in a simulated pageboy. No, it still looked better long, she decided as she let it drop down her back. Without meaning to, she remembered the way Kevin would bury his face in the onyx tresses after they had made love. Pushing away the bittersweet memory, she tucked her hair behind her ears and quickly made up her face. Nyen-Nyen, her beloved grandmother, wouldn't have minded if Debbie came in her jeans and wearing no makeup, but her father was coming tonight too, and he liked for her to look nice when she was with him. She gave her hair one last brushing and turned out the bathroom light.

Debbie opened her closet and pulled out a simple pair of brown slacks and a dusty pink blouse that did wonderful things for her skin. She pulled them on and was just about to put on her shoes when an impatient knock sounded on her front door.

Gordon Cheong was always five minutes early and in a hurry, and it wouldn't hurt him to wait a minute for her. Taking her time, she opened the door and faced her glowering father with a smile. "Come in," she said brightly. "You're a little early tonight."

Gordon Cheong tried to frown at his daughter, but before he could stop it his mouth had curved into a slight unwilling smile. "The traffic on the bridge is terrible," he declared. "We had better hurry if we intend to be on time." He leaned over and kissed her cheek gently. "So how have you been, Lotus?"

Debbie smiled at her father's endearment. "Just fine, Father," she said. "And you?"

"Same as always," Gordon replied. "Business is doing well and profits are gratifying," he said. After his retirement from the army, Gordon had opened a small shop in Chinatown that featured exclusive Chinese imports for the tourist trade. Although he had opened the shop more for something to do than to make a lot of money, the shop had proven to be quite a success, and he had been after Debbie for the last year or so to quit her job and work with him. Debbie had steadfastly refused, since she loved Gordon as a father but could never have gotten along with him as her boss.

"Are you ready to go?" Debbie asked as she picked up her sweater and her purse. Gordon opened the door for

39

her and shut it behind them, scowling at the five flights of stairs he was now forced to walk down. "Debbie, are you *ever* going to find a normal place to live?" he complained as they descended the stairs.

"Probably not," Debbie admitted cheerfully. She looked back up at her bird's nest apartment that was perched precariously on a Sausalito hillside. Since the town was so hilly, a number of apartment buildings were built up the sides of the hills rather than in conventional horizontal rows, which added to the picturesque flavor of Sausalito and afforded each resident a view of the bay. "I know it's a long way up, but I like it so much when I get up there."

Gordon Cheong nodded as he glanced at his daughter. Debbie smiled back as they walked down the last flight of stairs and got into Gordon's Buick, and she thought about the man who sat beside her. Gordon Cheong was a hard man, in some ways a cold man, and every inch a soldier; yet, buried deep within him there was love for Debbie, the child of his ill-fated marriage to a vain, selfish woman. He had been a strict disciplinarian when she was a child, demanding from her the traditional Chinese respect for her elders, but she had always known that Gordon loved her in his own hard, gruff, undemonstrative way. He did not understand Debbie's deep need for warmth and affection, or perhaps he did understand it but was unable to respond to it. He had raised her himself after her mother left. So if Debbie sometimes longed for a more gentle touch, more open affection, even a mother's love, she figured that Gordon had loved her the best way he had known how to, and she had been content with that.

Gordon drove through the narrow, twisted streets of Sausalito until he had reached the road that would take them across the bridge. "So you'd really rather live in your bird's nest in Sausalito and not move back in with me," he mused as Debbie chuckled.

"Father, you know that even that big house on Russian Hill isn't big enough for the both of us," she teased. "The first time I put on a Police album you'd go running out the door screaming." She glanced back at the pretty little town they were leaving behind. "Besides, where else am I safe on the streets practically all day and night?" She peered into the falling dusk at the looming bridge and the city outlined across the bay. "I love working in the city, though."

"So how is your work going?" Gordon asked. "And your friend, Jim? How is he?"

"Work's fine," Debbie said. "I'm doing a few more items of a sensitive nature these days and not so many propaganda rags." Her face grew thoughtful as she answered the second part of Gordon's question. "Jim is right back where he was a year ago," she said. "He sent Li the money, but hasn't heard a thing, and she isn't out yet."

Gordon shook his head in the dim car that was now racing across the bridge. "He should never have sent the money like that," he said. "He doesn't know whether she wants out or not."

Debbie sighed. "You sound just like Ben," she reproved him.

"Ben?" Gordon asked. "Who?"

"Ben Sako," Debbie said. "You remember. He was one of your soldiers in Nam."

Gordon nodded his head. "He was one of the best soldiers who ever served under me," he said, a trace of pride in his voice. "He was a killing devil, not reckless, but he could line up a Charley in his sight and pull the trigger and not even flinch. And he was a loyal soldier, loyal to his buddies and loyal to his country." Gordon was quiet a minute, then he turned to Debbie with a scowl on his face. "Are you and Jim up to what I think you're up to?" he demanded. "I remember telling you awhile back that Sako's a mercenary now."

"Jim is up to whatever, not me," Debbie replied indignantly, not bothering to admit her financial contribution to the project. "I only went because Ben knows I'm your daughter and that I'm not a government agent. I hope I never see the devil again."

"Wasn't the soul of gentility, huh?" Gordon said, laughing. "Well, he wouldn't be. That man has ice water in his veins." Gordon started to say more and stopped, turning his attention to the traffic on the bridge. Debbie's reporter's instincts told her that Gordon knew more than he was letting on, but she knew better than to press him.

Debbie asked her father a question about his shop, and they talked about his business the rest of the way into San Francisco. They drove through the business district, the streets filled with people even though it was evening. Gordon parked in a garage on the edge of Chinatown, and together he and Debbie walked into what Debbie thought was the most magical of places. When she looked at Chinatown objectively, Debbie realized that it was rundown and commercial, but when she shut her eyes and smelled the peculiar fried-food smell that she associated with the neighborhood, the dinginess and the tourists simply didn't matter. Chinatown was a special place, a child's wonderland and an adult's delight at the same time.

Debbie and Gordon walked down the crowded sidewalk past the myriad shops that sold everything from T-shirts and buttons to priceless Oriental antiques. She stopped to admire a jade bracelet in the window of a small jewelry store, and Gordon made a mental note to come back and get it for her birthday. The tantalizing odor of Chinese cooking drifted out of restaurant doors, and Debbie's mouth watered, knowing that Nyen-Nyen's cooking would be so much better.

Debbie and Gordon turned onto one of the side streets of Chinatown. They entered a side door of a building that housed a T-shirt shop, and after they climbed a narrow set of stairs, they knocked at one of the two doors at the top of the flight. In just a moment the door opened and Debbie moved into the open arms of her beloved grandmother. "Nyen-Nyen, *nay ho ma?*" she asked, slipping automatically into Chinese.

Nyen-Nyen hugged Debbie and then turned to her son. "I'm fine, Debbie. You are both looking well, I see," she said as she and Gordon bowed low to each other.

"I am well, *Mo Chen,*" he replied as he touched her hand lightly. "And you—are you well?"

"Yes, yes, I am well," Nyen-Nyen assured him. "Come and seat yourselves. Dinner will be ready in a minute."

"Can I do anything to help?" Debbie asked, knowing beforehand that Nyen-Nyen probably had everything under control. Cam Lee Cheong had been cooking for her family since she had married in China in 1919 at the age of fourteen, and although she had tutored Debbie in the art of Chinese cooking, tonight Debbie was a guest.

"No, dinner is almost ready," she said as she disappeared into her small kitchen. Debbie started to go after her, but Gordon laid his hand on her arm. "Don't," he said. "She takes such pleasure in doing for you," he said softly.

Debbie sat down and looked around at her grandmother's small apartment, the same apartment where her father had grown up. The furniture was Western, and the table was set with Early American pottery, but there were small mementos in evidence that hinted at how Chinese Nyen-Nyen still was. A Chinese calendar hung on her wall and the newspaper on the couch was in Chinese, and alongside the Western pottery Nyen-Nyen had set her chopsticks. Framed in one corner was a delicate watercolor, yellow and faded, of Nyen-Nyen's village in Canton. And although Nyen-Nyen's English was passable, she still preferred to speak Chinese when she could, and Debbie owed much of her linguistic talent to Nyen-Nyen's insistence that she learn the language.

Nyen-Nyen returned a moment later with several steaming bowls of food. They seated themselves, and Nyen-Nyen poured Debbie and Gordon each a small cup of very hot tea.

"Umm, delicious," Debbie murmured as she sipped the delicately flavored tea. "And you made Tun Ting Ha!"

"She makes your favorite at least every other week," Gordon teased as Nyen-Nyen laughed at Debbie's delight.

"That's all right. I make your favorite often too, son," Nyen-Nyen teased. Debbie took a generous helping of the delicately flavored shrimp and vegetable dish. They passed around another bowl of vegetables and fried rice, and Debbie burned her fingers on a hot egg roll. "Be careful," Nyen-Nyen cautioned Debbie.

They helped themselves, and Gordon asked Nyen-Nyen how her neighbors, the people he had grown up with, were doing. "Not well," Nyen-Nyen replied. "Their second granddaughter is dissolving her marriage and Toi Mae is heartbroken."

"Isn't she the one that married the doctor and bought the house on Russian Hill?" Debbie asked.

"No wonder Toi Mae's heartbroken," Gordon replied cynically.

"Gordon, where is your respect?" Nyen-Nyen demanded. "The young man's money was not the issue here. That marriage should never have been dissolved."

"Marriages come apart all the time, Mother," Gordon shrugged. "Look at me. Look at Debbie."

"What happened, Nyen-Nyen?" Debbie asked.

"The granddaughter doesn't think she loves the young man anymore," Nyen-Nyen said. "She says she made a mistake."

"Maybe she did," Debbie said quietly as she nibbled on an egg roll. "Goodness knows, it's easy enough to do."

"Unfortunately, you're right," Gordon agreed as he served himself a mouthful of rice. "I just hope you can avoid making the same mistake twice." His face twisted into a bitter grimace.

Debbie chewed her egg roll and swallowed it as she searched her father's face. "Do you think you've got the solution? Do you think I should stay single like you have?"

"No, Lotus, I don't mean that you should stay single," Gordon said, his face softening. "I have stayed single by choice, but I would not wish that on you. But I do hope that you make a wiser choice the next time than you did before."

"But I loved Kevin," Debbie protested quietly. "I really loved him and he loved me." She turned to Nyen-Nyen. "I tried to make my marriage work, Nyen-Nyen, but it was impossible."

"Oh, Lotus, I know that," Nyen-Nyen assured her. "I

wasn't talking about you, or your father either. You were both hurt badly."

*Father, hurt?* Debbie thought. She had never thought in terms of her father being hurt by the defection of his wife, but she guessed he had been. Debbie had felt so little love from her vain, selfish mother that she had missed her very little when she left. She had turned instead to Gordon, who had loved her the best way he could, and to Nyen-Nyen, who had done her best to fill the void in her granddaughter's life.

"Well, it's all water under the bridge," Gordon said.

"Yes, maybe I'll love more wisely next time," Debbie agreed.

Gordon shook his head. "No, that's where you made your mistake," he told Debbie. "Don't marry for love. It doesn't last, Lotus."

"Oh, Father, how can you say that?" Debbie asked.

"Well, it's true, isn't it? Sometimes I doubt whether there is such a thing. If it exists between a man and a woman at all, it goes out the window sooner or later. Your mother and I, you and Kevin. You would do better to settle for security the next time around."

"Father!" Debbie cried, horrified. "Do you have any idea how cynical you sound?"

"Of course, I'm cynical," Gordon replied. "But it's the truth. Love doesn't last."

"Oh, yes, it does," Nyen-Nyen replied forcefully. "Don't listen to my son, Debbie. He has been hard and cold for years, ever since Kay left him. Love does last, Debbie. Your grandfather and I loved one another for nearly fifty years."

"That isn't the same," Gordon protested. "You did things the old way. Your marriage was arranged."

Nyen-Nyen nodded. "Yes, that is so. But we did grow

to love one another, son, and your father was devoted to me until the day he died. He could have left me, or gotten a lady friend on the side like so many men do. But he didn't. He was devoted to me, and don't dishonor your father's memory by saying that love is impossible."

"Yes, Mother," Gordon replied, but Debbie could tell that he was unconvinced.

Debbie asked Nyen-Nyen about another relative, and they spent the evening talking about family and friends. Nyen-Nyen did accept help with the dishes, and then Debbie and her father indulged her in a game of Monopoly, one of the few American pastimes she had picked up. It was late when they left Nyen-Nyen, and Debbie promised to come by and see her one day next week on her lunch hour.

Gordon dropped Debbie off in front of her apartment building and waited in the car until she had flicked on the lights. As she sat down on the couch and sipped a soft drink from the refrigerator, her mind returned to the strange conversation she, Gordon, and Nyen-Nyen had shared this evening. Gordon was wrong, he had to be. He and Ben Sako were both wrong. There was such a thing as love between a man and a woman. She knew, because she had it once.

True, her love had not lasted. She and Kevin Delaney had been young when they had fallen in love and married against both families' wishes. Gordon and Nyen-Nyen had come around, after a fashion, but the very rich, very snobbish Delaneys of Belvedere had never accepted the thought of their heir married to the granddaughter of Chinese immigrants, even if her father did live on Russian Hill. After several years of constant pressure from his family, Kevin, too weak to stand up to them, had divorced her. But in the early days they had been wildly, gloriously happy with each other, and Debbie had reveled in the free expression of love that she had never known at home. She had missed that love in the last two years since her divorce. Although she was finally over Kevin, she still missed the warmth and caring that she had known with him.

And she would have it again, she promised herself as she sipped her soft drink, sneezing when the bubbles got up her nose. She wouldn't settle for her father's security. She wouldn't settle for the physical attraction that Ben Sako recommended. She wanted to be loved again, and she would be loved, the way Jim loved Li.

The shrill ringing of the telephone startled Debbie, and she spilled a little of her drink on the sofa. "Hello," she said when she picked up the receiver, wondering who could be calling her after midnight.

"Debbie Cheong?" a familiar voice inquired.

"Yes, Ben, this is Debbie," she said, fighting to keep her voice steady. "What are you—What can I do for you?"

"I'm not calling to agree to the mission," Ben said frankly. Debbie's face fell, and she was glad they weren't face to face. "I'd like to meet your friend tomorrow night to talk about this, and I want you there as well. I'll pick you up tomorrow night."

"Ben, this is between you and Jim," Debbie said quickly. "I'll introduce you, but then I'm bowing out."

"No, you aren't," Ben replied. "If you want me to consider this at all, you'll plan to be in on the entire meeting tomorrow. I'll pick you up at seven. What's your address?"

"I don't want you coming here," Debbie said through gritted teeth. "Besides, Jim won't like it. He considers this something between you and him."

"Tough. I'm calling the shots. I'll pick you up and you can take me to your friend." Debbie started to protest that she would meet him someplace else, but changed her mind. If she wanted him to find Li she couldn't antagonize him. She gave him her address and then hung up.

Oh, hell, she hadn't even told Jim she had upped the price! She mopped up the spilled drink and sat down on the dry side of the couch. Jim wanted to get Li out, but he also had his pride, and he might very well refuse to take her money. She had to call him tomorrow and persuade him to take the money somehow, because, as objectionable as Ben Sako was, he was the only mercenary on the West Coast that they knew of. And for that same reason, she would have to go to the meeting tomorrow, even though she didn't want to, and in the process be thrown into contact with a man that she didn't even like but for whom she had a dangerously strong attraction, a man who had announced to her that he had no use for love, just for lust. He was the very kind of man that she needed to avoid like the plague. Debbie shivered a little in the still dark night.

# CHAPTER THREE

Debbie stared into the mirror and, with fingers that trembled only a little, rubbed a little blush into her pale cheeks. Ben will be here in a few minutes, she thought as she dabbed on pink lipstick and tried to quell her nervousness. Just tonight, she thought as she dusted her nose lightly with translucent powder. She would leave everything in Ben's and Jim's hands and let them take it from there. She couldn't afford to be around Ben that much more, considering the way she was drawn to the hard, unloving man.

As she tugged on a mint-green dress, Debbie heard a loud knock on the front door. "Just a minute," she called as she found her shoes and fumbled with the straps of her sandals. She heard the knock again as she rushed across the room. "Coming!" she yelled as she threw open the door, irritation fading her nervousness somewhat.

Ben stood on her doorstep, dressed casually in a pair of jeans and a knit shirt. "So formal?" he asked as he took in Debbie's dress and stockings and the makeup that she wore. "Where are we supposed to meet this guy? The Imperial Garden? I thought we'd meet in a bar somewhere."

Debbie lifted her chin a little and motioned for Ben to enter. "As a matter-of-fact, we are meeting Jim at his home and dining with his family. At least I know how to dress for dinner."

Ben's face tightened as he stepped into her small apartment. He looked out the window at the view of the bay, but did not admire it as most visitors did. "I don't want to meet Jim at his home or have dinner with his family," he ground out. "Why didn't you set this up in a bar or something?"

"Jim insisted," Debbie said. "You called the time, he called the place and the circumstances. And if you don't like it, tough."

"His word or yours?" Ben asked.

"Neither. I just heard it recently," Debbie gibed. "Jim and his family are very sweet, very gracious people," she went on, the sarcasm gone from her voice. "If you do take on the job, they will feel very indebted to you. This is one way of letting their appreciation be known."

"I don't like it," Ben protested. "I prefer to keep my dealings purely business."

"Sure you do," Debbie said as she raised her eyebrow. "Like you have with me." She picked up a sweater and put it on. "Of course, if you'd rather throw their hospitality back in their faces, I'll be glad to call them and tell them so."

Ben shook his head. "You'd like that, wouldn't you?" he said. "That way you could turn your nose up at me just that much further. No way, Lotus. I'll go."

Debbie jumped a little at his unexpected endearment. Had he come up with it on his own, or had her father called her Lotus in front of his soldiers? "Uh, that's fine," she said as she picked up her purse. She followed Ben out the door and locked it behind them.

Ben started down the stairs, a wicked grin on his face. "I'm surprised you don't get nosebleed up there," he said

51

as he loped down the stairs two at a time. In her high heels there was no way Debbie could keep up with him, so she slowed her pace and let him wait for her on the bottom step. She expected a sarcastic remark when she reached the bottom, but Ben's face held no expression as he pointed to a beat-up Scout across the street. Debbie pushed a stack of vintner's magazines off the seat and got in. "Where do Jim and his family live?" he asked.

Debbie gave Ben an address in the North Beach area. "Jim moved into his parents' garage apartment so he could save money to send Li," she explained. "Translators do all right, but we aren't rich."

Ben shrugged and said nothing. They drove most of the way to the Anderson household in silence, and Debbie began to wonder if Ben had changed his mind about wanting her. She knew he had been attracted to her the other day, he would have had to be to kiss her like that, but tonight he had said nothing to indicate that he still desired her in any way. Maybe his passion had only been for the moment. Or maybe he was the kind of man who could turn it on and off. Debbie shrugged inwardly. Right now, all that really mattered was getting him to agree to rescue Li.

They pulled up in front of a ramshackle old two-story house. "How many are in the clan?" he asked as he arched his eyebrow at her.

"There's Jim, his parents, and a much younger brother," Debbie said. "His parents have been very much a part of the effort to bring Li out of Vietnam."

"You would think they would be just as glad if he forgot about her," Ben said mockingly. "Not too many red-blooded American types are just dying for a Vietnamese daughter-in-law."

Debbie stiffened at the crack. "You don't have to be

nasty," she said shortly. "Not everybody's like my former in-laws." She slammed the door of the Scout behind her.

Ben caught up with her as she reached the front porch. "I didn't mean it personally," he said. "But it's the truth and you know it." He looked at Debbie's face. "It still hurts you, doesn't it?"

Debbie turned haughty eyes in Ben's direction. "I don't think that's any concern of yours." She jabbed the doorbell with her thumb, surprised that Ben had the perception to tell that Kevin's defection still hurt.

An elderly, blue-eyed woman opened the front door. "Debbie, honey, come on inside and sit down," Mrs. Anderson said as she motioned Ben and Debbie to enter. "I swear, you look as pretty as a picture tonight!" Mrs. Anderson was from Georgia, and even after forty-five years in California she had not lost her Southern accent or mannerisms.

"Mrs. Anderson, this is Ben Sako," Debbie said as Ben shut the door behind them. "He's the—"

"Yes, I know, he's the man who's going to help Jim get Li out of Vietnam," Mrs. Anderson said as she extended her hand to Ben. Debbie glanced at Ben, expecting to see a scowl on his face, and was surprised to see Ben reaching out and taking Mrs. Anderson's hand. So he could be polite when the occasion called for it.

"I'm glad to meet you," Ben said as they stepped into the shabby old living room to one side of the entrance where Jim and his father were absorbed in the evening news.

Jim stood up immediately. "I'm Jim Anderson," he said as he extended his hand.

"Ben Sako," Ben said. The two men shook hands while they sized one another up. Though neither man was tall or physically imposing, each was tough and hard in his own way, Ben's physical strength and toughness matched by the inward strength and determination that years of loneliness and disappointment had given Jim. Debbie had the feeling that Jim just might be strong-willed enough to stand up to Ben if necessary and to get along with him.

Jim released Ben's hand and introduced his father. Mr. Anderson smiled cordially as he invited him to sit down. "So you're a soldier," he said to Ben.

"He's no soldier, he doesn't have a uniform!" a cheeky voice called down the stairs. "You don't look any different than I do."

"Oh, Johnny, hush," Mrs. Anderson said as a long-legged boy of twelve ran down the stairs. "Mr. Sako, this is my younger son, Johnny."

Johnny skidded into the living room and sat down crosslegged on the floor. "Are you really a mercenary? You sure don't look like one."

Jim looked uncomfortable and Debbie wondered how Ben would react to Johnny's outspoken comments. To Debbie's relief, Ben just smiled faintly. "Yes, Johnny, I'm a mercenary. And sorry to disappoint you. Not all of us look like Charles Bronson."

"Johnny, I could sure use some help in the kitchen," Mrs. Anderson said as she raised her eyebrows at the boy. Groaning a little, Johnny got up and followed her into the kitchen. "No, that's all right, Debbie," Mrs. Anderson said when Debbie started to get up. "Johnny and I can get everything just fine."

Ben and Debbie sat down on the couch. "I think Mother wanted to get him out of here before he let loose with any more of his questions." Jim laughed.

"You're much older than your brother," Ben observed mildly.

Jim's father answered the unspoken question. "We adopted Johnny when we were quite old ourselves."

"Very generous of you," Ben observed. Debbie searched Ben's face for any sign of cynicism or sarcasm, and to her surprise she found none.

They made small talk for a few minutes while they waited for Mrs. Anderson to call them into the dining room. Debbie was included in the conversation, but the warm and friendly Andersons talked mostly with Ben, although Ben's business with Jim was not mentioned. Much to her amazement Ben was responding to their friendliness with a little of his own. But Debbie also got the feeling that Ben, in spite of his outward behavior, was ill at ease in a social situation, and that surprised her. When she had met Ben the other day, he was the last one she would have expected to care enough to be ill at ease.

In just a few minutes Mrs. Anderson came to the door of the living room. "It's ready," she said as she wiped her hands on a dish towel. "Mr. Sako, I hope you like fried chicken and mashed potatoes. They're the family's favorites."

"That sounds fine," Ben said as they followed Mrs. Anderson into the big dining room with the scarred oak table and chairs. Debbie had always felt at home here the many times she had eaten with the Anderson family. As Ben held out a chair for her, she wondered if Ben had ever felt at home anywhere or with anyone.

"I guess you enjoyed a lot of Japanese cooking while you were growing up," Mrs. Anderson said to Ben.

Debbie could feel Ben stiffen slightly beside her. "Not really. I was brought up in a string of foster homes."

"Boy, that's the pits," Johnny volunteered.

"Oh, I'm sorry," Mrs. Anderson said.

"Don't be," Ben replied, his voice matter-of-fact, and Debbie wondered if she had imagined his earlier reaction.

There was a moment of awkward silence before Jim rushed to fill it. "I can hardly wait for Mom to taste some of Li's spring rolls. I used to eat them by the dozen."

"I'm looking forward to the day, son," Mr. Anderson said.

"That will be a happy day for all of us," Mrs. Anderson added.

Ben looked a little doubtful. "You're really looking forward to Jim's marrying Li?" he asked.

Mr. and Mrs. Anderson were prepared to answer honestly. "Yes, Mr. Sako, we very much are looking forward to Jim's marrying Li," Mrs. Anderson continued. "But I have to admit that we didn't always feel that way. At first, when Jim came home ten years ago, we hoped that he would forget this foreign girl and marry a nice American girl. But our son has not been a happy man for the last ten years. He's over forty and he still has no wife, no family, no one to come home to, because this woman is the only one for him. Yes, Mr. Sako, I will welcome her, because only she can make my son happy."

Debbie's thoughts were smug as she ate a bite of chicken. She and Jim weren't the only ones who believed in love. She glanced over at Ben's face but could see no expression other than vague cynicism there. Debbie would have loved to have known what Ben had thought about Mrs. Anderson's honesty.

They enjoyed Mrs. Anderson's apple pie with ice cream for dessert, and Ben complimented Mrs. Anderson on the delicious meal. Jim rose and looked over at Ben. "We can talk in the living room," he said. "Debbie, we won't be too long."

"Take your time," Debbie said. "I'll help your mother clean up."

"I'm sorry, but Debbie needs to be in on this," Ben said as Debbie stood up.

Debbie shook her head vigorously. "No, Ben. From here on out it's between you and Jim. I'll help Mrs. Anderson and Johnny."

"I said you need to come with us," Ben replied. "You need to be in on this talk."

"No, Mr. Sako, this is between you and myself," Jim said as he shook his head. "Debbie has done her part."

Ben stared at Jim, noting the determination that Jim was not trying to hide. Jim really didn't want Debbie involved, and he was ready to argue the point. "Jim, as badly as I hate to admit it, we need her if we're going to get Li out," Ben said, hiding his satisfaction when Jim backed down. He grasped Debbie by the arm and the three of them retired to the living room, where she and Jim sat on the couch across from Ben, who sat down in a beat-up recliner and pulled a cigarette out of the squashed pack in his pocket. "All right, I've come up with a tentative plan for getting Li out of the country, if you're willing to pay a second mercenary who speaks Vietnamese."

"I would do anything to save Li," Jim stated with determination, ignoring Ben's cynical expression. "I want her here with me."

"Then this is what I have in mind," Ben said. "Jim, where was your girl friend the last time you heard from her?"

"In Hai Thong, just a few kilometers outside Hanoi."

"All right. We leave next month, at the start of summer. Jerry and I will charter a boat in Hong Kong and sail through the Gulf of Tonkin to the coast of North

57

Vietnam. I know a couple of boat owners who do this all the time. The boat can let us off, then we can hike in and find her. We arrange for the boat and owner to stay in hiding with a member of the resistance—I have a family in mind who would be glad to get the extra money—until we return. And we sail back to Hong Kong. Now, Debbie, while the mercenary and I are in Vietnam, you're going to stay behind in Hong Kong and arrange for Li's legal entry into Hong Kong, then for her legal entry into the United States after her marriage in Hong Kong to Jim."

"I'm what?" Debbie demanded.

"You're going to be getting papers together for Li, buying her clothes, making arrangements for her and Jim to stay somewhere until she can get a visa—"

"Just a minute!" Debbie sputtered. "Where did you get the idea that I was coming with you?"

Ben turned steely dark eyes on her. "Where did you get the idea you weren't?" he demanded. "I told you to come tonight so I could brief you on your part in all this."

"Well, you can just rewrite your script," Debbie shot back. "What about my job? I have responsibilities here."

"Debbie's right, Ben," Jim said. "It's dangerous in that part of the world, and I won't have Debbie exposed to it. She's done enough for me already. Besides, I can do all that for Li."

"How's your Chinese?" Ben asked. "I was under the impression that you only spoke English and Vietnamese."

"I can get by with English in Hong Kong," Jim said stiffly.

"I'm not having this job bungled because you foul up on getting Li's papers," Ben said firmly. "You can wait around in Hong Kong if you want to, or you can fly over after Li gets there. I don't really care. But either Debbie goes or it's no deal. I'm not taking a chance on this falling through by not having things ready for Li's entry into Hong Kong, because the authorities will deport her. If Debbie won't go, I walk out that door and Li stays in Nam."

Debbie's mind was spinning, her heart torn in two by her friend's agony. If she said no, Li stayed in Vietnam, maybe forever. She looked from Ben's implacable face to Jim's miserable one. "Well, Jim, it looks like the soldier I found for you isn't that great after all, since he and another soldier together simply can't do this job without the help of a woman. But if he needs me that badly, I guess I can't say no. Sure, I'll come along and help you, Ben," she cooed, her eyes flashing with anger.

Instead of the anger she hoped to arouse in Ben, she was furious to see amusement shining out of his eyes. "I do most graciously accept your help, Lotus." His amusement faded and once again he was all business. He told them the injections they'd need to get and gave them a long list of things for Debbie to take care of while they were in Hong Kong.

Finally, after more than an hour, she and Ben rose to go. "About payment," Jim said. He had reluctantly agreed to accept Debbie's help with the upped fee, but only in the form of a long-term loan that would take years to pay off.

"Twenty thousand for me and ten for the other mercenary plus expenses, I believe it was?" Ben said. "Half when we leave for Vietnam and half when we return."

Jim glanced over at Debbie, who shrugged her shoulders behind Ben's back, glad he could not see the surprise on her face. "Fine," he said, his expression grateful. "Cash?"

Ben handed him an account number and told him to deposit the money in that account. "And Mr. Anderson," Ben said, "Jerry and I will see this through until we find her. No matter how long it takes us over there."

Jim nodded his appreciation of Ben's commitment to the task. Debbie sought out the Andersons to wish them good night before she followed Ben out of the house and to his car. *Back to your usual dour self, aren't you?* she thought as Ben glared out at the dark streets that were only lightly shrouded in fog.

They drove in silence across San Francisco and over the bridge, Ben concentrating on driving through the thickening fog and Debbie's mind in a spin. She and Jim both knew that Ben didn't really need her. Jim could have managed to do everything that was on Debbie's list of errands. So did that mean that he still wanted her after all? She bit her lip and looked over at the hard, unfeeling man, his face unreadable in the dark car. She would have to ask him, if she wanted to find out why he insisted that she come.

Debbie waited until Ben had parked in front of her apartment building, then instead of getting out, she turned and faced him. "Why drag me along on this trip?" she asked softly.

"I need you," Ben replied.

"You want me," Debbie said.

"Yes, I do," Ben said as he got out a cigarette and lit it, the light from the cigarette illuminating the long scar down the side of his face. "I could use your help in Hong Kong, but I admit that Jim could take care of getting her papers. I want to know that you'll be waiting there for me when I get there with your friend. You and I have something between us, Debbie," he continued. "Lust, physical attraction—label it what you will. But it's there, Debbie, and I want something to come of it. I want you to be my lover."

"No, Ben!" Debbie exclaimed, horrified. "I won't become your lover, not on this trip or on a thousand more. I told you the other day I don't believe in lust or in physical attraction as a basis for people to have an affair. I believe in love, and as far as I'm concerned, it's the only reason I'd go to bed with a man."

Ben rolled his eyes upward. "God deliver me from that kind of Victorian twattle," he said as he breathed out a lungful of cigarette smoke.

"I just don't believe in making love like that! There has to be caring, affection, respect—"

"Passion, desire, longing—put all the pretty words on it that you care to, Debbie, it's still sex and it's still between you and me and there isn't a whole lot you or I can do about it," Ben broke in as he ground out the cigarette in the ashtray and reached across the seat for Debbie. "Let me show you," he whispered as he pulled her close. "Let me show you what we have between us."

"No, you already—" Debbie whispered as he wrapped his arm around her neck and anchored her lips into place. His mouth came down on hers, gentle at first as he explored her lips with his lips and the tip of his tongue. Debbie moaned and tried to pull away, but although her mind recognized the danger she was in, her body failed to respond as it should, and Debbie could feel herself inching closer to the source of delight. Moving closer to Ben, she felt her hands slide up his arms and across his muscular shoulders, finally coming to lock across his nape.

Ben pulled his lips away from Debbie's and caressed her cheek tenderly. "It's there between us, you see?" he asked as he moved his lips back to her own. But before she could reply he had locked their mouths together, this time with a passion and urgency that Debbie had only imagined before. His tongue pushed against her lips until she opened all of her sweetness to him; their tongues fenced across the delicate divide. Ben's hands fell from the back of her head to her shoulders, touching and caressing her as she shivered from the intimate warmth of his fingers. He ran his hands down the length of her arms, savoring the softness of her skin under his calloused fingers, and slid one arm around her waist as the other one went to the top button of her shirtwaist. Slowly, so as not to alarm her, he eased open the first button and then the second.

Debbie shivered as Ben's rough fingers slowly unbuttoned her dress to the waist. Helpless to resist him, she made no protest when his lips left her mouth and began a slow, torturous journey down her neck and across her shoulders and finally traveled down to the border of her bra. Gently Ben pushed her down onto the car seat and partially covered her body with his own, unsnapping her bra and exposing the tender tips of her breasts to his eager gaze. He lowered his head and tormented one of her hardened nipples until it was tight with desire, then his lips traveled across her chest, one kiss at a time, until he found the other swollen peak. This one he grazed with his lips, rubbing it gently back and forth until it too was hard and proud in his mouth. Debbie moaned and clutched Ben's hair in her fingers, unmindful of anything except the delightful feel of Ben's body on hers, his lips on her breasts. All rational thought was forgotten as Ben kissed her and caressed her for long moments, the tension growing more taut between them as the moments passed.

It was the blaring of a car horn down the street that

finally roused them. Ben sat up suddenly, blinking his eyes, then he pulled Debbie's dress together with fingers that trembled a little. Debbie lay bemused by passion for a minute longer, then she too returned to the harshness of reality. Her face burning, she hooked her bra and buttoned her dress before she sat up in the car and put her head in her hands. "God, how could I—how could you?" she moaned, her head bent and her hair hanging in a cloud around her face.

"I don't know about you, but I can't seem to help it," Ben replied as he pulled out another cigarette and lit it. "Face it, Debbie. It's there between us whether we like it or not. It's never been like that for you before, has it?"

"No," Debbie replied bitterly.

"Well, it never has for me either. I haven't even wanted a woman for ages," Ben admitted as Debbie raised her head and stared at him in surprise. "All the fighting, all the killing—I thought it had me burned out. I thought I wasn't capable of desire anymore. And then you came along. Yeah, you're the first woman I've wanted to make love to in a long time, and I'll be damned if I'm letting that go."

"But what about the way I feel?" Debbie pleaded.

Ben shrugged. "What you feel isn't the problem—it's what you *think* that's holding you back for now." He sat quiet for a minute and smoked his cigarette. "It will be good for you, Debbie, I promise you that."

"No way am I getting involved with you," Debbie said. "I've been hurt once, I won't let that happen again."

"I won't hurt you," Ben said, but he could tell that Debbie didn't believe him. He took a deep puff on his cigarette. "We leave the middle of next month. You better go in. You have to go to work tomorrow."

Debbie scrambled out of her side of the Scout and

climbed the five flights of stairs as though she had the devil himself behind her. She locked her door behind her and stared out the window as Ben finished his cigarette and drove away.

Yes, she was attracted to him; they were attracted to each other. She would not—could not—deny that. And tonight's passionate exchange had given her a good idea of what Ben would be like as a lover. But what about love? She needed it and he didn't even believe it existed. If she had a brain in her head, she would be running away from Ben as fast as her legs would carry her.

But what about Li? She had no doubt that if she tried to get out of Ben's arrangement that he would scrap the entire mission and leave Li in Vietnam. He had no ethics she could appeal to in order to change his mind, and since he had gone back to the original price, she didn't think she could appeal to him with money either. She had no choice. She had to go to Hong Kong with Ben and Jim.

But that didn't mean she had to become his lover. She would have to steer clear of him, and at the same time she was sure Ben wasn't the kind of man who would take an unwilling woman. She just had to stay unwilling, in spite of the strong attraction that they shared, because she'd never get the love she needed from him.

Debbie sighed. In a way it was too bad that she had to say no to what Ben wanted, she thought as she wandered into the living room. If she had been a different kind of woman, she might have accepted the kind of loveless relationship he was offering and enjoyed it for its own sake. But she believed in love, needed it, craved it even, and she simply could not afford to get involved with a man who didn't believe it existed.

## CHAPTER FOUR

Debbie staggered through the door of her apartment, juggling the basket of freshly dried laundry in front of her, and dumped it on the couch. She had spent the day buying and washing a few new outfits that would be more suitable for the warm, humid climate of Hong Kong than her usual skirts and jackets, and now all she had to do was press out the wrinkles and put the dresses into her almost packed suitcase. The real estate agent that Jim had contacted had managed to locate a small apartment where she and Jim would be able to stay while they waited for Ben and Jerry Chan, the other mercenary who would go into Vietnam with him to bring Li back to Hong Kong. Debbie took out her ironing board and turned on her iron.

Opening her front window, Debbie picked up her first dress. The cool May breeze blew in off the bay, the fresh salt air tantalizing her nose. She was going to miss the breeze in Hong Kong. Jim had arranged for the two of them to take off from their jobs for as long as they needed to be gone, and in a rare moment of generosity Gordon had offered to pay for her airfare and Jim's to Hong Kong and also to help pay the exorbitant rent on the apartment. Ben and Jerry would only spend one night in Hong Kong before leaving on the small boat that would lead them through the Gulf of Tonkin and to the northern coast of Vietnam. She didn't know how much seducing Ben thought he could do in two days, but that was all the time he was going to get! She would stay and help Jim get Li's papers in order, of course, but she planned to be on the first plane back to the states once she had seen for herself that Li was all right.

Debbie tried to control the mounting combination of nervousness and excitement that was beginning to grip her. She wasn't sure whether it was the idea of flying halfway across the world, seeing Li after all these years of searching for her, or seeing Ben Sako again for the first time in a month, but she could feel a knot of tension tightening in her stomach.

She willed herself to stay calm. She had always wanted to see the Orient. Ben *would* get Li out. And if Ben had been all that eager to seduce her, he would have contacted her and not Jim about the trip. Ben had not called her or spoken to her in the last month, making all his arrangements with Jim instead, and after the last passionate embrace they had shared, Debbie was relieved that he had not approached her again. That last encounter had proven to her just how attracted he was to her, and how attracted she was to him in spite of the fact that he could bring her nothing but grief. If he had pursued her ardently, she was very much afraid that she might find herself in his arms and in his bed—the last place she needed or wanted to be.

As Debbie put a dress on a hanger, she looked out the window and noticed her father's Buick pulling up in front of her apartment. Knowing that it would take him a minute to climb the stairs, she picked up another dress and had it half ironed before Gordon had made it to the top of the stairs. "Hello, Father," Debbie said as she opened the door. Gordon leaned over and kissed her cheek. "It was nice of you to come and tell me good-bye." Debbie had not expected Gordon to drive out tonight, since she had seen him last night at Nyen-Nyen's, and he had wished her a good trip then.

Gordon shut the door behind him and pushed over the laundry so he could sit down on the couch. "I just wanted to see you one more time before you left," he said. "Go on with your ironing," he added as Debbie started to turn off the iron. "This may take a few minutes and I know you're trying to get ready to go tomorrow."

Debbie picked up a pair of shorts and put them on the ironing board. She looked over at Gordon and was surprised to find him looking a little uncomfortable. "What is it, Father?" she asked.

"Are you and Jim sharing that apartment in Hong Kong?" Gordon asked.

"Yes, but, Father, you know there's never been anything like that between Jim and me," Debbie said quickly. "He's so crazy about Li, I don't think he's even looked at another woman in the last ten years. I'm perfectly safe with him."

Gordon shook his head back and forth. "You don't have to defend Jim, Lotus. I'm glad you're staying with him. It wasn't Jim I was worried about."

"Then what were you worried about?" Debbie asked as she flipped over the shorts and pressed the backside. "My safety in a strange city?"

"Ben Sako," Gordon replied as he watched his daughter's face. "He hasn't come on to you, has he?"

Debbie's cheeks reddened. "Y-yes, Father, he has," she said, thinking that this was the first time she and Gordon had ever talked about a specific man's interest in her. "He's come on pretty strong."

"And that's why you're going on the trip," Gordon deduced thoughtfully. "He's practically dragging you along."

"How did you know that?" Debbie demanded.

Gordon smiled faintly. "I should have caught on before, but last night after you left, your grandmother asked me why you were even going on the trip, since Jim could have taken care of things in Hong Kong. You're a beautiful and desirable woman, Debbie, and I know Ben Sako. I put two and two together."

"He said he wouldn't make the trip unless I went along," Debbie said. "He told me very honestly that he wants me to become . . . well, he just wants me. And even Jim couldn't talk him out of taking me."

"That bastard," Gordon said under his breath. "Well, Debbie, I'm sure that Ben wouldn't hesitate to call off the trip even at this late date if you backed out, so I guess you'll have to go if you want to get Li out of there. But please, Lotus, whatever you do, don't get mixed up with the likes of Ben Sako."

"I have no intention of getting involved with him, Father," Debbie said softly. Her curiosity whetted, she turned off the iron and sat down across from Gordon. "I already know he's poison, but what do you know that has you concerned?"

"Well, if you've already decided not to get involved with him, then there would be nothing gained in my telling you about him," Gordon said slowly.

Debbie's face took on the determination that had made her a good reporter. "You could satisfy my curiosity," she said. "Why, Father? What do you know about him that has you worried about me?"

"Debbie, Ben Sako is one of the coldest, most ruthless men I have ever met in my life. He is capable of loyalty and tremendous dedication to a cause, and I admire him for that, but otherwise he is totally without heart."

"I had already figured out that much," Debbie said. "At first he refused to even go in looking for Li. He said that there was no way love could last the way hers and Jim's has, and that she just doesn't want to get out. We argued and he said that he didn't believe in love, period."

"Smart man," Gordon said. "No, Debbie, let's not get into one of our arguments over love tonight," he said as she opened her mouth to protest. "And that's not really my concern with you and Ben, anyway. You're a grown woman, and your sex life is really of no concern to me. If it was any other man and you wanted to have an affair, I would look the other way. But, Debbie, Ben's a user. I saw him do that over in Nam. He would take a woman and then discard her as though she were a used tissue."

"But that was during a war," Debbie said. "Do you think it would be any different now?"

"No, I don't," Gordon said. "And I'm not saying that he was physically cruel or anything. But sometimes Ben would see a woman, desire her, and have her. Just like that. And then when he got tired of her, he would drop her. He never seemed to care how the women in question felt, not that any of them seemed to care all that much either. And I don't want that for you, Lotus. You deserve better than that."

"Father, do you have any idea why Ben's the way he is?" Debbie asked.

"Yes, I have an idea, although Ben never said anything about it himself. I saw the psychological profile they wrote up on him when he applied for the Green Berets, and apparently his childhood years were devastating."

"He said something once about being brought up in foster homes," Debbie mused.

"He's the product of the ill-fated marriage of an immigrant Chinese mother and an immigrant Japanese father," Gordon said. "Haven't you noticed how Chinese his eyes look?"

Debbie nodded. "Anyway," Gordon continued, "apparently neither of his real parents had much use for him, and when he was four and his father took off, his mother's people said they would take her back in but not her half-Japanese child. It was right after the war, and a lot of people still hated the Japanese. So she turned him over to the state, and he spent most of the next thirteen years bouncing from one foster home to another. It's obvious that his mother didn't love him, and there was reason to suspect that he might have even been abused as a child by her."

"How awful," Debbie murmured.

"Yes, it was," Gordon continued. "And apparently he had a pretty rough go of it in the foster homes. So he never managed to learn anything about kindness or compassion, but he did learn a tremendous amount about using other people before they used him. And to make matters worse, he went straight from that to the army, and volunteered for the Green Berets. The Green Berets as a whole are loyal Americans and dedicated soldiers, but not big on the gentle emotions. And that's my point, Lotus. I'm not hung up on that dream of love like you are. But I don't think he's the man for you. He knows how to be loyal to a job or a cause, but not how to be loyal to people."

"Thank you for telling me about him, Father," Debbie said. "It makes me understand him a little bit better now."

"I didn't tell you to get you feeling sorry for the man,"

Gordon said. "I meant to warn you off him. Stay away from him, Debbie. I mean that. He'll just hurt you."

Debbie swallowed. "I know that," she said. "Believe me, if I didn't know it before I know it now. I'll stay away from him, honestly I will."

"Please do that," Gordon said as he stood up. He squeezed Debbie's hand. "Have a safe trip, Debbie. I'm sure that Ben will get Li out of there."

"I will, Father. And thanks," she said as she walked him to the door. She wouldn't get involved with Ben. Or at least she would try not to. She watched as her father drove away. She had no desire to get involved with a man like Ben, yet her body couldn't seem to keep from melting into his arms every time he came near. She would just have to stay away from him.

And how was Ben going to feel about that? she wondered as she turned back to her ironing. He was a ruthless man, determined to get his own way. And she was just as determined that he not have his way with her. . . .

Debbie got out of the cab and struggled to carry her heavy suitcase to the ticket window. She, Jim, Ben, and the other mercenary were to meet here this morning to take the flight to Tokyo where they would spend the night before flying to Hong Kong. When Debbie had protested to Jim that they could fly straight to Hong Kong, he had said that Ben wanted to have a day to ease himself and Jerry into the time change; also they could see a few of the sights in Japan. Debbie seriously doubted whether or not Ben cared about sightseeing, but she could understand his need to become accustomed to the time change before going into Vietnam.

Debbie turned around when she heard Jim calling her

name. "Hey, Debbie, wait a minute," he said as he carried his suitcases into the airport. He traded her heavy suitcase for one of his lighter ones and fell into step beside her as they made their way through the bustling airport to the ticket window. After her talk with her father, Debbie's knot of tension had disappeared and she looked and felt calm, but Jim's face revealed a mixture of excitement and nerves as he fumbled around in his wallet for his ticket. They checked in Jim's luggage and were processing Debbie when Debbie spotted Ben and another man, both dressed in conservative business suits, coming across the airport. Debbie's heart leapt to her throat and she swallowed back her sudden nervousness. She reminded herself of her father's warning. All she had to do was say no. He wouldn't force himself on her.

Since there was no line at the ticket window, Ben stepped up directly behind Debbie and set his suitcase on the floor. She stiffened and tried not to notice the tantalizing fragrance of his after-shave, or that his body was a mere foot from hers. "Hello," he said gravely as he stared into Debbie's eyes, but he could read nothing in her expression. He felt the pull toward her that he always did when he glimpsed her tall, fragile body, and it was all he could do to keep from kissing her right in the middle of the airport. He had to have her sooner or later, he thought as she turned around and spoke to the ticket agent. He really couldn't make himself care what she thought or felt. He had to possess her body at least once, to free himself of his obsession with her. His lips thinned into a grim line, a line that Debbie did not miss as she turned back around. Startled by his intense expression, she stumbled backward into a large college student and had to apologize for stepping on his sandaled toes.

Debbie watched as Ben and his companion stepped up

to the ticket window and handed in their bags. "George Hirohito and Tom Wang," Ben said as he got out his wallet. Debbie turned her head quickly and tried not to look surprised when Ben pulled out a book of traveler's checks made out to George Hirohito and signed one. She walked to their terminal and sat down beside Jim on one of the plastic chairs. "Ben's traveling under another name," she said under her breath. "And so's the other one."

Jim's eyebrows shot upward. "I didn't know he had tangled with the authorities over there."

"I haven't," Ben said quietly as he sat down beside Debbie. This close, she could feel the warmth coming from his body, and she unconsciously leaned closer to Jim to take herself away from the threat he represented. "I always travel under an alias. I don't want anyone ever questioning why a vintner would make three or four trips to the Orient every year. Jim, Debbie, I'd like you to meet Jerry Chan. He's going to be my interpreter on this trip."

*"Anh khoe khong?"* Debbie asked.

*"Thua khoe,"* Jerry replied before he switched to English. "I really can speak it, honestly. My mother was Vietnamese. And I'd like to compliment you on your accent. You sound like a native."

"Why, thank you," Debbie said, trying to mask her surprise at Jerry Chan. She was expecting another tough, aloof mercenary like Ben, but Jerry was an older man who was quite plump and who smiled readily.

Ben sat quietly while Jim, Debbie, and Jerry made small talk. Their flight was called in a few minutes, and Debbie was quick to sit down next to Jim, leaving Ben and Jerry to take the seats that were across the aisle. She tried to ignore the sardonic smile Ben sent her way before he took a book out of his pocket and opened it. He knew she was avoiding him and he thought it was funny! As she remembered her father's warning, Debbie shivered at Ben's supreme confidence in his ability to seduce her before their rescue was over. She turned her head away and buckled her seatbelt before she got out a book of her own.

The flight to Tokyo was long and uneventful. For most of the trip, Debbie managed to ignore Ben and read a couple of exciting mysteries, occasionally relieving the stiffness of her legs with a walk up and down the aisle. Jim appeared to be reading, but Debbie could sense that his mind was far from the printed page. She would have to think of ways to distract him in Hong Kong to keep him from worrying while Ben and Jerry were in Vietnam. Across the aisle, Ben and Jerry alternated periods of reading with quiet, intense conversation, and she wondered if they were talking about the rescue. According to what Ben had told Jim, they planned to sail down the Gulf of Tonkin and land on the coast of what used to be North Vietnam. They would hike into the village where Li had been heard from last, and bring her back to the coast. Debbie was not aware of the particular details of the mission, and she figured that Ben might have felt it was better if she didn't.

It was afternoon in Tokyo, and there were still several hours of sunlight left when the plane finally landed. Debbie watched and was not surprised to see Ben open a passport under the name of "George Hirohito" with Ben's picture on it. Jerry also had a fake passport, and Debbie would have loved to have known where they had the passports made up. As they went through customs, Debbie wondered where the special clothes and equipment Ben and Jerry would need were, since they appeared to have only the clothes that a businessman would need. And did they intend to carry a gun? Surely they would need one.

Debbie reclaimed her luggage and fell into step beside Ben. "Won't you need some special things to take in with you?" she asked.

Ben's eyes narrowed. "Been peeking while we went through customs?"

"Yes, as a matter-of-fact I did," Debbie replied. "I admit to being curious. Will you need special clothes to wear and a gun or something?"

"No, I'm going to take in George's American Express card and wear a business suit. Come on, Debbie! Do you honestly think I would bring Vietnamese peasant clothing and a .38 through customs? They would be down on me in no time flat!"

"So where do you get the stuff you need?" Debbie asked.

"Hong Kong," Ben replied as he moved away from her, unwilling to answer any more questions. Well, that was one way to get rid of him! Just ask him about his work.

Jim caught up with Debbie and together they stepped out of the airport terminal onto the busy sidewalk, and Ben hailed a taxi that would take them to their hotel in the middle of downtown. Debbie found herself wedged in between Ben and Jim with not an inch between them, and Ben's warmth seared her as it had in the airport in San Francisco. She tried to ignore the reaction that rippled through her body but was unable to do so. So she turned her attention away from Ben and hoped that he couldn't feel the quickening beat of her heart.

As the taxi pulled away from the airport, Debbie looked out the window and stared out at the modern city that bustled around them. "You know, except for the signs being in Japanese and everybody being Oriental, this could be Los Angeles," she commented.

"All large cities are alike," Ben murmured.

"I disagree," Jim said. "Saigon was different."

Ben thought a moment. "You're right," he said. "But Saigon was a third-world city then. God knows what it's like now."

"The last time I saw the place, it was a living hell," Jim said.

"The whole country became a living hell when the Communists took over," Ben said bitterly. Taken by surprise by his bitterness, Debbie glanced over at Ben, but could not tell by his expression what he was thinking.

"I don't see how it could have gotten much worse," Jerry Chan said. "It was pitiful when we were stationed there."

Ben said nothing and Debbie returned her attention to the city they were passing through. It was a lot like Los Angeles, large and flat and sprawling, with a forest of high-rise office buildings and hotels filling the downtown area. Being used to the Oriental culture in San Francisco, Debbie felt right at home in this large, modern city. She pointed out the strange X-shaped frames on the sides of the buildings and Ben said that they were put there to reinforce the buildings in case of an earthquake.

Their cab pulled up in front of their modern hotel and in just a few minutes they were checked in. Tired from the long plane ride, Debbie longed to lay down across her bed for a short nap, but Jim wanted her to go and see a little of the city before they had to get ready for dinner with Ben and Jerry. Debbie drank a cup of coffee and changed her shoes, and she and Jim spent the better part of two hours wandering up and down the streets of downtown. They saw the moat that surrounded the Imperial

Palace, an island of antiquity surrounded by the rest of the city. The outside of the moat must have been the most popular place in the city to jog, for it was surrounded by dedicated joggers dressed in snappy jogging suits.

After a refreshing shower, Debbie dressed in a sleek black sheath that made the most of her slender curves, and wound her hair up on top of her head, letting little tendrils escape to trail down her long, slender neck. She put on more makeup than usual and was waiting for Jim to take her to dinner. He was a little late and she was beginning to wonder where he was when she finally heard a knock on the door. "It took you long enough," she said as she threw open the door.

"My apologies," Ben said as he stepped into her room. Dressed in a fresh sport coat and tie, he was more compelling than he had ever seemed before, and Debbie immediately sensed the danger that he represented to her. "And here I thought you were trying to avoid me." He grinned wickedly at Debbie's startled reaction.

"I thought you were Jim," she said. She picked up her purse and started toward the door. "We better get on down to the restaurant. It's getting late."

Ben smiled faintly, but made no move to step away from the door. "What's the matter, Lotus, afraid to be alone with me?" he asked. "Still feel it, don't you?"

Debbie didn't pretend not to understand. "Yes, I still feel it, Ben, but I'm not going to give in to it. Now, let's go eat."

"Not before I get my appetizer," Ben said as he reached out and grasped Debbie by the shoulders. "I've wanted to kiss you for the last month."

Debbie's protest was muffled as Ben's lips descended to hers. He held the back of her head firmly as he teased and tantalized her mouth, drawing from its sweetness before he plundered her depths. Willing herself not to respond, Debbie clenched her fists at her side, fighting the longing to raise her arms and bury her fingers in the thick black hair at his nape. She could not help it, however, when her lips softened and responded to the tenderness and the passion of Ben's sensual caress. He did not move his hands from her head and her shoulder, he did not press their bodies closer together, but he made love to her with his lips and his tongue for long moments before he pulled back, his breathing as ragged as hers. He glanced down at her clenched fists and his face twisted into a frown. "I don't know why you're being so hardheaded," he snapped. "It could be good between us, you know."

"I've tried to explain my objections, but you're apparently totally incapable of understanding them," Debbie shot back. "Let's go." She stepped out the door of the room.

"Debbie." Debbie turned back with what she hoped was a haughty expression on her face. "Your lipstick is smeared."

Debbie swore quietly as she repaired her makeup and hoped that she didn't look quite so thoroughly kissed by the time she got down to the dining room. To her surprise, Ben offered her his arm. Debbie didn't realize what a handsome couple they were as they walked across the floor and sat down at the table with Jerry and Jim. "Thanks for meeting Debbie for me, Ben," Jim said, a smile on his face as he turned to Debbie. "Jerry and I were ready early and wanted to come down here and have a drink before dinner."

So that was why Jim was so relaxed. Ben pulled out a chair for Debbie. This was the first time all day Jim had unwound even a little. "Don't drink too much tonight," she cautioned him, although she was smiling when she said it. "I wouldn't want to have to put you to bed like I did that time before."

Ben glanced over at her with a disapproving expression as Jim broke into laughter. "No chance of that tonight, Debbie! I don't want a hangover for the flight tomorrow." He turned to Ben and Jerry. "I got falling down drunk the day I got my first letter from Li after almost seven years of not hearing from her. I took Debbie and her ex-husband out to celebrate, and I must have gone through two bottles of champagne by myself. I was a happy man that day."

Ben smiled sardonically but Jerry laughed out loud. "Seven years! That's an awful long time to go without even hearing from her."

"I didn't know where she was for six of those years," Jim admitted. Jerry opened his mouth to ask another question, but the waiter brought menus, and he turned his attention to that.

Debbie had planned to order a traditional Japanese meal, but she gasped when she read the prices. Even the simplest meal was over fifty dollars in American money. Biting her lip, she glanced over the Chinese menu before raising her head to see if the others had come to the same conclusion she had. "Well, is it going to be Chinese tonight?" she asked.

"I guess it better be," Ben said as he closed his menu. "Jerry, Debbie, we'll defer to your superior knowledge of Chinese cuisine."

After a little good-natured wrangling, Debbie and Jerry selected several Chinese dishes that the four of them could share. After the waiter took their order, Jerry turned back to Jim. "How long has it been since you've seen your fiancée?"

"Ten years and one month," Jim said. "I was in Saigon when it fell. We were within a few minutes of getting to the airport when the Communists attacked her neighborhood and put her on a truck."

"I'm surprised they didn't kill you," Ben said.

"They thought they had," Jim admitted. "They shot me in the shoulder. Li was smart enough to pretend I was dead. She screamed and cried over me for a minute while she whispered for me to get out and go to Debbie. She managed to save my life that day."

"Sounds like quite a lady," Jerry commented. Debbie glanced at Ben, who had a bored expression on his face, before she looked over at Jerry, whose face shone with lively interest. Debbie had expected Jerry to be cut out of the same mold as Ben, cold and uncaring, and his warm, smiling interest continued to surprise her. "So how did you find out that she was alive?" Jerry asked.

The waiter brought glasses of water and a pot of tea. Debbie poured them each a small cup of tea and sipped a little from hers. "Debbie has some Vietnamese friends who are in contact with the underground over there," Jim said. "They found her up north in a work camp and smuggled a letter in to her and another one back out to me."

Jerry sipped his tea thoughtfully. "I'm surprised she hasn't gotten out sooner. Why didn't she get on a boat in 1979? I know three families who got out then."

"She tried," Jim said. "But remember, she was a general's daughter and she was watched. They caught her and threw her into prison for four months before they sent her back to the work farm. I finally saved up enough last year to send her gold coins to bribe her way out, but I guess that didn't work either."

"So we're your last resort," Ben said as he lit a cigarette.

"Something like that," Jim admitted. "If this fails for some reason, I don't know what I'll do next."

"Call it quits?" Ben asked softly.

"Like hell," Jim said quietly. "I'll spend the rest of my life trying to find her and get her out, if that's what it takes." He fingered the dragon ring on his little finger. "I'm going to put this on her finger again."

Jerry whistled under his breath. "You sure must love her," he said.

"You bet I do," Jim said. "She's the other half of me."

At that moment the waiter brought their steaming plates of food and placed them on the table. As they passed around the delectable Chinese dishes, Debbie glanced over at Ben, wondering what he thought of Jim's deep love for Li. Had anything Jim said impressed Ben?

As they shared the delicious meal, Jerry plied Jim with questions about Li and their ill-fated romance. Jim told Jerry how he and Li had met when he was a journalist in Vietnam and she was just seventeen, how her father had at first violently disapproved of her budding romance with an American, how, after he and Li had become serious, her father had insisted she spend a year in school in America, and of their last few months together in Saigon before it fell. Jim's eyes shone with love as he spoke. Only a fool would deny the existence of love, Debbie thought.

Jerry in turn told them about his wife and young son in Los Angeles, and he too seemed deeply in love. A wistful expression crossed Debbie's face as she wondered why she and Kevin couldn't have shared a love like that.

Ben saw that expression and his lips tightened just a fraction. She was taking it all in. She was wishing she had what those two jokers were sitting there professing to. He bet Jerry wasn't going to tell her about that hot little number in the barrio that he messed with twice a week, and you couldn't convince him that Jim had lived the life of a monk for the last ten years! Ben considered for a moment feeding Debbie some of that romantic garbage himself, if it would make him welcome in her arms, but dismissed the idea. He might be ruthless, but he was honest. Besides, if he tried to tell her of his undying love, he would probably laugh in her face.

Jim picked up the tab for dinner and invited them all into the bar for a drink. Jerry immediately accepted and Debbie glanced over at Ben. The flight and the long day were beginning to catch up with her, and she had no desire to stay awake any longer, but neither did she want Ben to escort her up to her room. The decision was taken out of her hands when Ben put his arm around her waist and started to guide her to the door. "You two clowns can close the bar if you want to," he said. "Debbie looks like she's about to go to sleep here in the restaurant, and I'm feeling a little tired myself. See you in the morning."

Reluctantly, Debbie let herself be escorted from the restaurant. "Presumptuous, aren't you?" she asked. "What if I had wanted to stay?"

Ben immediately dropped her arm. "Fine, go back and listen to Vietnam war stories all night," he said. "That's what they're going to do, you know. Sit there and fight the war all over again. Jerry did two tours over there and he can spin tales all night."

Ben grinned when Debbie continued toward the elevator. "What's the matter, don't you want to fight the battle of Hamburger Hill again?" he teased.

"No, thanks," Debbie said as they stepped onto the elevator. They rode in silence as the elevator took them to Debbie's floor. "Although I didn't mind listening to them this evening. Jim needs to talk about Li some-times." She stepped off the elevator and got out her room key. "His devotion to her is something else, isn't it?"

"It sounds like a pile of baloney to me," Ben said.

"Damn it, Ben, how can you say that?" Debbie asked, so caught up in the argument that she didn't notice as he followed her into her room. "You sat there and heard him. You sat there and heard Jerry, too, for that matter. Now how can you insist that there's no such thing as an enduring love?"

"Why don't you ask Jerry's girl friend just how de-voted he is to his wife?" Ben scoffed as he paced the floor with his hands in his pockets.

Debbie shrugged. "A lot of seemingly devoted men have women on the side," she said softly. "I know that, but there are others that don't."

"And do you really think your friend, Jim, has been totally without women for the last ten years?" Ben asked. "From the looks of the guy, he's no wimp."

Debbie arched her eyebrow at Ben. "As to the particu-lars of Jim's sex life for the last ten years, I don't know, and I don't ask. But I think he's been loyal to Li."

"And why do you think that?"

"Because at one time I was hurting and lonely and in need of some masculine affection, and Jim could have had me if he'd wanted to," Debbie said softly. "But he didn't. He stayed loyal to Li."

Ben stared over at Debbie. "Then he's capable of more devotion than I would be," he admitted as he reached out and loosened the hair coiled around her head. "Because if you offered yourself to me, Debbie, I couldn't have turned away." He unwound the hair from its tight knot and ran his fingers through it as it cascaded down her neck. "Kiss me, Debbie," he said as his lips met hers in a wild explosion of passion.

Touched by Ben's admission, Debbie let herself go in his embrace, for the first time meeting his passion without holding back, letting him feel the depth of emotion that she was capable of. Her lips opening to his, Debbie drank in the hard masculinity of Ben's mouth as his tongue raked the perimeters of her teeth before probing deeper. Ben placed his hands on her shoulders and gently pushed her down onto the bed. Debbie's hands found and stroked the coarseness of the thick hair at his nape as his hands ran down the sloping softness of her shoulders and onto the softness of her breasts, where his finger found one tip and stroked it into a knot of desire.

Moaning, Debbie was not even aware that she had thrust herself closer to his roaming fingers, but Ben was aware of the delightful willingness of her body to touch and be touched. He moved his lips away from hers, but when she would have protested he proceeded to forge a trail down the side of her face, planting warm, moist kisses that drew shivers of desire from her. "Oh, Ben," she gasped as her fingers found the hard muscles of his shoulders. "I can't touch you through this jacket."

Ben sat up and tore off the jacket and tie. "The better to touch me with?" he asked as he picked up Debbie's hand and kissed each of her carefully manicured fingers before he lowered his gaze to her bodice. "And the better to see you with," he said as his fingers slowly unbuttoned the front of her dress. Debbie shivered as Ben found the front closure of her bra and unfastened the tiny hook, baring her small, high breasts to his gaze. "Ah, beautiful," he said as he lowered his head and touched one of her breasts with the tip of his tongue.

Debbie arched her breast to his passionate touch as she

ran her hands down Ben's shirt-covered torso. Her fingers found one of his flat male nipples under the shirt and she tormented it with her finger until it was hard to the touch. She was on fire for Ben. She had never desired a man so much—not even Kevin. And instinctively she knew that it was the same way for Ben. No matter how many women he had desired and taken in the past, he had never shared this kind of passion with any of them. "You're wrong, you know," she said as Ben's lips found and tormented her other breast.

"I'm wrong about what?" Ben asked as he drew a circle around her breast with his tongue.

"You would be capable of Jim's kind of devotion with the right woman," she said softly. "You just don't know it."

"Damn it, are we back to that?" Ben said and sighed as he sat up. "Do you *have* to justify sex between a man and a woman with all that romantic hogwash? Can't we just go to bed?" Impatiently, he pulled on his coat and slung his tie around his neck.

"It's not hogwash!" Debbie shouted as she sat up and tried to pull the dangling ends of her bra together. "It's real and it's important!"

Ben tipped her head up so that he was looking into her eyes. "It's lust, Debbie, pure and simple. That's all it is between you and me, and that's all it is between any other man and woman, even your friends. I told you that I wasn't capable of the kind of devotion that you think your friend Jim has shown to his precious Li. What I didn't bother to tell you is that I wouldn't even try to be devoted like that. It's a waste." He let go of Debbie and walked out the door.

Debbie stared at the closing door, her cheeks burning with shame as she recalled how she had practically thrown herself at Ben. How could she have been so uninhibited, with a man who only wanted to possess her body? Her father's words came back to her and she supressed a slight shiver. Ben was a user, and he had come close to using her tonight. She had been a fool for even thinking that Ben would even be capable of feeling more for her than the simple lust he thought was all they needed. But then, why was she so surprised? She certainly felt enough lust for him!

When he got back to his room, Ben sat down on the edge of his bed and lit another cigarette. *Naive little fool,* he thought as he inhaled deeply on the cigarette and let the smoke fill his lungs. Just as they were starting to get somewhere, she had to start prattling about love and devotion. Why couldn't she just accept good sex for what it was and stop trying to make something more out of it?

But he still wanted her. Ben cursed the basic honesty that had kept him from lying to her and taking her tonight. But no. He would wait until she was able to admit that it was desire alone, pure physical pleasure between a man and a woman that they shared, before he would take her to bed. He was in no hurry. She could think about it while he was in Vietnam, and then he would have a good two or three weeks back in Hong Kong, while her friends made their arrangments, to bring her around to his way of thinking. He could feel the desire she had for him, and she wouldn't be able to fight it forever.

## CHAPTER FIVE

"Jim, I can't see the harbor from here," Debbie complained as she leaned over him and tried to peer out the window. The plane was about to land in the Kowloon airport, and Debbie found herself more excited than she had been since the trip had begun.

"Look, by all means, don't let me get in your way," Jim said as he rubbed his bloodshot eyes.

Debbie peered down at the blue harbor for a minute before she sat back down. She glanced across the aisle at Jerry, careful not to look at Ben. "Did you two close the bar?" she asked.

Jim nodded. "I didn't get drunk, if that's what you're thinking," he said. "We did a lot more talking than we did drinking." Jim lowered his voice. "Jerry Chan's an all-right guy. Not like that friend of yours."

Debbie's head shot up. "Who said he was my friend?" she asked sardonically.

"Well, he did walk out of the restaurant with his arm around your waist," Jim teased.

"Believe me, after last night that joker's the last man I'd claim as a friend!" Debbie hissed.

Jim's teasing smile faded. "What happened, Debbie? Did he try something? Do you want me to talk to him?"

Debbie's cheeks reddened. How could she tell Jim that

Ben had pulled away from her, and not the other way around? "No, don't try to talk to him," she said. "He didn't try anything, at least not what you're thinking. I just don't like him, that's all."

She didn't like him, but she would like to go to bed with him, she thought as the jet circled for the landing. Ben was right about the feelings they shared. It was all just physical desire between her and Ben. Debbie was sure of that, but she had in no way changed her mind about becoming Ben's mistress. Even if the sex between them was good, she would only be hurt in the long run. She needed more in her life than simple physical satisfaction. She needed to be loved, and Ben could never provide her with that.

They went through customs for the second time in two days, and Debbie noticed that Ben and Jerry were careful to travel under their aliases. Debbie stared out the window of the taxi at the distinctively Chinese architecture of the houses and shops. The city was nothing like Los Angeles, she thought as she caught another glimpse of the harbor. And to think that she was going to have a month or more to explore it! For the first time she was glad that Ben had insisted she come with them on the trip.

They checked into the hotel and freshened up, then Debbie and Jim called the real estate agent who had located an apartment for them. She agreed to pick them up and take them to the apartment later that afternoon. As Debbie left her hotel room to meet Jim, she spotted Ben and Jerry at the end of the hall, dressed in faded peasant clothing and looking totally disreputable. They were leaving by the fire well, and Debbie correctly surmised that Ben and Jerry did not want anyone to associate the two scruffy peasants with the well-dressed businessmen who had checked in just a little while ago. Jerry had said earlier that he and Ben were going to get their provisions for the trip this afternoon, and Debbie guessed that was where they were going. For the first time, real fear trickled down her back, fear both for Li and for the men who were trying to save her. So many things could go wrong! Shutting her mind to the fear she felt, Debbie stepped into the elevator and let the door shut behind her.

The smiling real estate agent greeted them in the lobby and drove them in her small car to an old Victorian mansion that had been divided into apartments. The apartment the agent showed them had two spacious bedrooms and was decorated in a combination of charming old wicker furniture and Oriental pieces, and Debbie immediately fell in love with the quaint place. They paid her a deposit and said they would move in tomorrow.

It was late in the afternoon by the time Jim and Debbie trudged back to the hotel. Ben had left a message at the desk for Jim to call him as soon as they arrived, so Jim used a house phone and dialed Ben's room. In a minute he turned around to Debbie. "Ben wants us to meet them in the lobby in an hour for dinner."

Debbie made a face. "You go ahead and meet them," she said. "I'm tired." She didn't want to spend another evening with Ben Sako. He had shown her a taste of paradise last night before he had turned away from her. And she wasn't sure what she resented most—his passionate caresses or the fact that he had rejected her when she had mentioned devotion.

Jim turned from the telephone and covered the mouthpiece. "He says you need to be there. This is more of a business meeting than a night on the town. He's going over everyone's part in this for the last time."

Debbie shrugged as Jim uncovered the mouthpiece. "Tell his lord and master I'll be there."

Jim said something into the speaker, paused a minute, and laughed. "Ben says that the lord and master expects you to be on time. He has reservations on a floating restaurant."

Debbie stuck out her tongue at Jim as she punched the button for the elevator. She showered and washed and dried her hair, deciding tonight to let it fall free to her waist. She dressed in a deceptively demure designer dress and left the room ten minutes early, lest Ben decide to escort her to dinner again.

She needn't have worried. The men were waiting for her when she arrived, and together the foursome made their way down the crowded sidewalk and across several bustling streets to the ferry that would take them over to the island of Hong Kong. Debbie stared out at the harbor at the junks floating in the sunset, each junk housing one or more families. "It's so beautiful and yet they're so poor," she said to no one in particular as a small child held her hand out to Debbie for a coin.

"No, don't give her money," Ben said sharply as Debbie reached for her purse. He waved the ragged child away.

"Why not, Ben?" Debbie demanded angrily. "These people are so poor, and I wouldn't have missed the coin."

"Because we'd be mobbed, that's why," he said as he took her arm. "Don't feel too sorry for them, Lotus. They have a lot more than many people have."

"No, they don't!" Debbie protested. "They're horribly poor. They must not make any money at all."

"You can't always measure what a man has by his possessions," Ben said. Debbie thought that Ben was trying to tell her something, but she wasn't sure just what.

A small motorized ferry took them from mainland Kowloon to the island of Hong Kong. They walked down the busy dock to one of the floating restaurants in the harbor. Debbie forgot all about the poverty on the junks, her antagonism with Ben, and her worry about the success of their mission as she gazed out at the hauntingly beautiful Hong Kong harbor as the sun set on it. She was so caught up in the spell of the harbor that Jim had to speak to her twice to tell her that Ben had taken the liberty of ordering a specially prepared Peking Duck for them to share. Debbie nodded absently and stared out at the harbor, letting the men's conversation drift over her as they waited for their meal.

Later, Ben got out a notebook and tore off several sheets of paper for Jim and Debbie. "I want you to write down what I want you to have done by the time we get back with Li," he told Debbie. "And I'm also going to tell you and Jim our exact plans for this mission, which I do not want you to write down, but to remember. If something happens and we don't get back in three or four months, you need to have a general idea of what our plans were so you can put your friends in the underground to work finding us. That is, if we're alive to find." Debbie gasped softly and Jim winced.

The waiter brought a pot of tea and Debbie poured them each a cup. "Now listen carefully. Tomorrow morning we're sailing down through the Gulf of Tonkin to the coast of North Vietnam. The owner of the boat is going to dock the boat and stay in the house of a member of the underground until we get back with Li. Jerry and I are going to hike through the forest to Hai Thong and try to stay out of the way of the Communists. Jim, do you have that letter written to Li ready yet?"

Jim pulled a piece of paper out of his pocket and

handed it to Ben along with a frayed snapshot. "Here's a picture of her. It was taken just before we were separated."

Ben studied the picture carefully and handed the picture to Jerry, who stared at it thoughtfully. "This is all well and good, but she probably doesn't look like this anymore," Jerry said. "Ten years of the life she's led is bound to have taken its toll. You don't look like that anymore either." He handed the picture back to Jim.

Ben took the picture back from Jim and studied Li's smiling face. "The bones don't change," he said to Jim as he memorized Li's face in the picture. "She probably hasn't changed all that much."

"It wouldn't matter to me if she has," Jim said. "I love that woman, and I don't care if she comes out of there looking like an old hag, as long as she comes out." Ben handed the picture back to Jim.

"What are you going to do if she's not there?" Debbie asked softly.

"If anybody has any idea where she's gone, we'll try to track her down," Ben said. "There's usually somebody willing to talk in a situation like that."

"And if there isn't anyone?" Jim asked tensely.

"We'll persuade them," Ben said as he smiled just a little bit cruelly. Debbie was sure that he and Jerry would not hesitate to apply a little painful "persuasion" if a bribe didn't work, and she shivered a little in spite of the warmth of the night.

"Anyway, we track her down and we bring her out if she wants to come," Ben continued. "I'm not bringing her out if she prefers to stay," he added firmly to Jim.

Jim looked Ben straight in the eye. "That's no problem. She'll want to come with you."

"Debbie, you and Jim need to visit the American consulate and get an application for an immigrant visa and a form for a medical exam. Line up some official who will perform a marriage on short notice, and get Li all those things women think they can't live without. She'll probably be coming out with the clothes on her back. We'll bring her back to the coast and sail back up the Gulf. We'll see you in anywhere from one to three months, depending on how long it takes us to find her." He looked around at the three solemn faces at the table. "Everybody understand?"

They all nodded. "We'll drink a toast to our success when we get back," Ben said, smiling faintly. "Let's go back to the hotel."

They walked down the crowded dock and got on the ferry that would take them back to Kowloon. The warmth of the night surrounded Debbie, and the salty, tangy, fishy odor of the harbor wafted over her. Her lips curved into a slight smile. Ben had been overconfident of his powers of persuasion. He was leaving tomorrow, and he was no closer to being her lover than he had been back in San Francisco. In fact, after last night, she was more determined than ever to keep her distance from him.

The ferry docked on the Kowloon side of the harbor. They stepped off the boat and the four of them started to weave their way across a busy street that would lead them back to the hotel, she and Jerry leading the way and Jim and Ben talking earnestly behind them.

Suddenly, Debbie was conscious of the sound of a car bearing down on them, a woman's muffled scream, and the imprint of two strong hands as they grabbed her and pushed her out of the way and flat down on the sidewalk. Her mind registered the sound of an impact of some sort, and Debbie gasped as her unprotected palms and knees made contact with the sidewalk. She lay still a moment, face down where she had fallen, as Ben lifted his body from hers. "Debbie, are you all right?" he demanded harshly. "No, don't move her! She might have a fracture and that would just make it worse."

Debbie pushed herself up and stared around groggily. "I think I'm all right," she said. "What on earth happened?"

"A car came bearing down on you and Jerry," Ben said. "You nearly got hit. Here, let me take a look at those hands and knees."

Debbie extended her hands and let Ben look at them. When he had let them go, he pulled her torn pantyhose to one side and gently probed the scraped flesh of her knees. "You'll be all right in a day or two," he said as Jim stepped up to them.

"We have a problem," Jim said. "The car hit Jerry and he's hurt pretty badly."

Ben muttered a curse under his breath and helped Debbie to her feet. They made their way through the thickening crowd to where Jerry lay in the middle of the street, his face contorted with pain. "It's my legs," he said in an agonized whisper. "I think they're both broken."

The next couple of hours were a blur to Debbie. A policeman arrived on the scene, followed shortly by an ambulance, which took Jerry to the nearest hospital. Ben hailed a taxi and the three of them followed the ambulance to the hospital. Debbie and Jim stood in the hall of what she supposed was the emergency room and waited while Ben talked to the doctor in passable but accented Chinese. The doctor was saying that he wasn't sure of any other injuries, but that he was certain that both of Jerry's legs were fractured. Jim swore under his breath and Debbie hung her head in misery. To have come this far and to have it fall through because of a brutal accident! She swallowed a lump in her throat and willed herself not to cry.

The doctor returned to Jerry and a sister handed Ben a couple of forms in Chinese. "Come over here, one of you," Ben said as he sat down on the beat-up old rattan couch in the waiting room. "I can't read Chinese."

Debbie stepped into the waiting room and took the paper and a pencil from Ben. Together they filled it out as best they could, using Jerry's alias but otherwise sticking to the facts. They left blanks in the spaces of which they had no knowledge, such as any medications that Jerry might be taking, and told the sister she would have to get those facts from him the next day. Debbie sat back down on the couch in the waiting room, staring into space while Ben stood at the window and smoked a cigarette.

The doctor returned an hour later. They had x-rayed Jerry and there were no internal injuries, but both of his legs had suffered fractures from the impact of the car's bumper. Jerry was being taken to a room, and they could see him in a few minutes. They waited until the sisters had settled Jerry into his room before they trooped in and shut the door.

Jerry lay back on the pillows, both his legs encased in thick plaster casts. "I'm sorry about this," he said thickly, his speech impaired by the pain-killing drugs he had been given.

"Better here than in Nam," Ben said.

Jerry turned pain-filled eyes to Debbie's stricken face and Jim's unreadable one. "The doctor said it will be several months before I can walk without crutches," he said.

Since there was really nothing they could do for Jerry, Jim and Debbie left and waited out in the hall while Ben talked to Jerry for a few more minutes before he too left Jerry to rest.

The three of them walked out of the hospital into the warm, muggy night. "We'll refund your money and absorb the airline tickets as our loss," Ben said to Jim. "We can try again next summer."

Debbie grasped Jim by the arm. "I'm so sorry," she said as her eyes filled with tears. "I had so hoped that they would make it."

"There will be no need to refund the money for the rescue," Jim said calmly. "Sako, you're going on tomorrow as planned."

Ben stopped walking. "What was that, Anderson?" he asked quietly.

"I said that there was no need to refund the money," Jim said. "You can go into Vietnam tomorrow after Li."

"No way in hell," Ben said. "I'm not going in there without Jerry. Look, Jim, I'm sorry and we'll plan to go back in when—"

"Can it, Sako," Jim said harshly. "We've already come this far, and you can't tell me you really needed him to get Li out of there. He couldn't have helped you do a damn thing. You're going on alone, Sako. You promised you would see the job through."

"No, I promised that *we* would see the job through. I wasn't taking him along for the physical help!" Ben snapped. "I was taking him along as an interpreter. I don't speak very good Vietnamese, and I can't read it at all. I take him on all my Vietnamese missions." He took Debbie by the arm and started down the street. "He's crazy if he thinks I'm going in there alone."

Several quick angry strides caught Jim up with them. "Li speaks English," he argued. "You wouldn't need to speak Vietnamese to her."

"And will the Communist soldiers who might detain me speak English to me? And how about the peasants at the roadside stands where I plan to buy food? And how about the people I may have to question to find Li? Are they all going to speak English to me? I'm sorry, but the mission is out of the question until next summer."

Jim walked quietly for a few minutes, deep in thought. Debbie wondered what was going through his mind as they trudged nearer and nearer to their hotel. Jim said nothing more as they walked up the steps and went inside, but as soon as they were in the lobby, Jim spoke. "I want to talk to you both," he said.

"Jim, I'm tired," Debbie said. "In the morning."

"Now," Jim said harshly. In all the years she had known him, Debbie had never heard that kind of desperation in his voice. They silently went to his room. Debbie sighed as she entered and sat down on the edge of the bed. Ben followed her in and stood by the window. Jim shut the door behind him and sat down on the only chair in the room. His eyes burned in his face, and Debbie compared his expression to those she had seen on the faces of religious fanatics.

If Ben recognized the desperation on Jim's face, he gave no sign of it. "I don't know what good talking to us is going to do," he said as he lit a cigarette. "Jerry's hurt and that's that. We'll refund your money and try again next summer."

"The *hell* you will!" Jim thundered suddenly. "Damn it, Li's not living in that Communist hellhole for another year. Find another mercenary who speaks Vietnamese," Jim said.

"Sure. Of course, I know literally hundreds of mercenaries who live here in Hong Kong, are fluent in Vietnamese, and who can be ready to sail for North Vietnam by morning. Anderson, come on! Jerry is the only mercenary I know of who fills those conditions, and he's out of commission."

Jim looked slowly from Ben to Debbie. "So who said your interpreter had to be a mercenary?" he asked slowly.

Debbie started to shake her head back and forth. "If you're thinking what I think you're thinking, forget it, Jim. I can't go in there with him."

"Why not?" Jim demanded. "You speak it like a native, and Sako as much as admitted that all he needed was an interpreter."

"Why not?" Ben asked sardonically. "Mostly because I say why not, that's why. There is no way I'm taking a woman on that kind of mission with me."

"You will if I say you will," Jim said harshly, his eyes glittering as he looked from Ben to Debbie. "I would go in myself, gladly, if I wasn't so damned Caucasian. But I am, and I would be dead in forty-eight hours. The two of you could pull it off, and by God, you're going to."

"Don't you tell me what I'm going to do or not do!" Ben said as he started across the room.

"And what gives you the right to demand that I put my life in danger?" Debbie demanded as she too stood up. "I could get killed in there. But that doesn't matter to you, does it?"

"Of course it matters," Jim said. "And if it were any other person on the face of this earth, even my own mother, I wouldn't ask it. But this is *Li*, Debbie! I have to get her out of there, and you can help him do it. Besides, don't you think she would do the same for you?"

Debbie sat down on the side of the bed and held her head in her hands. "Moral blackmail isn't fair, Jim," she said, her hands muffling her voice.

"I'm beyond being fair," Jim admitted. "And she would have done it for you. You know she would."

Debbie remembered Li and nodded her head. "I know that."

"Haven't you forgotten somebody, Anderson?" Ben asked quietly. "You can make Debbie feel guilty all night if you want to, but I'm not susceptible to all this garbage about sentiment and loyalty. And, no, don't bother to offer me any more money," he continued. "That won't change my mind either."

"Then how about a little out-and-out blackmail?" Jim asked softly. "I bet the Hong Kong authorities would sure wonder why you and Jerry are traveling under false passports that you got God knows where, wouldn't they?" Jim pointed toward the telephone. "You walk out on this project, and I'll be on the phone before you can get back to your room. Even if you get away, your buddy, Jerry, is going to be in deep trouble."

"You bastard," Ben said through clenched teeth. But he was whipped and he knew it. He had enjoyed too many years of coming and going without suspicion to land himself in the Hong Kong police department's computer terminal, his face and his fingerprints permanently on record. And even if he did get away in time, he owed it to Jerry not to blow his cover. He would have to take Debbie and just hope to God she didn't get hurt. "All right, you bastard, you have me over a barrel. I'll take her, and I'll try not to let her get killed on this trip. But let me tell you something, Anderson. If anything does happen to her, and it very well could, you can have the privilege of telling her father that she's dead, and that you're the one responsible."

Debbie raised frightened eyes to Ben. "You mean you're really going to take me?"

"Your so-called friend here hasn't left me much choice," Ben said as he glared at Jim.

Jim stared at them both calmly. "Debbie, I realize that I'm putting you into danger, and I'm sorry. You know how much I care for you. But Li has waited long enough. You have to go in there and try. She's your friend, too."

Debbie strode past Jim and opened the door. "Thanks a lot, Jim," she said as she left the room.

Ben followed her out in the hall and slammed the door behind him before he closed his hand around her arm. "Why in the hell did you say yes?" he demanded. "If you had said no, he couldn't have blackmailed me."

Debbie shook her head back and forth. "If I had said no, he would have blackmailed you anyway," she said. "Ben, in all the years I've known him, I've never seen him like this. He's beyond reason. You saw the look in his eyes. I think he's a little crazy right now."

"I think he's a whole lot crazy to think of sending you in with me," Ben said. "I'd rather go alone."

"Fine! I'd rather you went alone too!" Debbie snapped as Ben unlocked the door of his room and pushed her inside. "The idea of traipsing around in a Communist country doesn't exactly turn me on. In fact, why *don't* you go on without me?"

Ben rummaged around in a sack on the bed and pulled out a shirt and threw it toward Debbie. "Here, put this on and let's see if you can pass as a boy," he said.

"But why can't you go in without me?" Debbie wailed as she put on the shirt.

"Because I can't speak Vietnamese, damn it!" Ben snapped. He glared at Debbie in the shirt. "You're too damned feminine to go as a boy," he said. "I'll have to go out and find some women's clothes for you. Now, get to your room and try to get some sleep. I'll bring you the clothes in the morning."

Debbie returned to her room and got ready for bed, but sleep was a long time coming. Cold fear enveloped her as she realized that she was committed to entering a Communist country illegally and smuggling out one of its citizens. She could refuse to go, of course, but if she did, Ben would have to go alone or risk being turned over to the authorities by Jim. Debbie believed him when he said that he couldn't speak Vietnamese, and she realized that without her, his chances of finding Li were nil. So, if she wanted Ben to bring Li out of there, she had no choice but to go along and help him.

A frisson of fear trembled down her back as she remembered the way she and Ben set each other on fire. She knew the Communists were not her only danger in Vietnam.

## CHAPTER SIX

Debbie shut her makeup case and paced nervously up and down the room. She jumped when a knock sounded on the door. Thinking it was Ben with her peasant clothes, she opened the door to greet Jim, who looked embarrassed and uncomfortable. "May I come in for a minute?" he asked.

Debbie shrugged and stepped aside so Jim could enter. "Debbie, I'm sorry for the way I acted last night," he said as he shut the door behind him. "You were right. I have no right to demand that you put yourself in that kind of danger, even for Li."

Debbie sat down on the edge of the bed. "That's all right, Jim," she said. "I understand. You're desperate to get her out of there, and we're the only two people who can do that for you at this point."

"You don't have to go in, Debbie," Jim said. "I'm sorry for what I said last night. I didn't mean to put you in that kind of position. Sako can find another mercenary."

Debbie shook her head back and forth. "No, he can't, Jim. Not here, no one he knows he can trust. And besides, he doesn't have time. The boat sails this morning. If you insist that he go, I'll have to go with him."

Jim ran his hands through his hair and took a deep

breath. "Then I'm going to rephrase my demands of last night. Debbie, I'm pleading with you to go with him, but if you say no, I'll call it all off and wait."

Debbie felt tears start to well up in her eyes. She could have denied another demand, but she couldn't refuse this anguished plea from the heart. "Jim, I'll go." She wiped her tears away. "I'll go find her."

Debbie stood up and Jim enveloped her in an equally fearful embrace. "Thank you, Debbie," he said and sniffed. "I'll be grateful to you for the rest of my life."

Debbie hugged him tightly for a moment before she pushed him away. "Now get out of here before Ben gets back," she said with a smile. "He'll back out of it if he has any idea you've changed your mind."

"God be with you, Debbie," he said as he left her room and shut the door behind it. Debbie composed herself and was waiting calmly ten minutes later when another knock sounded on the door.

"These were the best I could do on such short notice," Ben said as he tossed her a couple of strange-looking garments. "Get them on. We're due at the dock in fifteen minutes." He glanced around at Debbie's suitcases. "What are you doing with all this?"

Debbie shrugged. "I guess Jim will get them later when he checks out."

"Have you seen Romeo this morning?" Ben asked. "I had hoped he would change his mind about this ridiculous idea."

"No. But I really didn't expect to." Debbie was amazed at how easily the lie fell from her lips. She went into the bathroom and stripped down to her underwear. Ben had handed her two articles of clothing, a dresslike garment and a pair of pants that looked like pajama pants. She put on the pants first and pulled the dress on

103

over them. The pants and the skirt of the dress, both of which hit her mid-calf, were baggy, but the bodice of the dress fit snugly. Debbie stared into the mirror of the bathroom. With no makeup and the rough clothing, she looked no different from the poor women who thronged in the streets below.

While she had been in the bathroom, Ben too had changed into the rough black shirt and baggy pants of the Vietnamese peasant. Debbie put on the crude but sturdy sandals and the palm-leaf hat that were waiting for her on the bed and tried not to laugh at Ben's ridiculous-looking pith helmet. He handed Debbie a cloth backpack, which proved to be heavier than it looked. "I wish we could take in aluminum backpacks, but that would be a dead giveaway," he said as he showed her how to fit the pack over her shoulders. Debbie started to protest, but stilled her complaint when he shouldered one that was probably twice as heavy as hers. "Let's go," he said. "Down the back stairs."

"Just a minute," Debbie said. She picked up a small bundle and handed it to Ben. "Shove that in my pack, will you?"

Ben grinned as he pushed in a bottle of shampoo and two changes of lacy underwear. "Not going to be a native on the inside, huh?" he asked.

Debbie shook her head. "We'll have to go days without washing these peasant clothes. I'm going to be as clean as I can be."

"Ah, civilization," Ben teased as they left her room and used the fire stairs to get to the street. "I've done some thinking," he said as they made their way down the busy street toward the Kowloon side of the harbor. "In Vietnam it's very unusual for a man and a woman to travel together or to do much together in public, and it's

104

almost unheard of for a woman to speak for a man. So any time you have to do the talking, pretend that I'm deaf. Make hand motions to me or something."

Debbie nodded. "Deaf. That's as good a cover as any." They walked across the street and got on the ferry. "How long will it take us to sail to Nam?"

Ben shrugged. "Several days, a week, it depends on the wind and the speed of the boat. I've motored in with this man once before and it took six days."

They got off the ferry on the Hong Kong side and walked down the long dock, past the junks that were teeming with women and small children, to an area that seemed populated mostly by small, bedraggled fishing boats, some with sails and some with small motors. Ben approached one with a motor that was a little larger than most and looked around. "Kwan, where are you?" he called out in accented Chinese. He stood in front of Debbie, partially shielding her from view. "We're here."

In response a small, wiry man came out of the cabin. "Sako, I was beginning to think you weren't coming," he said. "Are you ready?"

"Yes, we're ready," Ben said as he started to step on board.

Kwan's eyes narrowed as Debbie came into full view. "What's this, Sako? You told me there would be you and another man on this mission."

Ben stepped up on the deck of the boat. "Our plans had to be changed. I'm taking the woman instead."

Kwan shook his head vigorously. "No way, Sako," he said. "I agreed to take two men on this trip. No women. She's not getting on my boat."

"You know there's a woman coming out," Ben argued. "What's the difference?"

"This one is an American she-devil," Kwan said. "You can't bring her."

Ben glanced around the dock. "Then give me back the money I paid you yesterday. I'll go find another boat."

Kwan licked his lips. "It's gone," he said calmly. "It's gone, and I'm not taking the she-devil on this boat. You can pay another boat owner."

The knife appeared in Ben's hand before Debbie realized what was happening. "That won't be necessary, Kwan," he said as he pointed the long, sharp blade at Kwan's midsection. "We had a deal, Kwan, and I've already paid you half what you have coming. Now, does the she-devil come on board or do I carve you up and throw you overboard to feed the fish?"

Kwan's eyes widened as he stared down at the knife so carefully poised at his midsection. "Bring your she-devil on," he said as he shot Debbie a look of pure hatred. Swallowing back her fear, Debbie stepped up onto the deck of the boat. "Go down below," Ben told her in English. "Get out of his sight for a while until he cools off."

Debbie took one look at Kwan's furious face and rushed to do Ben's bidding. She went into the dim, dirty one-room cabin and peered out a crack in the wood. She could feel Ben and Kwan poling the small boat away from the dock before Kwan started the motor. Even through the narrow crack, the Hong Kong harbor was a breathtaking sight as they puttered out of the harbor and toward the open sea.

Debbie stayed in the hot cabin most of the morning, trying to let Kwan get over his anger at being forced to take her on board his boat. By the time the sun was directly overhead, they had left the harbor behind them and were out on the open sea, heading south toward the

Gulf of Tonkin. Debbie stepped out of the cabin and approached Ben, who was sitting in the stern whittling on a piece of wood. Debbie sat down crosslegged on the deck beside Ben. "Is he over being angry by now?" she asked.

Ben shrugged. "It doesn't matter whether he is or not," he said. "But I would stay away from him. Even if he looks like he's all right, you never know what those Chinese are thinking."

Debbie put her hand up to her mouth to keep from laughing. "Well, it's true," Ben said.

"They could say the same thing about us," Debbie observed.

Ben shook his head. "No, not really. You, at least, are an open book most of the time. Like this morning. Jim talked to you before I got there, didn't he?"

Debbie jumped and her face turned red. She realized her escape to the bathroom that morning hadn't been quite fast enough. "What of it?"

"He offered to let us off the hook, didn't he?"

Debbie nodded, her face a picture of guilt. "So why didn't you call it off?" she asked.

Ben shrugged. "I have my reasons," he said as he fiddled with his pocketknife. Debbie glanced at his face, but could tell nothing of his thoughts. Was he planning to use this mission to make her his lover, or did his reason for going ahead with the mission have nothing to do with her? Maybe she should have gotten out of this while she still could have, but the look of anguish on Jim's face and the thought of Li having to stay in Vietnam had been more than she could bear. Her decision had been made, and she would have to take her chances with Ben.

"Hey, is that she-devil any good at cooking?" Kwan asked. "I'm hungry."

"Yes, the she-devil cooks pretty well," Debbie called

out in Chinese before Ben could reply. She got up and approached Kwan. "What would you like me to prepare?" she asked more modestly.

Kwan's face split into an evil grin. "So the she-devil can make herself useful," he taunted. "Rice is in there." He flipped his thumb toward the cabin.

That was all? Debbie thought as she found the rice stored in an old burlap sack. She burned her finger a little but managed to light a small fire under the wok, and in a few minutes she had prepared them each a steaming bowl of rice. Kwan ate his rice and made no more taunting remarks, but as the afternoon wore on and they sailed farther and farther from Hong Kong, Debbie noticed that he watched her more and more. She couldn't tell what he was thinking, but somehow she didn't think his thoughts were benevolent toward her. She sat on the deck near Ben and watched him as he whittled, or she stared out at the bright blue waves of the ocean.

"Bored?" Ben asked late in the afternoon. "I wish we could have brought you a book or two, but I didn't dare risk being found with them."

Debbie shook her head. "I'm not bored. I've always loved to sail. My mother's parents would take me sometimes."

"Where's your mother?" Ben asked. "The colonel never mentioned her."

Debbie shrugged. "She left when I was seven and I honestly never missed her."

"Yeah, I know the feeling," Ben said as he returned his attention to his whittling. Debbie stared out at the ocean, conscious that for the first time she and Ben had communicated on more than a superficial level.

The evening meal was rice again, only this time Debbie prepared a fish that Ben had caught and skinned. They ate their meal as the sun disappeared over the horizon and the winds stilled. Kwan lowered an anchor and he and Ben sat in the stern of the boat, talking softly. Ben was smoking a cigarette, and Kwan was smoking a strange-smelling concoction in his pipe. Debbie figured he must have gotten over his anger and she decided that he meant no harm to her.

Tired from the long flight and two sleepless nights in a row, Debbie went into the cabin and unrolled the pack that Ben had given her. As she had expected, she found among other things a lightweight sleeping bag. Debbie didn't remember there being a mat in the cabin, so she unrolled the sleeping bag onto the bare wood floor and wadded up the outer covering of her pack to use as a pillow. It wasn't the most comfortable bed in the world, but she would be sleeping on it for the next month or more, and she guessed she better get used to it. She lay awake a few minutes, listening to the murmur of the men's voices, but the lapping of the water and the gentle motion of the boat lulled her into sleep.

Debbie wasn't sure just what brought her up out of a sound sleep. Maybe it was the creak of a wooden board nearby. Maybe it was the almost imperceptible rustle of clothing, or maybe it was just that she could sense the danger she was in. Whatever it was, Debbie's eyes flew open in the darkness as she sensed another's presence in the cabin. She looked around and saw the figure at the end of the room. "Ben?" she called out quietly in the night, lest she wake Kwan.

The figure moved closer to her. "No, Ben," she whispered before she realized that the figure moving toward her wasn't Ben.

Before she could call out, the figure leaped across the room and he slammed his hand across her mouth. "No,

I'm not Sako, she-devil," Kwan's voice grated harshly in her ears. "Sako's asleep out on the deck. No, don't bother to call out to him," he sneered as Debbie squirmed to free her mouth. "After the little powder I slipped into his coffee, he won't be coming even if you did call him. No man brings a she-devil on my boat and holds a knife to me and gets away with it," he continued. "Even if she is a beautiful she-devil." His dirty hand snaked up and touched her breast. "I'm going to have fun with you to-night, she-devil, before I throw you overboard and your sleeping friend after you."

*God, no,* Debbie thought as she kicked and squirmed beneath Kwan's hard, foul-smelling body. He pinned her arms up over her head with one hand and moved over her. She had to stop him. Frantically, without hesitating for a second, she jerked upward with her knee and hit him hard in the groin as her mouth opened and she bit his hand. He let out with a roar of pain as Debbie screamed under him. "Ben!" she cried as she tried to push Kwan off her.

Kwan grunted as he tightened his grip on her. "Good try, she-devil," he taunted as he clamped his hand back over her mouth. It was going to happen. A wave of nausea rushed over her. She couldn't stop him. But at that moment Ben crashed through the door of the cabin, swaying and groggy, and picked Kwan up off Debbie's body. Ben's fist made a sickening crunch as it crashed into Kwan's nose. Kwan fell backward and sprawled helplessly on the floor.

"Tie him up, Lotus," Ben said as he crumpled to the floor. "It took everything I had in me to hit him. Whatever he gave me sure knocked me for a loop."

Debbie found the flashlight and the rope in her pack and tied the unconscious Kwan's hands and feet as fast as her own trembling hands could work. "Are you all right?" she asked Ben as she sank to the floor beside him.

Ben nodded. "I only drank half the cup," he said. "I should have known he would put something in it. I'm sorry, Lotus. Did the bastard hurt you?" His eyes were filled with hatred as he looked across the cabin at the unconscious man.

"I'm all right," Debbie said, but as the realization of what almost happened rushed over her, her head swam and her stomach churned. She had come within an inch of rape and death tonight, and if Ben had finished his cup of coffee, Kwan would have killed him too.

Debbie felt gentle hands rub her shoulders gently. "Oh, Debbie, this was all my fault," Ben said as he tucked her head into his shoulder. "I should have been more cautious. I should have known that he was up to no good."

"Don't blame yourself, Ben," Debbie said as they both swayed. "Uh, we better sit down or something."

"Over here," Ben said as he pointed her toward his sleeping bag that was spread out on the deck. Debbie stumbled to the sleeping bag and fell facedown on it, tremors of fear still shaking her body. Ben lay down beside her and threw his arm over his eyes. "I'll have to keep him tied up for the rest of the trip," he said. "Can you help me sail this thing?"

"Yes," Debbie whispered. "I'll do anything, just don't let that stinking bastard touch me again like he did tonight."

"Where did he touch you, Lotus?" Ben asked, his voice low as he turned her over. "Did he hit you?"

Debbie shook her head. "No, but he hurt my wrists." She touched the tender places on her wrists and realized

111

that she would have bruises tomorrow. "And he touched my breasts. I feel dirty. Are you okay now?"

"My head's still spinning," Ben admitted. "But I'll be all right. Here, I'll hold you," he said as he cuddled her to him. "You're still shivering."

Debbie nodded as she snuggled closer to Ben. He cupped her head in the palm of his hand and brushed her lips ever so gently. Tenderly, he kissed her, willing her to calm down and to stop shaking like a leaf in his arms. For long moments he kissed her lips as he murmured words of comfort to her in the night, until she had stopped trembling and was still. Her arms curled around his neck and she pressed herself closer to him, meeting his lips with her own as her need for comfort and her desire to give Ben comfort overcame her horror at what had nearly happened to her tonight. Her tender, caring fingers stroked back the hair on Ben's forehead as her lips caressed the stubbly skin of his face. There was nothing passionate or sensual in their embrace, just two human beings reassuring each other that everything was all right.

"Thank you for stopping him, Ben," Debbie whispered as she snuggled close to his hard, warm body. "When he said he had drugged you, I was sure I was done for. I fought, but he was too strong. You pretty well know the rest."

"It's all over now. We better get some sleep, Lotus," he said. He sat up and pulled his shirt up over his head for Debbie to use as a pillow. Debbie shoved the shirt under her head as Ben pulled her up to him and cradled her face against his smooth, hard chest. "Try to sleep," he said as Debbie's eyes flickered shut. She had thought she would never be able to sleep again, but Ben's arms were warm and comforting, and before long she was asleep, safe in them.

Ben stared, wide-awake, into the starry night. The drug Kwan had given him was wearing off, leaving him clearheaded and angry. His carelessness had almost gotten Debbie raped and murdered. He cursed himself for his carelessness as he stared down at the face of the woman who slept beside him, using his chest as a pillow. In spite of the drug, he had almost killed Kwan tonight, and would have done so with pleasure if Debbie had not been there.

But it was his motivation that had Ben confused. He was angry, but he was more angry with Kwan for trying to hurt Debbie than he was for planning to drown him. If he had killed Kwan, it would have been on Debbie's behalf, not his own. He felt more than just responsible for Debbie—he felt very protective toward her, he wanted to take care of her and make sure she was all right. Ben couldn't understand why he should feel this way. He had never felt protective toward a woman before in his life, and the feeling was very new and very strange to him.

Debbie sat at the bow of the boat and gazed out at the blue water. She could not see it, but she knew that the coastline of North Vietnam was just a few miles away. They had been on the boat over over a week now, and according to Ben they would reach their destination on the North Vietnamese coast in another day or two. Debbie dreaded leaving the safety of the high seas and sneaking into a Communist country, yet at the same time she looked forward to getting off the boat and away from the bound Kwan. Not daring to trust him after the first night on board, Ben had kept him securely bound by his hands and feet except while he was eating, and then he stood over him with a knife, daring Kwan to make one false move. Debbie wasn't sure, but she sensed that Ben was dealing with Kwan much more mildly than he would have if she had not been on the boat. Kwan said nothing, but he looked at them both with such hatred in his eyes that it gave Debbie cold shivers down her back. They had left Kwan alone in the cabin and the two of them had pretty much lived up on deck, Debbie's golden skin darkening to a deep chestnut brown, and Ben's face and chest becoming even darker.

Debbie glanced over at Ben as he gazed toward the coastline. She had wondered, the first morning after Kwan had attacked her, how they would manage to pilot the boat to North Vietnam, but Ben had cranked up the motor and after a few hours Debbie realized not only that Ben was an excellent sailor, but that he knew his way down the coast of China. He had piloted them through the Gulf of Tonkin, managing to stay out of the way of the Chinese patrol boats as well as the huge shipping boats and tankers that populated the gulf. Debbie wondered how many times he had made the trip before.

"Hey, Debbie!" Ben called from the rudder.

"Hmm?" Debbie asked, loathe to interrupt her musing.

"Here, do me a favor." Ben threw her his shirt and untied the sash around his pants. "Rinse these out over the side, will you? And you might want to do your own as well. If this wind is anything to go by, we should be there by morning." He stood up and stepped out of the pants that had fallen around his ankles, leaving him naked except for his briefs.

"*Ben!*" Debbie said as her cheeks reddened at the sight of Ben's nearly nude body. "I can't just take off my clothes in front of the two of you."

Ben rolled his eyes. "Shut the door of the cabin so Jack the Ripper won't see you. And as for me, I'll stay back here. The cabin will shield you from my lascivious stare. Go ahead and wash your things, Debbie. They're getting dirty and it will be your last chance for a while."

Debbie arched her eyebrow. "Are you implying that I'm just a wee bit smelly?" she asked, but she couldn't help but smile. "Well, all right. But you stay *over here.*"

Ben nodded his head. Debbie walked toward the front of the boat, earning herself a hateful glare from Kwan when she shut the door of the already stifling cabin, and positioned herself so that the cabin was between her and Ben. She stripped out of the dress and pants and one at a time, so as not to lose a garment in the ocean, she rinsed out her outer clothing and Ben's, along with her underwear and Ben's briefs from yesterday. Although he had laughed at her for bringing spares, he had done the same, which had earned him a little teasing from Debbie.

Debbie spread the wet garments out on the deck to dry in the hot sun. She dipped a cloth in the water and rinsed her face and her body, letting the water soak her underwear until it was nearly transparent. She would have loved to have rinsed her hair, but she knew that the salt water would leave it even worse than it already was, so she put that off until she could clean it with fresh water in Vietnam. She stretched out on the hard wood deck and was about to doze off when she heard the sound of Ben's footsteps on the deck. Quickly, she flipped over, an embarrassed stain on her cheeks as Ben stared down at her nearly naked beauty. "You said you wouldn't come over here," she said tightly.

Ben shrugged. "I heard the sound of you splashing yourself, and I thought it seemed like a good idea." He grinned as Debbie tried to twist around so that he couldn't see quite so much. "Come on, Debbie, you probably show more than that at the beach."

"Not nearly," Debbie said through clenched teeth. "My bikini's not transparent."

"Shame," Ben said as he picked up the cloth. He dipped the towel in the water as she had done and let the water trickle down his bare body, clad only in a pair of briefs which were quickly soaked. Debbie couldn't help but stare at the hard muscles of his thighs and calves before her gaze traveled upward to his smooth, hard-muscled chest. Ben rinsed himself as thoroughly as he could and sat down on the deck a few feet away from Debbie. Ben tossed her the cloth. "Cover yourself and sit up. You look miserable."

Debbie draped the long cloth down her breasts to where it stopped mid-thigh. "Ben, how many times have you made this trip?"

Ben thought a minute. "Once while I was in the army and maybe, oh, five or six times since '75."

"Do you work just in Vietnam?"

"Are you sure you're not still a reporter?" Ben asked. "You ask a lot of questions."

"Sorry," Debbie mumbled. "If you prefer not to talk about your work, that's okay. I understand."

"That's all right, Lotus, I can talk about it with you. I work anywhere in the Orient where I can pass as a native. I've been behind the curtain in China, Cambodia, and Korea. And I've done a mission or two in Japan."

"Japan?" Debbie asked.

"Sure. I've rescued the kidnapped children of a couple of American businessmen, and once I kidnapped the daughter of a Japanese politician on the eve of her wedding."

"Why?" Debbie asked, astonished.

"Her father had information that the fiancé was marrying her strictly to further his own political career.

When the man's daughter wouldn't believe him, he hired me."

"Was it true?" Debbie asked. "What happened when you let her go?"

"Yes, it was true, and I turned her over to her father. I collected my money and left. I don't know what ever happened after that."

Debbie stared across the water. Their state of near undress gave her a feeling of secret sharing, a feeling that prompted her next question. "Have you ever killed anyone?"

Ben lifted his eyes and looked into hers. "You mean assassinated them?" Debbie nodded. "Only once, Debbie. And the cruel monster deserved it. But it left such a bad taste in my mouth that I swore off that kind of thing." He got up and picked up his nearly dry clothes. "It's getting close to sundown. Better fix us some more of that damned rice."

Debbie's face puckered into a frown as she pulled on her pants and dress. She wasn't surprised that Ben had assassinated a man before, but she was surprised that it had bothered him to do it. Maybe he wasn't as cold and heartless as she had thought him to be.

They ate their supper of plain boiled rice, Debbie swearing that once they landed she was going to steal and cook the biggest chicken she could find. Ben untied Kwan long enough for the man to eat, and as the sun went down and the stars twinkled out, Debbie cleaned up their dishes and unrolled their bedrolls, placing them side by side but with a couple of feet between them. Since the first night, when Ben had held her to comfort her, they had slept with a few feet between them, but still close enough for Debbie to feel safe. Miraculously, it had not rained on them while they slept, but had rained mainly in the daytime.

Ben returned with Kwan's bowl and chopsticks. "This is the last night you have to share a boat with him," Ben said.

"Yeah, tomorrow I'm sharing the dry land with a nation full of Communists," Debbie said curtly. She flopped down on her bedroll and stared out at the stars.

Ben stretched out on his back beside her. "Don't feel like that, Debbie. Most of them aren't Communists, but very unfortunate people caught in a situation that was not of their making." He turned over on his stomach and shoved his shirt under his face. "Go to sleep, Debbie. Tomorrow's going to be a long day."

Debbie nodded and turned over, wondering why Ben hadn't made a move toward her since they had been on the boat. He had teased her, yes, he had looked at her with longing a few times when he thought she couldn't see, but he had made no move to make her his lover. Debbie had expected him to do something long before now. Had he changed his mind? Had he decided that he didn't want her as his lover? Or had she finally gotten her message across? Debbie wasn't sure, but she did know that she should have been a lot more pleased with his actions than she was.

Ben stared at Debbie's delicately curved back, its even rising and falling indicating that she had fallen asleep. His eyes darkened with desire as he remembered the way she had looked in her soaking wet underwear. It had been all he could do not to take her into his arms and make her his then, but he sensed that she wasn't yet ready. That bastard, Kwan, had given her a good scare, and she had been jumpy and nervous for several days afterward. After what Kwan had tried to force on her, she wasn't ready to go willingly to a man's arms. But it wouldn't be long, he thought as he closed his eyes in the darkness. He would get her off this boat, and then he would have her alone in the beautiful rain forests of Vietnam, a place that to him was one of the most beautiful on earth in spite of what the war had done to it. Yes, in the beautiful forests of Vietnam, under a canopy of teak, there he would make her his.

Debbie stared out at the rapidly approaching coastline. "Are we getting off here?" she asked. "There's nothing around but that old shack over there."

Ben steered the motorboat through the shallow waters, forcing a school of fish to part in the middle. "That's the whole point, Debbie," he said patiently. "There's no one around to see us coming in."

"But there's no place to hide the boat," she protested.

"Kwan will go down another thirty miles or so to a little fishing village on the coast. We're getting off at the nearest point of entry for us. That will save us several days of hiking in the beginning."

Debbie glanced behind her at Kwan's bound figure. "Do you trust him?" she asked.

Ben ignored her question and squinted at the beach. "We're getting closer," he said. "Get your things together. We'll be off this thing in an hour."

Debbie had already rolled up her bedroll, and she made quick work of putting it into the cloth pack. In spite of her growing aversion to rice, she poured a generous quantity into a large square of cloth and stuffed it into her pack in case she and Ben couldn't buy or steal food every day. "You steal my rice, she-devil," Kwan said suddenly.

Debbie jumped and turned startled eyes on the man.

119

"You did worse to me, or tried to," she said, trying to mask her fear. "Let's call it a repayment of debt."

"I'll get you, she-devil," Kwan said as Debbie gathered up the rest of her and Ben's things, staggering a little under the weight as she returned to the deck. They were much closer to the beach than they had been, and Ben was staring down the coast at a small vessel bobbing at the edge of the horizon.

"What is it?" Debbie asked.

Ben shrugged. "I can't tell, but I don't like it," he said. "You and I are getting off here now."

"But we're a quarter of a mile from shore!" Debbie protested. "What about the packs?"

"We'll have to dry everything out once we get there," Ben said. "And you may as well put back the rice you packed. It'll just weigh you down. And we can get some soon."

Reluctantly, Debbie tossed the rice out on the deck. Ben went into the cabin and loosened Kwan's hands a little, so that he could work himself free eventually. "Be waiting for us in Ho Nan," he said. "If you know what's good for you."

Kwan turned his head away. Debbie glanced over at the boat and saw that it was a little closer, but not within hailing distance. She and Ben put their shoes in their packs, and together they lowered themselves over the side of the boat, swimming through the water slowly, the weight of the packs and their clothes slowing them down quite a bit. Foot by foot they made their way to shore, swimming through the choppy waves that felt as thick as molasses. Debbie's lungs burned and her arms and legs felt like lead weights, but when she felt herself falter, Ben would reach out and give her a push through the water.

Debbie almost sobbed with relief when she could feel

120

her feet touch sand. She and Ben staggered toward the shore, intent on nothing more than collapsing on the beach, when Debbie heard the sharp crack of a rifle and a ping as a bullet hit the sand in front of her. "Son of a bitch, the bastard's shooting at us!" Ben snapped as he reached out and grabbed Debbie's hand. "Run for the shack!"

Debbie scrambled out of the water and the two of them sprinted toward the building, dodging bullets as Kwan fired shot after shot. Good God, were they really getting out of this alive? she asked herself as Ben finally threw open the door of the rundown old shack and pushed her in behind him. She had been sure on the beach that they were both done for. Ben pushed her face down on the floor and lay down beside her as Kwan peppered the little building with bullets. "Is he going to come after us?" Debbie asked, her breath uneven from fear and exhaustion.

The shooting stopped abruptly and Ben raised his head. "I doubt it," he said. "That boat's approaching him pretty fast."

Debbie raised her head just a fraction and looked out a slit where there was a piece of wood missing. The boat, which appeared to be a patrol boat of some sort, had stopped about fifty yards from Kwan, who was standing on the deck gesturing wildly toward the beach. "He's telling them about us," she whispered, her heart in her throat. "What do we do if they come this way?"

Ben looked behind them at the flat coastal plain covered with rice paddies, which would not hide them, and back over at the patrol boat with the North Vietnam insignia on its flag. "We kill everyone on that boat," he said as he withdrew a large pistol that was strapped to his leg and removed it from its waterproof pouch.

Debbie gasped but said nothing. They watched for a moment as Kwan continued to talk and gesture. Suddenly, the captain of the boat gave a signal and a small cannon was whirled around. Debbie watched, fascinated, as the captain signaled the gunner to fire. She flinched and shut her eyes when Kwan's fishing boat was engulfed in a ball of flame. The captain of the patrol boat watched the wreckage burn for a few minutes before the boat turned around and sped down the coast in the other direction.

"Well, what do you make of that?" Ben said. "They didn't believe him!" He turned over and lay on his back.

Debbie dropped her head to the floor and shut her eyes. "So how are we going to get out of this place?" she asked.

To Debbie's disgust, Ben started to laugh. "Surely you didn't really think he was going to wait around for us?" he asked. "He wouldn't have been around even if they hadn't blown up the boat."

"So how are we going to get out of here?" Debbie asked. "Once we find Li."

"We do what thousands of refugees have done," Ben said as he raised his arm and put it over his eyes. "I hope you like to hike, Debbie. We're walking out through Cambodia."

## CHAPTER SEVEN

Debbie swore as she stumbled on a wide vine and lost her footing. "Damn!" she muttered as she fell into the soft yellow clay. This was the third time she had tripped over one of the thick vines today, and she was sure that Ben was tired of picking her up and dusting her off. "Wait a minute, Ben," she said as she scrambled to get back up.

Ben turned around and walked back to where Debbie was trying to brush the dust off her hands. "Get tangled up in a wait-a-minute?" he asked, referring to the small vines with the sharp thorns that would catch in clothing and produce an inevitable "Wait-a-minute!" from Debbie.

"Not this time," Debbie said as she pointed at the huge vine at her feet. "I tripped on that."

Ben shook his head back and forth. "And to think that the first time I saw you, I marveled at your grace!" he teased as he grinned at her.

Debbie blushed. "I'm sorry if I'm delaying you," she said. "I'm doing the best that I can."

Ben picked up the hem of her dress and wiped her face with it. "I haven't fussed at you, have I?" he asked. "You've done fine. A lot better than I expected."

"Thanks," Debbie said as she straightened her pack and trudged after Ben. She had found the hiking very rough going, tangling regularly with the huge vines and the nasty wait-a-minutes of the tropical rain forest they were making their way through, and she had been surprised and grateful that Ben had been as patient as he had. He had let her set the pace and stopped for frequent rests for the first few days, as Debbie gradually got adjusted to the hours of hiking. Debbie thanked her lucky stars that they had spent the first few days walking across the coastal plains and that they had not had to tackle the rougher hiking of the mountains until just three days ago.

Debbie hurried until she was just a few feet behind Ben. "How many more days until we reach Hai Thong?" she asked.

"If my memory serves me correctly, we're only about a day or two away," Ben said. "Less than a day if we had bicycles and could take the road." Bicycles were the most common form of transportation in Communist Vietnam.

"I'm surprised you didn't bring some in with us," Debbie said musingly.

"I would have, if I had known whether or not Li had a bicycle too," Ben said. "But this is probably better. On the main roads, the soldiers stop travelers pretty often for a travel pass."

Debbie nodded and said nothing more, saving her energy for the strenuous hike. They had traveled parallel to the major roads, if you could call the dirt or gravel paths roads, staying about fifty yards to one side or the other. They had seen several groups of soldiers stopping hapless travelers, and turning back all who didn't have a travel permit. The first couple of days they had seen a lot of people, either working the farms or traveling on the roads, but as they climbed higher and higher in the mountains, the population level fell off and they only saw a few persons every day, usually the women in the markets where Debbie went to buy food. Each village had a "market" in the middle of town where the women of the farm families brought their rice, vegetables, and poultry to sell, and since the men of the villages were never seen in the markets, Debbie would slip into town, leaving Ben hiding on the outskirts, and buy a couple of days' worth of food. When she had asked Ben why the Communists had not put an end to this show of free enterprise, he said that it probably wasn't frowned on in Communist Vietnam.

Debbie took off her hat and fanned herself. "Ben, was it this hot when you were in the service?" she asked.

Ben shrugged. "It didn't seem as hot, I guess, but we soldiers were notorious for running around without our shirts on. Hey, put that hat back on! I don't want you getting heatstroke or something."

Debbie put her hat back on her head and pulled the sash down around her neck. She reached out to grasp a tree limb for support, and just a few seconds later felt the insistent tug of the wait-a-minute vine. "Wait a minute!" she cried as she started to unwind the prickly, tenacious vine from the skirt of her dress.

Patiently, Ben helped her unwind the vine. They trudged on in the late afternoon heat as they made their way through a ghostly forest of dead teak trunks, some still standing and some rotting on the ground.

Debbie tried to picture what the countryside might have been like before the war had damaged it so. It must have been a place of enchanting beauty, especially in the summer, since the land was still beautiful, even with the scars of war that it bore.

"Are we going to make camp soon?" Debbie asked as the sun dipped lower in the sky. They usually hiked until about sundown or until Ben found the right place for them to sleep. They had stayed one night in the barn of one of the members of the resistance, but most nights they had slept out in the open or in an old bomb shelter, carved out of the mountainside.

"I remember an old abandoned shack on the other side of this hill," Ben said. "Let's try to make it that far."

Debbie nodded and followed Ben on the circular path that ringed the hill, stumbling after him as she grew more and more tired. She spotted the rundown shack and her face broke into a smile of relief. "That ugly old shack looks as good as the Hilton," she said as she looked up the steep path at the little building.

Ben started up the path. He reached up to hold on to a tree trunk for support but bellowed in pain and snatched his hand back. "Son of a bitch, that hurt!" he said as he cradled his hand in his other hand.

"Ben, what did you do?" Debbie asked as she reached out and tried to take his injured hand.

"No, don't touch it!" Ben said as he sat down on the steep path. "I guess it's Black Palm."

He opened his hand and Debbie gasped when she saw the sharp, porcupinelike thorns that studded Ben's palm and fingers. "I'm going to have to take those out," she said.

"How?" Ben demanded.

"Did you think to bring a pair of tweezers?" Debbie asked.

Ben nodded and jerked his thumb toward his backpack. Debbie found a pair in his waterproof medicine case and sat down beside Ben, cradling his hand in hers as she slowly and patiently picked out the offending barbs. Ben was silent, but his face was pale, and Debbie knew that he might be in quite a bit of pain. She squinted in the fading light and removed the last of the thorns before she smeared his hand with antiseptic. "Better?" she asked.

Ben nodded. "Thanks, Lotus," he said as he smiled. This was the first time she had seen any vestige of tenderness on his face, and the impact of that smile shook her to the bone. She returned the kit to Ben's backpack and extended her hand to his good one. "Come on, we better get up there before it gets too dark to see," she said.

Together they made their way up to the abandoned house, its former occupants probably killed in the war. Ben made a fire so that Debbie could cook the rice and the vegetables they had bought earlier that day.

When she finished she handed Ben a full bowl and chopsticks. "Do you think we'll get there tomorrow?" she asked. "I want to see Li so badly!"

"Yes, I think we'll get there," Ben said. "But Debbie, please don't get your hopes up about Li."

"What do you mean?" Debbie asked. "About not getting my hopes up?"

"The last word you and Jim had of Li was over a year ago," Ben said. "She might not be there anymore. Or—"

"Or what?" Debbie demanded.

"Or she may not want to come out with us," Ben finished. "I meant what I told Jim. If she isn't a hundred percent willing to come out, she stays."

"Ben, why do you insist on trying to discourage me?" Debbie asked peevishly. "I know Li, and believe me, she'll want to come out, if for no other reason than to be with Jim. She loves him, Ben."

Ben rolled his eyes. "I'm just warning you, Debbie. If she doesn't want to go, I'm not forcing her. Got that?"

Debbie nodded. "But she'll want to come, you just wait."

They finished their meal in silence, watching the sun

disappear behind the next hill, and the reds and purples of dusk gave way to the darkness of night. Since they would be up with the dawn, Ben worked the pump until the water seemed clean and washed the dishes while Debbie washed yesterday's underwear. Since the night was hot and her clothes would dry by morning, she took off her long top and pants and rinsed them too, leaving them draped over a tree branch to dry. She offered to wash Ben's too, and in just a few minutes his were hanging beside hers. She sponged herself off and lay down on her sleeping bag, barely noticing when Ben came back inside and lay down on his own sleeping bag a few feet away.

Exhausted from her day of hiking, Debbie slept deeply that night and was ready to resume hiking in the morning. They walked through the mountainous forest for most of the day, circling the city of Hanoi, and finally reached Hai Thong late in the afternoon. Debbie bought food in the marketplace, a little extra in case Li would be sharing their evening meal and, as casually as she could, asked where the work farm was, explaining that she had a brother there she wanted to visit. One of the younger women pointed to a narrow dirt road that went north.

Debbie paid for the food with the money Ben had brought with him, and rejoined him in the forest. "Up that road there," she said. "I don't know how far."

Ben started up the road and Debbie followed, hoping they could find the farm before dusk. They walked a couple of miles up the road, and Debbie was beginning to think they would have to stop for the night when they rounded a bend and spotted a cluster of shacks surrounded by cultivated fields. "There it is!" Debbie whispered.

"It's guarded," Ben said as he took Debbie's hand, and

pulled her off the road into a grove of trees. "You'll have to sneak in there."

*"Whoopee!"* Debbie said under her breath. She followed Ben as he made a wide circle of the camp, guarded by a tall fence of barbed wire. They got just as close to the wire as they could, watching as the workers left one old rundown building and wandered toward what looked like a couple of dormitories. "What will I do?" Debbie asked.

"Just look in the windows of the women's dorm," Ben said. "They'll have lamps on. See if you can see her."

"How will I get through the fence?" Debbie asked.

Ben reached into his backpack and removed a pair of wire cutters. "You thought of everything, didn't you?" she whispered as they made their way to the fence. Ben cut the bottom two wires and held them long enough for Debbie to roll under the fence.

Forcing herself to remain calm, Debbie sneaked around the men's dorm and peered into the large building where the women were housed. She strained her eyes in the dark, studying the faces of the thin, tired-looking women she saw there. Were any of them Li? She stared at them one by one, but only one of them bore the faintest resemblance to Li. Could it be she? She didn't know, but she had to find out.

Debbie made her way around the building to where the young woman was sitting, reading what appeared to be an old magazine. Debbie tapped on the glass, hoping the woman would not become frightened. Instead, her face brightened as she got up and put the magazine down. Casually, she walked toward the door and stepped out of it. "Phuong?" she asked in Vietnamese. "Is that you out there?"

"No, it's me," Debbie said as she stepped out of the shadows. "Li? Is that you?"

The woman looked startled. "Li? I am not Li. I'm Anh. What do you want with Li?"

Debbie strained to look at the woman's face in the moonlight. No, this woman was too young to be Li, and she was a bit too tall, although her voice was similar to Li's. "I want to talk to her," Debbie said. "I heard she was here and I wanted to see her."

Anh thought a minute, then answered. "She doesn't live here anymore," she said slowly. "What do you want with her?"

Was Anh a friend or a foe? "I wanted to help her," Debbie said carefully.

"You have more money?" Anh asked. "She got money last year and used it to get out of here."

"Where did she go?" Debbie asked. "How did she get away?"

"She used it to bribe them to transfer her to a farm outside Phu Bai," Anh said.

Debbie repeated the words to herself as she reached in her pocket and gave Anh a couple of coins. "Don't tell anybody I was here," she cautioned Anh. "Please."

Anh looked down at the money and nodded. "I never saw you, friend-of-Li," she said as she turned away.

Fighting her feelings of disappointment that Li was no longer there, Debbie hurried back to the fence and pushed aside the barbed wire. Ben came out from behind the trees and held the wire so that Debbie could get under the fence. "That didn't take long," he said. "What did you find out?"

"She bribed them to transfer her to another farm," Debbie said. "In Phu Bai. Where's that?"

130

"South of Hue," Ben said. "About thirty miles. Come on, I found a place where we can stay tonight."

Debbie stumbled behind Ben as they made their way through the moon-dappled grove of trees to the bank of a small stream. "Is this far enough away from the camp?" Debbie asked.

Ben shook his head. "No, they could see the fire from here. Look over there," he said as he pointed down into a small valley. "We'll fill our canteens and go down there. We ought to be able to find shelter under those trees."

They crossed the stream, splashing as little as possible, and hurried down the side of the hill to the small grove of trees that would shelter them for the night. Luckily, the moon was full and they could see pretty well where they were going, although Debbie got tangled up in another wait-a-minute vine and Ben had to untangle her. They walked into the grove of trees, far enough in so that the trees would hide the brightness of their campfire. These trees had somehow escaped the defoliation that had spoiled so much of the Vietnam forests and provided a canopy under which they could take shelter. Debbie removed her backpack and held a flashlight while Ben made a fire for them from the dried wood on the ground. She set their tiny wok in the middle and got out the rice and the fish she had bought in Hai Thong earlier. "We're going to eat well tonight," she said. "I bought extra in case Li was with us."

Ben smoked a cigarette while Debbie prepared the rice and fish. "I'm down to one pack," he observed as he puffed the last of his cigarette and pitched the butt into the fire. "Cigarettes are the only part of civilization I really miss."

Debbie dished out a bowl of rice and fish for Ben and handed it to him. "I miss long hot showers," she admitted. She served herself a generous bowl of food and sat down on the ground beside Ben.

"Tell me everything the woman told you about Li," Ben said as he sampled the steaming rice.

Debbie repeated the conversation as best she could. "She said that Li had bribed her way out of the camp and into another camp in Phu Bai. Where's Hue?"

"In the central part of the country," Ben said. "There was a lot of fighting around it during the war." He sighed as he took another bite of his meal. "I knew she didn't want to get out of the country when I took on this ridiculous search," he said as he set his unfinished bowl of rice aside. "Now we have to go chasing halfway down the damned country to hear it from her."

"Ben, you don't know that!" Debbie exclaimed.

"Then why isn't she out by now?" Ben demanded. "She's had the money for nearly a year. That's plenty of time to bribe her way to London if she'd wanted to. But instead of leaving the country, she uses her money to get onto another work farm. What sense does that make?"

"I don't know," Debbie replied hotly, setting her own unfinished bowl of rice on the ground and unrolling her sleeping bag. "How do refugees usually get out?"

"Either through Cambodia like we're going to, or if they can get hold of a boat, they sail to Indonesia." Ben got out his own sleeping bag and unrolled it next to hers.

"And to do either of those things she would have had to have gone south, right?" Debbie demanded.

"Yes, but—"

"But nothing!" Debbie said. "She was headed toward freedom. She just didn't make it that far."

"So what happened?" Ben challenged Debbie as he stripped off his outer clothes and rolled them up to use as a pillow. Debbie shivered a little as she looked at his nearly naked body in the light of the moon. She had seen him in this nearly nude state a number of times in the last week and a half, and she had memorized the tough, sinewy lines of his masculine body. "Why did she get that far and no further?"

"I don't know," Debbie admitted as she lay down on her sleeping bag. "But something happened to stop her, I know it did. She loves Jim and would want to be with him."

"Are we back to that again?" Ben scoffed as he lay down and propped his head on his hand. "Come on, Debbie, it's been ten years since she's even seen the man, and he probably never even made love to her. She's become a woman, with a woman's needs, and she's probably found a man to meet those needs."

"All you ever think in terms of is sex," Debbie said tightly, yet at the same time she had to admit to herself that at the moment those were exactly the terms she was thinking in. Ben's bare body, just a foot or so from hers, invited her to touch it and caress it, to feel his hard muscles underneath his smooth dark skin. She saw the flame in Ben's eyes and knew that he was taking in the way her hair drifted down the sides of her face and her back, the way the bodice of her dress hugged her breasts, and that he was remembering the way she looked when she took off her clothes to wash them. With effort she dragged her eyes away from Ben's strong chest and stared at his face. "There's more to life than just sex, Ben," she added softly. "Maybe you don't know that, but Jim and Li do."

"And you? Do you know about that, Lotus?" Ben asked as he rolled over to her sleeping bag and took her by the shoulders. "Do you know all about this so-called love between a man and a woman, or do you know about this?" he demanded as he pulled her to him and covered her lips in a searing embrace of raw passion.

Debbie gasped as her mouth opened to Ben's sensual invasion. *Yes, yes, I know about this,* she thought as her arms crept up his shoulders and around his neck, locking together behind his head. She knew about the passion of which he spoke. He had taught her about that passion. As their mutual awareness exploded into a flaming embrace, Debbie moaned and shifted so that Ben could cover her body entirely with his own. She desired him, wanted him to ravish her body with his own strong one. Whimpering softly, she opened her lips and let Ben sample the sweetness of her depths, letting him draw all the sweetness she had within her. "Ben, Ben," she murmured as he broke their kiss and pulled her up. "Why—what?"

Ben reached out and with careful fingers unbuttoned the bodice of her dress. "This has to last the whole trip, and I don't want to tear it off you," he said as he unfastened her long top to the waist. With tender fingers he pushed it down until it was bunched down around her hips. "Beautiful, so beautiful," he murmured as he stared at Debbie in the moonlight, naked to the waist except for the delicate lace bra concealing her high, firm breasts. Ben's fingers trailed down a path from her shoulders to her breasts, touching every sensitive nerve ending along the way. When he reached the lace barrier of her bra, he removed it carefully, laying it on the side of the sleeping bag before his fingers found and caressed the tender tip of one of her breasts. "Let me kiss you there," he said as he gently pushed Debbie back down onto the sleeping bag and found her breast with the tip of his tongue.

Spasms of delight shot through Debbie as Ben's tongue caressed the tip of her nipple, stiffening it into a hard peak of delight. His hand found her other nipple and tormented it until it too was hard in his hand. Debbie moaned as her hands found the hard warmth of Ben's chest and caressed it, finding his two small masculine nipples and tormenting them until they were hard to the touch. "Do you like this, Debbie?" Ben whispered as his breath came in little puffs against her breast.

"You know I like it, Ben," she moaned as Ben's questing lips traveled lower. "It's beautiful."

"That's good, Debbie," Ben said as his lips found and caressed the sensitive skin of her waistline, just at the edge of her dress. "Touch me, Debbie," he whispered.

With eager fingers, Debbie stroked the hard, velvety skin of his back and his sides, finding and touching a couple of scars on his back that she had noticed before. "How did that happen?" she asked as she fingered a short hard ridge on his side. "A bullet in the war?"

Ben chuckled as his fingers caressed the tender skin of her waist. "No. Would you believe a bar fight in Singapore?" He laughed. "We were fighting over a woman."

And how many women had he fought over in bars? Debbie asked herself as she continued to touch and caress him. How many women had he fought over for the privilege of having sex with? Because that's all it was to him. Just sex. It could be her, it could be a lady of the night, it wouldn't make any difference. Almost of their own volition, her fingers continued to touch and to stroke the body of the hard, unloving man she held in her arms, but in her mind, Debbie had pulled away from Ben.

Ben raised his head and, looking into her troubled eyes, pushed her into the blankets and covered her lips in a hard, punishing kiss that left her senses reeling but her heart cold. "It's beautiful, Debbie," he whispered as he could feel her spirit withdrawing from him. "It's good and it's right, you and me under a canopy of trees in the night."

Debbie's fingers touched the slightly softer skin of his stomach. "And what about the other?" she asked, more to herself than to him, as she continued to stroke and caress his strong body.

"There is no 'other,' " Ben said harshly as he held her face between his palms. "This is it, babe. This is what there is, this is all there is. A man. A woman. Sex. Period."

"No, Ben," Debbie said as she wrenched herself out of his arms and sat with her head buried in her hands. "I don't believe that sex is it. Period. There was more at one time for me, and there has to be more than that now, at least for me."

"So you're going to turn it off like a fountain because I won't say the right words, aren't you?" Ben scoffed. "All right, let's see how long you can hold out for love." He framed her face between her hands and kissed her hard and passionately, pushing her down into the sleeping bag and covering her body with his own. Her traitorous body responded in spite of her will, and Debbie's arms slowly crept back up around Ben's neck. She held him tightly, mindlessly, and she was taken totally by surprise when Ben pulled himself away from her. "There, how does it feel?" he taunted when Debbie murmured in protest. "How do you like it when I turn it off?"

"You're heartless, Ben Sako," Debbie whispered.

"I could have had you tonight and we both know it," Ben said as he lay on his back and willed his breathing to return to normal. "I could have taken you tonight, but I want you to come to me willingly."

"That will be a cold day in hell," Debbie said dryly.

"Sure it will," Ben taunted. "If I hadn't told you about

136

the bar fight over the woman, you would be in my arms right now, and your haughty eyes would be glazed over with passion. You aren't going to be able to hold out much longer, Debbie. We both know that." Ben whirled around to face her. "And that was the point I was trying to make about your friend. She's had ten years to learn about passion, ten years to forget about the chaste lover of her youth."

"You're wrong," Debbie whispered vehemently. "Wrong about Li and wrong about me."

Ben shrugged and turned over to face away from Debbie. "We'll just see about your friend," he said. "But it won't be long until you change your mind, Lotus."

Debbie found her bra and put it back on, but decided that it was too hot to put her dress back on. She lay awake in the darkness for long hours, trying to still the restless longing her unfulfilling encounter with Ben had generated within her. She had kept up a brave front, but inside she had her doubts. What if Li had gotten involved with someone else, and had just used Jim's money to join her lover? Debbie was able to reassure herself that Li and Jim's love had not died, but she seriously doubted her own strength of will. How much longer would she be able to fight her own growing attraction for Ben? Would she be able to hold out until they found Li and were out of the country? Or would she give into the attraction she felt for him and allow him to become her lover? She knew that a loveless affair would only hurt her in the long run, but she was beginning to wonder if the kind of affair she and Ben would have just might be worth the inevitable pain it was bound to inflict on her when it was over.

## CHAPTER EIGHT

Debbie squinted at the crudely lettered sign that pointed south. "What does it say?" Ben asked as he shifted his pack from one shoulder to the other.

"It says that Hue's another one hundred kilometers," Debbie said as she did a little mental arithmetic. "That's sixty miles, and another thirty miles to Phu Bai," she said.

"Well, I guess we better get moving," Ben said as they started back down the dusty road. An afternoon rain shower yesterday had taken the dust out of the air for a while, but the effects of the storm had worn off and the dust had returned full force. Since the area they were passing through was mostly farm country, they were having to use the roads instead of sneaking through jungle, and although they had been detained only once, Debbie became nervous every time they came upon the khaki-clad Communist soldiers. Debbie had been terrified, but Ben had pulled a piece of paper out of his shirt pocket and told Debbie to say something, anything, about their pass. She had babbled something about a weekend pass to the country and handed it back to Ben, who had proudly shown it to the soldier. The illiterate soldier had taken one look at the paper and waved them on through. Still, they never knew whether the next soldier to detain them would be that ignorant, and Debbie hoped to get off the roads and back to the forests very soon.

"Where are we going to spend the night?" Debbie asked as dusk began to fall. They had spent last night on an old American base that still had a couple of buildings standing, but there appeared to be no such accommodating structure around for them tonight.

Ben gazed around him as they walked past a water buffalo with a small girl, naked but for a shirt, sitting astride the buffalo's wide back. "I used to come by here in the middle of their winter, when it was fifty or sixty degrees outside and rain pouring down, and see little kids dressed just like that out playing in the rain."

Debbie gazed around at the cluster of rundown shacks that constituted yet another small village. "You know, it almost reminds me of the country around Monterrey, Mexico," she said. "The beautiful rain forests and right in the middle is an impoverished village. Was it always this poor, Ben?"

"Always this poor in material possessions," Ben said. "Not always this poor in spirit."

Debbie opened her mouth to ask Ben to elaborate, but at that moment he pointed to a small shack a little removed from the rest of the houses. "We can stay there. It's owned by a woman I knew in the war."

Debbie followed Ben to the door of the shack, the deepening dusk sheltering them from any prying eyes that might be following them. Ben knocked twice, sharply. After a moment the door was opened by a boy, maybe fifteen years old, with dark hair and Oriental eyes but with the strong cheekbones and jaw of a typical Irishman. He stared at them in the gloom of dusk for a moment before he threw open the door. "Mom, it's the soldier again," he said as he gestured for Ben and Debbie to enter.

A tiny, birdlike woman came out of the back and bowed formally to Ben. "I am honored that you join me in my home, Ben Sako," she said in English, with the cultured tones of an educated city dweller. "Will you want to stay the night?"

"Yes, Tian, my companion and I would like to spend the night," Ben said as he returned her formal bow. "Debbie, I'd like you to meet Tian and her son, Van."

Debbie bowed low to Tian. "I'm pleased to meet you and to be a guest in your home," she said in Vietnamese.

Tian looked surprised for a moment. "You are Ben's new interpreter?" she asked, also in Vietnamese.

Debbie glanced over at Ben. "Just for this trip," she said before she switched back to English for Ben's benefit.

"And Van, how are you?" Ben asked.

The boy hung his head. "Very well," he said in accented but clear English. Debbie stared at the Irish bones in the boy's face and the freckles that dotted his nose. He was the love child of Tian and a G.I. Was the father a good friend of Ben's? Debbie could feel her usual curiosity starting to grow about these two people, and it was all she could do not to blurt out her questions right there.

Although she had not been expecting Ben and Debbie, Tian was able to prepare a delicious dinner from the chicken and vegetables she had on hand. Van said very little throughout dinner and asked to be excused as soon as the meal was over. Ben told Tian a little bit about the mission he and Debbie were on, neglecting to tell her that he didn't really think Li wanted to be rescued, and Tian sent her best wishes to Jerry for a speedy recovery.

Although Tian was plainly curious when Ben and Debbie unrolled their sleeping bags and placed them side by side, she asked no questions and Debbie volunteered no answers, since she didn't know the answers to those questions herself. Since the night almost two weeks ago when they had found out that Li had gone south, Ben had not touched her, except in the most impersonal way. Yet Debbie was more achingly aware of his appealing masculinity than ever. He made no effort to hide his body from her, stepping out of his underwear with casual abandon and on a couple of occasions swimming in the nude, taunting her with his masculinity; yet, he had made no move to claim her as his lover. Debbie should have been pleased by Ben's passivity, but strangely she was not. More than once in the last two weeks she had wished that Ben would take the decision out of her hands by taking her into his arms, but he seemed content to wait until she gave a sign that she was ready. And Debbie could not bring herself to do that, to make a conscious commitment to a loveless affair that was bound to bring her pain.

Debbie watched with interest as Ben talked to the woman and her son. Although Debbie could detect no particular warmth or familiarity on Ben's part toward either the woman or her son, he was polite and kind to them both, and she saw him slip Tian and the boy each a little money the next morning before they left. Debbie's curiosity was eating her alive by the time they left Tian and Van, and she barely waited until they were out of town before she turned to Ben, her eyes bright with unspoken questions. "Who is she?" she whispered as they walked down the road that led south. "And what is she doing out in the country?"

Ben gazed over at Debbie. "Her son's an outcast, you know," he said. "And because she refused to give him up, she's an outcast too."

"Is it because he's part-Caucasian?" Debbie asked.

Ben nodded. "The Vietnamese, except for the most highly educated and sometimes even them, look down on a child of mixed parentage as something lower than an animal. Most of the G.I.s' love children were abandoned as very small children and forced to roam the streets in order to survive. Tian thinks she loved the soldier that fathered her child, so she refused to abandon him and moved up here to hide from her family."

"Was Van's father killed in the war?" Debbie asked.

"Hell, no, he's a Colorado businessman," Ben said. "He knows about Van, but has never lifted a finger to help either one of them. Some of us Green Berets helped her a little when Van was a baby, and now she helps me whenever I need a place to stay."

Debbie walked beside Ben in silence for a minute. "If Jim and Li had been able to stay here and marry, would their children have been looked down on?" she asked.

"Yes, in many circles they would have," he said.

"That's terrible!" Debbie said. "That's mean and cruel."

Ben shrugged. "Would it have been so different if you and Kevin had had a child?" he asked. "Your child would have been a half-breed too. A lot of people in America wouldn't have accepted him."

"Starting with my in-laws," Debbie said dryly. "They made cracks about squint-eyed grandkids until the day Kevin walked out my door. You're right. Our society's no better." She fell silent, remembering that Ben's grandparents had rejected him because he was half-Japanese. "What will become of Van?" she asked.

Ben shrugged. "He'll be an outcast all his life."

They walked south for most of the morning, passing cultivated fields and children playing while their mothers worked in those fields. Since there was no market as such nearby, Debbie stopped at one farm and bought a little rice and some dried water buffalo meat. She did not notice the way the farmer stared at her as she paid for the food, and at Ben as he stood at the edge of the field waiting for her. Debbie ran up to Ben and showed him the meat. "I've got real meat for tonight," she said as she tucked the food into her backpack.

They got back on the road south and had walked another mile or so when Ben spotted the familiar green pith helmet and cheap khaki uniform of the Communist soldiers. "Quick, give me that piece of paper," Ben said as the soldiers blocked the road and pointed their rifles at Ben and Debbie. Ben held out the piece of paper and made a gesturing motion with his hand.

The soldier read the paper and his face hardened. "This is no official document," he said to Ben. "This is forged."

Ben looked properly unconcerned, shrugging when the soldier repeated the statement to him. He turned to Debbie and gestured wildly toward his ears and his lips as the soldier thrust a gun in his ribs. "He's deaf," Debbie told the soldier in the colloquial accent she had heard for the last month.

The soldier ignored Debbie and spoke to Ben again. "This paper is a forgery," he repeated loudly. "And the farmer said that he saw the man talk to you." Again Ben gestured wildy at the men and Debbie.

Debbie fought to keep the trembling out of her voice. "He can't hear a word you say," she said. "He lost his hearing in the war." A nervous film of perspiration covered her upper lip.

The two Communist soldiers looked at each other. "Let's take him over to the hut and talk about this little document of his," the older one said. They grabbed Ben by the arm and propelled him toward the door of the hut by the side of the road. As the first soldier threw open the door, Debbie knew that if the soldiers opened that backpack, she and Ben were both goners. "We'll talk to him for a little while before we search that bag," he said as he jerked the bag off Ben's shoulders and tossed it down on the porch.

As soon as the door was shut behind them, Debbie ran to the porch and sat down beside the pack, her mind racing as she tried to remember all the incriminating things Ben was carrying. Her trembling fingers unearthed the American medicine kit and the wire cutters pretty quickly, but she had a hard time finding the pistol and the three knives she had seen Ben with. She put those into her pack and removed several more items that were of a suspicious nature. She was about to make a final check when the door flew open and the younger of the soldiers stepped out. Without even glancing her way, he picked up Ben's pack and took it inside.

Afraid that her pack would be next, Debbie retreated to the road and scurried down it a half mile or so to a small grove of trees. Since the trees had not been defoliated, she clambered up one, the now heavy pack cutting into her shoulders as it bounced against her. What were they doing to Ben? Were they torturing him, trying to make him talk? Were they going through his backpack? Had she forgotten to take something out of his pack that would give them both away? Reaction setting in, she shook with fear and dread as she stared up the road at the hut. She didn't dare return lest they decide to search her bag too. Her best bet was to wait here until Ben was released. Surely, if she had removed everything that was incriminating from the pack, they would let him go in a little while.

Debbie's fear mounted as the afternoon sun traveled across the sky and started sinking in the west. What could they possibly be doing with Ben for so long in there? Debbie's overactive imagination came up with all sorts of scenarios, each one more gruesome than the last. They could be torturing him in there, trying to get him to answer their questions. Debbie wondered if any of them spoke Chinese or English and could interrogate him in a language that he did speak. Debbie started once to load the gun and take her chances with the two soldiers, but just as she had worked up her courage, two more soldiers got off their bicycles and entered the building. Her heart sank and she put the gun back in the backpack. She might have had a chance with just two, but there was no way she could outshoot four soldiers. What were they doing to Ben? Was he all right? Strangely, Debbie only thought of her own safety once during the entire unending afternoon, and she was able to reassure herself that she would be all right even if something did happen to Ben, once she found Li. It was Ben's safety that worried and frightened her on that hot June afternoon.

Debbie squinted her eyes into the glare of the late afternoon sun as she spotted movement at the hut where Ben was being held. She stared at the hut, damning the glare off the metal roof that was making her eyes water, as she tried to see what was happening. The door had opened, but to her disappointment only a single soldier came out. No, the door was opening again and a black-clad figure emerged clutching a familiar backpack. It was Ben! They had let him go after all!

Debbie put her fist to her mouth to keep from calling out to Ben and giving herself away. She scurried down the tree, scratching her shin in the process, and waited at the edge of the grove of trees, behind a large teak tree.

Ben looked up and down the road before he spotted the sheltering grove of trees. He walked slowly toward the trees, searching them with a practiced eye, and stepped into them just a few feet from where Debbie stood. "Debbie? Are you in here?"

"Ben!" Debbie cried softly as she hurled herself toward him. "Are you all right? Did they hurt you? Oh, Ben, they gave you a black eye!" she said as she took in the shiner that graced Ben's right eye.

"That's all right, Lotus, I have a few more bruises in the gut," Ben said as he folded his arms around her and held her to him tightly. "But that's all. I guess you know you managed to save both our lives today," he said. "When they brought in that backpack I knew I was done for!" He cradled Debbie's shaking body against his. "Thank you for getting that stuff out of there. How did you manage it?"

"I worked fast," Debbie said as she cradled Ben's face between her palms and stared at his bruised eye. "Oh, Ben, I was so scared! I kept picturing all these awful things they might have been doing to you! I wanted to come after you, but then the other two soldiers came, and I knew I couldn't take them all on." She clung to him and rained feverish kisses all over his face. "I'm glad you're all right."

"I'm glad you're all right too," Ben said as he pulled her closer to him. "I was afraid they might go after you, especially after my bag was clean, and I knew you had that stuff with you." He gave her a long, passionate kiss that left her senses reeling. "Come on, we can't stay here tonight," he said as he pointed down the road. "We have another hour or so of light. Let's get away from those Charleys in case they change their minds about me."

Debbie shouldered the heavy backpack, and they

walked swiftly down the road, lest their lingering presence encourage further investigation. "What happened in there?" she asked as she trotted after Ben, her shoes kicking up dust in the road.

"I'm not sure," Ben said. "Since I didn't understand very much of what they were saying, it was easy to just keep playing the part of a deaf mute. They went through the pack and took my cigarettes and lighter, but since both are pretty common over here on the black market, they weren't particularly alarmed by those. They kicked me and punched me around a little, and then the four of them sat down over my little paper and tried for three hours to decide whether or not it was really a traveling permit. They must have decided it was, because they gave it back to me and let me go."

"Thank goodness," Debbie breathed. She was tempted to reach out and take Ben's hand, and only the knowledge that it was highly improper in this culture to do so stopped her. Still shaken by their experience of the afternoon, Ben and Debbie walked at an almost breakneck speed for the next hour, glancing over their shoulders for the familiar khaki uniform. They groaned when they could see up ahead another hut with the Communist flag flying. "We might not be so lucky this time," Ben said as he pointed into a cultivated field. "We're ducking this one."

They ran across the field, praying the soldiers at the patrol station would not notice them, and ran into another grove of trees. "Let's go a little deeper in here and set up camp," Ben said. "I guess it will have to be under the stars again."

"No, maybe not," Debbie said as she pointed at a small, painted building that was barely visible in the gathering dusk. "What's that?"

Ben took a couple of steps toward the building. "Well, I'll be," he said. "It looks like an old Buddhist shrine." They walked toward the quaint old building and stepped inside. It had been beautiful once, with the typical pagoda shape of the roof and intricate tiles inside, and even the ravages of age and the damage done by the war had not destroyed its charm completely. "We're staying here," he said.

"But Ben, this is a *church!*" Debbie protested. "We can't stay here."

"Why not?" Ben argued. "It's a sanctuary, Debbie, a place of peace and of rest. And I really need a place of peace and rest about now. Thank God, we're finally safe!" he said as he drew Debbie into his arms and tipped her face up to his lips. "I was horrified they'd catch you and hurt you."

Debbie pushed Ben's backpack off his shoulders. "I was terrified of what they were doing to you in there," she said as she started to pull the peasant shirt over his head. "Now I want to make sure you're all right. Are you sure that's all they did to you?"

"Yes, I'm sure," Ben said as he shrugged out of the shirt.

"They did, too, hurt you," Debbie said softly as she took in the black and blue spots on his chest and stomach. "They beat you pretty badly."

Ben looked down at the marks on his body. "I've had worse," he said as he fingered the scar on his face. "Want to kiss them all better for me?" he asked.

Debbie looked into his face, but could see none of the cynicism she had expected. Instead, Ben looked eager and almost hopeful that she would want to touch him. She shrugged out of her own heavy backpack and, with gentle fingers, caressed one of the marks on his chest before she bent her head and lightly touched the tender bruise. "Is that better?" she asked.

"Much," Ben breathed.

Debbie bent her lips to another spot and kissed it lightly before she moved to another. One by one she ministered to the bruises the soldiers had left on Ben, tasting and kissing and nibbling the smooth, slightly salty skin of his chest and stomach. She could feel Ben's breathing becoming rough and ragged, and her own was coming in labored gasps. As she kissed the last mark on his stomach, Ben put his hands on the side of her head and raised her lips to meet his. Hungrily, their lips met as their bodies melted together, their fears for each other and their relief that all was well erupting in a wild, explosive embrace.

Their mouths met and mingled for long moments, as they touched and tasted with starved eagerness. Debbie moaned and pressed herself closer to Ben, taking in the hardness of his body and the surprising softness of his mouth. Her eager fingers stroked his back and shoulders, and unmindful of the bruises on his stomach and chest, she pressed herself closer to his body, feeling every mesmerizing ridge and sinew. Now, finally, she was ready for what Ben had wanted for so long. She was ready to become his lover, to join her body with his and give and take freely with him. He was right—they did belong together, it was right for them to come together, even if her reasons for doing so and Ben's were not the same. Ben released her lips and trailed a string of feather-light kisses across her face. "Are you really all right, Lotus?" he asked softly.

Debbie smiled tenderly at Ben. "I'm all right now, but I'm going to be even better later," she said. "And so are you. Make love to me, Ben. I need that tonight. We both do."

Ben pulled back and looked into her eyes. "Are you sure, Debbie?" he asked.

Debbie's eyes widened. "Have you changed your mind about us?" she asked.

"No, but I want you to be very sure," Ben said. "I don't want you to come to me unwillingly, and I don't want you to feel any regrets in the morning for what we've shared. I want you to want this as much as I do."

Debbie stared into Ben's eyes and tried to hide her amazement. Was this the same Ben who had earlier announced his intention to have her for his lover, no matter what? The same man who had forced her to go with him to Hong Kong? Was this caring man and the other, callous one the same Ben Sako? Debbie cleared away her surprise and took Ben's face between her palms, kissing him lightly. "Yes, Ben, I'm sure. I've never been quite this sure of anything in my life."

"Then nothing is going to come between us tonight, Lotus," Ben said as he stepped away from her. He got out his sleeping bag and spread it full width on the wooden floor, and spread hers on top of his, making the makeshift bed surprisingly comfortable. He got the flashlight out of her backpack and wrapped his shirt around it before he set it next to the sleeping bags, bathing the shrine in a soft, muted glow. "I want to see you when I make love to you," he said as his gentle fingers slowly unbuttoned the bodice of Debbie's dress. He pushed her top off her shoulders and down her hips, leaving Debbie bare to the waist except for her lacy scrap of bra. He drank in the sight of her loveliness for a moment before he tucked his thumbs into her pajamalike pants and pushed them down her hips and legs.

Debbie braced herself on Ben's shoulders as she stepped out of the pants, her body naked but for the lacy underwear. Ben gazed at her body, tenderness and desire in his expression. "You better get those off yourself," he said. "I don't want to tear them in my eagerness."

Debbie unhooked the bra and pulled it off. Her panties joined her bra on the floor, and she stood before Ben. She stood boldly, not shy as she had been the first time Kevin had seen her nude. It was as though her body had been created for Ben to see, to enjoy, to possess. Ben stared at her for a moment, taking in the sleek lines of her naked body before he pulled off his pants and his briefs and stood before her.

Debbie had seen Ben naked before, since he had made no particular effort to hide his body from her, but this time, knowing that she would be able to touch him, to feel him—Debbie stared at the naked symmetry of his hard, scarred body for a moment before she opened her arms to him. Ben stepped into her arms, and they pressed their bodies together, softly and tentatively at first, as they explored the sensation of their bodies touching. Ben enveloped Debbie in his arms and they clung together, Debbie's breasts pressed into Ben's hard chest, her stomach nudging his, their legs entwined. Debbie could feel the evidence of Ben's desire for her, the same desire she felt for him, and had for so long. "Take me, Ben," she whispered as Ben lowered the two of them to the sleeping bags. "I want you so. I want you to be my lover."

"I want you too, Lotus," Ben said as he rained kisses down her face and onto her shoulders. "I wanted you the first time I laid eyes on you. The very first time." He found the tip of one of her breasts and explored it with his tongue.

"I know," Debbie whispered. "You made it very clear that you wanted me."

"No, Lotus," Ben said. "I wanted you years ago, when you came to me for an interview. You were another man's wife then, and I still wanted you so badly that it made me ache inside. I got you out of there as quickly as I could." His lips moved to her other breast and touched it lovingly.

"You wanted me then?" Debbie asked as her fingers played down the hard muscles of Ben's back and down his hips.

"Yes, I wanted you then, and I want you even more now," Ben said as his lips traveled down Debbie's midriff to her tiny waist. "I've lain awake, Lotus, and watched you sleep at night, and it was all I could do to keep from reaching out to you and taking you in your sleep."

"I've wanted you too, Ben," Debbie whispered as her hands stroked the hard flesh of his buttocks. "But I was scared."

Ben's grip tightened on her. "Don't be, Debbie," he said as his lips tormented her navel. "I'm not going to hurt you. I'm going to make this special for you." His fingers touched her tenderly, intimately, and when he could tell that she was ready for him, he eased his body over hers and made them one.

Ben was still for a moment, letting her body adjust to the presence of his, and the first of his movements were slow and gentle. Debbie relaxed in his embrace, letting herself go to the pleasure of his touch, whimpering a little with delight as Ben moved within her. When he saw that she was ready for his passion, his movements increased in strength and intensity, transporting Debbie to a place where she had never been before. She moaned and gasped beneath him, twisting herself so that Ben would be able to possess her most fully. Higher and higher they swirled, together on a plane that Debbie had never reached before, crying out together when the ultimate overtook them both. Ben's moan of pleasure was masked by Debbie's startled little cry, and they collapsed together, a damp tangle of arms and legs, as they slowly drifted back down to earth.

Debbie ate the last of her dinner of rice and meat and set the bowl down beside her. She and Ben had finally roused themselves after a second session of lovemaking and prepared a very late supper, which was probably no better than anything else they had eaten on the trail but certainly seemed so. They sat together, crosslegged and naked as the day they were born, on the sleeping bags that they would share tonight. Debbie smiled at Ben as she took his hand. "Well, you finally got what you came for on this trip," she said. "I'm your lover now."

Ben stroked the back of her hand. "Are you sorry?" he asked.

Debbie shook her head. "No, I'm not sorry," she assured him.

Ben thought a minute. "I have a confession to make," he said slowly. "I wasn't lying when I said you were wonderful," he said when Debbie turned startled eyes on him. "You were." He leaned toward Debbie and kissed her lips tenderly. "But I didn't come ahead on this trip just to make you my lover."

"You didn't?" Debbie asked. "Even after you realized that Jim had changed his mind about blackmailing you?"

Ben nodded his head. "If making you my lover was all that I had cared about, I would have gone on back to San Francisco and kept seeing you there. With or without your cooperation," he said as Debbie started to sputter. He silenced her with another kiss.

"Then why did you come on this trip?" Debbie asked.

For a moment Debbie thought he wasn't going to answer her. "For the money," he said finally. "It's my living."

Debbie uttered a rude word and shook her head. "Come on, Ben, after what we've shared tonight, I deserve a more honest answer than that. Really, why do you do it? Brave the hardship, put yourself in danger time after time? You could make a lot more money doing something else. For that matter, you could have made a lot more money on this trip, but you didn't."

Ben looked uncomfortable for a minute. "For freedom," he blurted suddenly. He turned to Debbie and his eyes were blazing. "I may not believe in much in this life, but I believe in freedom, Debbie. I believe that people ought to have the freedom to come and go as they please, to hold the job they want to hold, and to say and believe what they want to. And the people over here don't have that anymore. Your friends weren't the only ones who were separated or thrown into prison or worse by the power that's now in control here. I can't fight that whole power, but I can do something to get a few people out from under that kind of tyranny."

"And Li?" Debbie asked.

Ben put his arm around Debbie. "Lotus, I don't give a damn about your friend's love life, but if I can get her out from under Communist domination and into a land of freedom, then I'll do it. It was a land of freedom that gave me a chance, and I want that for other people too." He and Debbie shared a long, lingering kiss. "Now, come on and lie down beside me. We better get some sleep."

Ben put out the fire and they lay down together, but

154

Ben sat up in less than five minutes. "We're far enough south so that we're going to have to sleep under this from now on," he said as he covered them both with mosquito netting. "I don't want that delectable body of yours covered with red welts."

Debbie snuggled up beside Ben. " 'Night, Ben," she said softly in the darkness. She lay quietly in the still of the night, listening to the peculiar night sounds of the forest. Debbie had been surprised that Ben believed so passionately in freedom, although she admitted to herself that the signs had been there all along. He was more than just a believer—his opinions bordered on being almost idealistic. And for his beliefs he risked his life on a regular basis.

As Debbie thought, she tried to reconcile the cynical, hard-nosed man who did not believe in love with the idealistic freedom fighter who had made love to her so tenderly. Perhaps Ben wasn't the impossibly cold and hard man she thought she knew. Maybe he was capable of deeper emotion than he thought he was. Maybe, just maybe, he was capable of the love that he put down so frequently. Was she the woman who could teach him to love?

As Debbie's eyes drifted shut, another thought occurred to her and her eyes snapped back open. In her passion for Ben, she had completely forgotten about taking any precautions, although out here in the forest she really couldn't get any to use. And she knew from the contents of Ben's backpack that he wasn't prepared either, since he hadn't expected to bring her or any other woman along on this part of the trip. Oh, well, it would probably be all right. She and Kevin had tried to have a child, and nothing had happened. She probably wasn't all that fertile. It wasn't the right time in her cycle for conception and in any event, there wasn't really anything she could do about it at this point, anyway. She shut her eyes again and in just a few minutes she was asleep.

Ben stared down at the sleeping woman that he cradled in his arms, a troubled expression on his face. Well, he had finally done it. It had taken a good scare and a couple of Communist soldiers to help him, but he had made Debbie Cheong his lover. After weeks of frustration, his body was finally sated, but the peace of mind he expected had not come. He was still frustrated and unsatisfied, and the worst part of it was that he didn't know why. He knew that he wanted more, but he didn't know what more he wanted or why he wanted it, or even if there was more to be had. They had become lovers, as he had wanted them to. They had achieved the ultimate possible between a man and a woman. What more was there to achieve?

## CHAPTER NINE

Debbie stared across the sparkling blue waters of the Perfume River. "It's so beautiful," she said as she gazed at the foliage-covered banks of the famous river. She turned to Ben, a wide smile on her face. "This whole land is simply enchanting," she said. "In spite of the war and the Communists, it's gorgeous."

Ben put his arm around Debbie and squeezed her shoulders. "I've always thought it very special," he said. "That's why it nearly killed me when the Communists took over. So, are you ready to go across?"

Debbie nodded. "I sure wish I could see Hue," she said as she glanced in the direction of the ancient walled city where the Imperial Palace was found.

Ben stared at her in astonishment. "You have to be kidding!" he said. "I thought you just wanted to get in, get Li, and get out."

"Well, I don't have any desire to hike to Saigon, but it's a shame to get this close and then not get to see any of it."

"You're right," Ben said as he took her hand and pointed back up to the road. "Let's go play tourist."

Debbie's face lit up in a smile. "You mean we're really going to do it? We're really going to see Hue?"

"We might as well," Ben said. "It's only about an hour

away on foot. We can see the city today, camp on the other side of the river, and make it to Phu Bai sometime tomorrow. Just keep your mouth shut once we get inside the walls."

Debbie nodded, and just to be on the safe side they put on the Communist soldier uniforms Ben had stolen the morning after he had been detained by the soldiers. Cursing himself for not thinking of it earlier, he had hiked down to the second hut and slipped inside for a moment, and he and Debbie substituted their peasant clothing for the unisex, khaki uniforms. Now they traveled boldly down the roads, Debbie waving papers and saying something vague about a message from Ho Chi Minh City any time they had to go through a road block. They had made faster time in the uniforms, but in order to avoid suspicion they would change back and travel every so often as peasants.

They were waved through the entrance to the ancient walled city without hesitation. For the next two hours, Ben walked Debbie through the narrow streets of the old city, and Debbie marveled at the beauty and grace of the ancient Vietnamese architecture. They were both grateful that the ancient shrines had not been destroyed, and Debbie was enchanted by the Imperial Palace and the spacious grounds that surrounded it. She had to hide her amusement at Highway 1, the only paved highway in Vietnam. It ran the entire length of the long, narrow country, and consisted of two narrow lanes clogged with bicycles, funny little English cars, and the occasional American jeep left over from the war years. When Debbie had seen her fill of Hue, they were waved back out the exit, and they crossed the Perfume River and managed to hike to within ten miles of Phu Bai before nightfall.

Ben found an old American campsite that was far off

the road and spread their sleeping bags in an old body pit, a depression that wasn't much more than a hole in the ground but that would allow them to drape their mosquito nets while they slept. The mosquitoes were an increasing problem as they traveled farther south, and Ben had found that mosquito nets were much more effective than repellent. Debbie prepared a meal and she and Ben sat side by side on the sleeping bags, clad only in their underwear, the mosquito net suspended over them. "I'm excited," Debbie admitted as she put her empty bowl down and sat crosslegged beside Ben. "I just have a feeling about tomorrow."

"You were excited last time, Lotus," Ben cautioned her. "We don't know that she's in this camp either. We may chase around this country all summer looking for her."

"We've been here nearly a month already," Debbie said. "What is it—about the fifteenth?"

Ben shrugged. "I've lost count," he said. "Anyway, it doesn't matter."

"You could have made better time with Jerry," Debbie said. "I've slowed you up."

"Well, maybe a little, but you also saved my life," Ben said as he took Debbie into his arms and pushed her down onto the sleeping bag. "Besides, traveling with you has certain compensations that traveling with Jerry never had." He covered her lips in a hard, sweet kiss.

"Oh, and what compensations are those?" Debbie asked as she linked her arms around Ben's neck. "Does Jerry do this to you?" she asked as she feathered soft kisses across his chin and down his neck. "Or this?" she asked as her gentle fingers held him close to her. "Or this?" she asked as her hips thrust upward to meet his.

Ben chuckled as his fingers found the closure of her bra

and snapped it open. "No, I can't say that Jerry ever did," he said as he lowered the cups of her bra and sampled the sweetness of her breasts. "And I must admit that I would prefer to have you do these things to me. Dear God, Lotus, you feel so good when you do that to me!"

The rest of their underwear was swiftly removed, and before long they were sharing the tenderness and passion that had become so much a part of their relationship. Debbie reveled in the passion that Ben had brought out of her, passion that even Kevin had left undiscovered. Debbie in turn brought out in Ben a tenderness and a gentleness that he had not known he was capable of. He continued to be amazed at the tender, protective, caring emotions, completely separate from sex or passion, that she inspired in him. At times Ben felt confused by his feelings for Debbie, but he was enjoying their affair too much to spend time worrying about it.

Afterward, Debbie lay in Ben's arms, lulled by the even rise and fall of his chest beside her. She wondered, as she sometimes did in the quiet of the night, if this affair was going to hurt her in the long run, but there was no way she could go back to the way things were before she became Ben's lover, nor did she really want to. Ben was a passionate and demanding lover, but he was gentle at the same time, and with him she had climbed the mountains and soared the skies. In spite of her father's warning about Ben, a tiny seed of hope was growing within her, a hope that maybe Ben someday could throw off the dehumanizing effects of his loveless upbringing and learn to love, if not her then another woman. If his compassionate treatment of her since they had left Hong Kong was anything to go by, he had the potential to love within him. It was just a matter of developing that potential. And when they found Li, and he could see for himself that Li's love had lasted as well as Jim's, maybe he would let himself learn to care.

Debbie finally drifted off to sleep and slept deeply, but she was awake instantly the next morning when Ben shook her shoulder. "If we hurry, we can be to Phu Bai by the middle of the morning."

Debbie stood up and took fresh underwear out of the pack. "What are we wearing today?" she asked. "The uniforms?"

Ben thought a minute and shook his head. "Uh, I don't think so. It's one thing to wear one on the road where they just wave you through, but it's another thing entirely to try to pass yourself off as one of them for any length of time. We would be better off going as peasants." He knelt on the sleeping bag and soaped and shaved the sparse beard that he grew.

"I don't know why you bother," Debbie teased as she pulled on the peasant outfit and wound her hair up on her head. "Most fellows wait until their peach fuzz gets a little thicker."

"At least I never scratch your face," Ben quipped before his face sobered. "But really, does a beard and all that turn you on?" He glanced down at his smooth, hairless chest and stomach.

Debbie knelt beside him, surprised by the insecurity on his face, and kissed his shoulder. "You turn me on," she told him. "Everything about you—your face, your hair, your body, even this scar on your face." She kissed the long scar that ran down the side of his face. "Get this in a bar fight, too?" she teased.

"No, I got that on my last mission in China," he said as he fingered the scar she had just kissed. "Thanks, Lotus. You can say a few words and make a man feel wonderful." He kissed her once, hard, and returned to his shaving, leaving Debbie to wipe soap suds off her face. "Are you about ready to go?"

Debbie nodded, and together they walked down the muddy road that led to Phu Bai. It had rained the day before and a heavy thunderstorm in the morning drenched Debbie and Ben to the skin. It was over quickly, and in the moist heat their clothes soon dried. The humidity was high, and Debbie thought that she had never been so hot in all her life.

Debbie got directions to the farm in Phu Bai, and she and Ben walked the four miles to the farm, skirting the road and cutting through woods and fields. There was a guard posted at the entrance to the farm, but as they circled the farm, they realized that part of the farm was unfenced. Ben commented that this farm must not be of the same quasi-prison variety as the farm in the north, and his supposition was confirmed a few minutes later when a couple of workers walked out in full view of the guard, who made no move to stop them.

"This farm should be fairly easy to get Li out of," Debbie whispered as she glanced out at the workers in the field. "She can just walk out after dark."

"That is, if she wants to," Ben muttered, earning himself a dirty look from Debbie. They waited until there were just a few workers in the fields and no guards nearby before they walked down to the field. They received a few curious stares, but no one seemed too surprised to see them.

Debbie stepped up to a very young girl who was working with a hoe and tapped her on the shoulder. "Excuse me, can you tell me if a woman by the name of Nguyen Li Ha is at this camp?" She did not see the young man who was kneeling several yards away, or the way his eyes narrowed when he heard Debbie's question.

"Nguyen Li Ha? No, I know no Li at this camp. But I've only been here a few weeks and don't know very many people yet. But he might know." She gestured over to the young man. "Hung! Come here a minute!" she called.

The young man named Hung got up off the ground and walked over to Debbie and the young girl. Ben stood quietly a few feet away. "Hung, this lady is looking for a woman named Li. Do you know anybody by that name here?"

Hung nodded. "Of course, Nguyen Li Ha. Her father was an important military officer in the old regime."

"Yes, that's Li!" Debbie said excitedly. "Where is she? Can I see her?"

"Madame, I'm so sorry you have come here for no cause," Hung replied quickly. "Li left here several weeks ago."

Debbie's face fell. "Do you know where she was going?" she asked.

Hung shook his head. "No, I don't," he said, but at that moment he glanced back at Ben's intent stare. "No, wait! She said she had asked to go to the People's farm, up close to the Ashaw Valley. And with the money she had to pay the officials, I'm sure they sent her there."

"I see," Debbie said, fighting the tears that were stinging her lids. "Thank you." She and Ben walked out of the field and back into the woods adjacent to the farm. Debbie sank down on a fallen log and buried her face in her hair. "He said she had gone to the People's farm up close to the Ashaw Valley."

Ben uttered a sharp curse word. "Hell, she's either trying to learn every farming method utilized in Vietnam, or she's looking for somebody," he muttered. "Come on. We're going to have to retrace our steps a little."

It was a tired and dispirited Debbie who followed Ben back up the countryside that afternoon. They had changed into their soldiers' uniforms and a peasant woman unexpectedly offered them a ride on her cart, so by nightfall they were already back to the Perfume River.

Sitting on the bank of the wide, serene river, Debbie went over in her mind the conversation she had earlier with the young man named Hung. Something had not been right. Hung had been too quick to say that Li had gone, and he had been about to say that he didn't know where she was before he changed his mind for some reason. And he had been too quick to identify her as her father's daughter. Debbie motioned Ben over and patted the ground beside her. "You're going to think I'm crazy, but I want to go back to Phu Bai tomorrow and look around," she said. "I don't think Hung was telling the truth."

Ben lay back on the ground and closed his eyes. "Tell me exactly what was said in the conversation and also the way it was said."

Debbie shut her eyes to think. "I asked if he knew anyone named Li, and he immediately said that he knew a Nguyen Li Ha and that she was a general's daughter."

"Go on," prompted Ben.

"Well, I asked if I could see her and he said that she had moved, that with the money she had they had probably moved her where she wanted to go. At first I thought he was going to say he didn't know where she was, but he suddenly said she was at the People's farm near the Ashaw Valley. Ben, I don't know what it is, but there's something suspicious about that. Or am I just grasping at straws?" She looked over at Ben. "Do I just want to find her so badly I'm seeing things like I want to see them?"

Ben shrugged his shoulders. "I'll tell you what I'm seeing, but you're not going to like it."

"I'm probably not," Debbie agreed. "So tell me—what do you think's going on?"

"I think she put him up to lying for her."

Debbie thought a minute. "That won't hold water," she said. "How did Li know to have him lie for her? How did she know anybody was coming for her? She didn't know we were coming, so she could hardly have made arrangements with him to send us away."

"You're right," Ben conceded. "She couldn't have known." He thought a minute. "I know you're not going to like the other possibility, either."

"You think he's her lover," Debbie said dully.

"Bingo. Yes, I do think she's involved with him," Ben said. "He knew who her father was, and he knew that she had money. The question is, if they were just casual acquaintances, how did he know so much? And why did he want to get rid of us so badly? I don't think he has any idea who we really are, I just think he's very jealous of his girl friend."

"No, Li couldn't have gotten involved with him," Debbie said defensively. "Not after Jim wrote her and sent her the money. She wouldn't do that, Ben!" Debbie clenched her hands in front of her.

"What other explanation is there, Debbie?" Ben asked.

"What if the affection's all on his part?" Debbie demanded. "You know, he loves Li and Li loves Jim. It's entirely possible, you know."

"Anything's possible," Ben conceded. "But I do think you're right about him lying to us. How would you like to pay another visit to the historic old metropolis of Phu Bai?"

"And if she's there?" Debbie asked.

"I'll ask her what she wants to do and abide by her wishes," Ben replied steadily. "And if I get a chance I leave Hung minus a few teeth for lying to me. No, Debbie, I wouldn't really do that," he said when her eyes widened in horror. "I'm not about to do anything that will draw attention to us. Now, I'll make the fire and you make the rice."

"Yes, Tarzan," Debbie teased as she got up and found the wok in her backpack.

Ben finished the last of his supper and pushed the bowl aside. "I get so sick of rice on these trips I could scream," he admitted as he got a couple of vitamin pills out of the medicine kit and gave one to Debbie. "Here, we don't want you getting scurvy." He fiddled with his hands while Debbie finished the last of her rice and took her vitamin pill.

"They didn't give back your cigarettes?" Debbie asked as she gathered up their bowls. "Can you buy any over here?"

"No, they didn't, and I don't know if there are any available locally on the black market." Ben picked up the wok and followed Debbie to the bank of the river. They rinsed out their dishes and put them in the backpack. "We better wash our clothes, too, as soon as it gets dark," Ben said.

"Why not go ahead?" Debbie asked.

Ben pointed to a flat-bottomed boat coming down the river. "I personally don't care to be anyone's peep show, but if you don't mind . . ."

"I'll wait." Debbie laughed. They sat on the bank, soaking in the peace and beauty of the meandering river, as dusk colored the sky and the water. As the sun drifted below the horizon, the huge yellow orb of the full moon rose in the east, bathing the river in silver splendor. Debbie and Ben said little, and when they did speak, they avoided the topic that was uppermost in Debbie's mind. Was Li in Phu Bai? Had she become involved with another man, or had she remained loyal to Jim? Debbie desperately wanted to believe that Li had been faithful, but she was honest enough with herself to admit that Li could very well have become involved with someone else in the intervening years. But Debbie simply could not believe Li would take Jim's money if she didn't intend to come out of Vietnam. Li had a basic integrity that would not have allowed her to do that, even if her heart now belonged to another man.

Ben glanced over at Debbie's strained face. She was fretting about her friend again, when she should have been enjoying the beauty of the night. He reached out and squeezed her hand. "It's dark enough now to wash our clothes," he said as he stood up and stripped the peasant clothing from his body. "And the other set, too. Those uniforms look a little seedy."

Debbie stood up and peeled off her dress and pants. "I wish we had some soap to use on these things," she grumbled as she stepped into the river and waded out to where the water was up to her waist. She scrubbed the two garments together and wrung them out as she waded back to shore.

"I think we ought to save our soap for us," Ben said as he took her clothes and wrung them out a little better. He handed her his clothing to wash and then the Communist uniforms, and wrung them for her and spread them over clean rocks to dry in the heat of the night.

Debbie waded out to where the water lapped her chest. Carefully, so as not to lose them in the meandering current, she took off her underwear and scrubbed them together. The pale moonlight gently painted her body in its silver glow as she waded into the shallower water and handed Ben the undergarments. "Put these with the others, will you?"

Ben took the underwear from her, his gaze never leaving her body as she stepped out of the water and felt around in her backpack. She had to be the most beautiful woman he had ever laid eyes on. She was slender but not too thin, and the tips of her breasts turned up just a little. Ben felt the familiar rush of desire he had known every time he had seen her naked, which had been pretty often in the last two weeks since she had become his lover. She was not in the least bit modest or embarrassed about her body—in fact, she seemed to enjoy the pleasure he took in seeing her naked beauty, and he knew that she took pleasure in seeing him nude. Ben could understand the physical desire he felt for this beautiful woman, of course, but he could not understand why it seemed to grow, and not slacken, as he had thought it would once they had become intimate.

Debbie found the small bottle of shampoo she had insisted on bringing with her and stepped back in the water. "Have any of your soap left? I don't know about you, but I feel like getting really clean tonight." She smiled at Ben provocatively, and he didn't miss the invitation in her eyes.

Ben felt around in his backpack until his hands closed over the small bar of soap. By the time he had waded out to where the water was up to his chest, Debbie had dipped her head in the water, and her hair was plastered to her neck and her back. "Here," she said as she handed him the shampoo. "Squirt in a little of this, will you?"

Ben took the shampoo from her and squirted a little into her hair. Debbie raised her arms and started to rub the soap into a lather. "Hey, Ben, I need a little more shampoo," she said as she pulled the ends of her flowing hair up out of the water. "I have a lot of hair, and it's pretty dirty."

Ben squirted her another stream of shampoo and ducked his own head in the water. He squirted a little shampoo in his own hair and tossed the plastic bottle up on the bank. "So what exotic wildflower am I going to smell like this week?" he teased as he rubbed the shampoo into his own hair.

"Mountain daisies." Debbie giggled as she worked the suds down her long black tresses. Ben just watched her for a moment, as her graceful fingers soaped her hair, but the desire to touch her was too great. His hands buried themselves in her hair, gently touching and soaping, his fingers caressing the sensitive nerve endings of her scalp. Debbie shivered as she lowered her own hands, only to raise them again and bury them in the soapy thickness of Ben's hair. Her fingers found the sensitive skin down close to his nape and she caressed it, deliberately teasing and arousing him with her touch.

Ben shivered a moment from the sensuality of her caress. "Are you sensitive there too?" he asked as he found and touched the same place on the back of her head. He stroked her there for long moments, touching and caressing, as he brought Debbie to the same pitch of arousal that she had brought him to. He piled the soapy mass of hair high on her head, fashioning it into a crown. "You look like a princess, Debbie. A beautiful Chinese princess."

"Does that make you my prince?" Debbie asked as her fingers framed his face. Ben pushed her down into the water and with gentle fingers rinsed the soap from her hair, leaving her hair a wet, wild tangle down her back.

He ducked his head under the water and quickly washed the soap out of his own hair.

Ben fingered the rough features of his face and the scar that ran down one side of it. "Would you believe the frog?" he asked ruefully.

Debbie responded swiftly to his self-deprecating remark. "Ben, you're the most attractive man I've ever known," she said as she framed his face in her hands. "I wish you could see yourself through my eyes."

"Thank you, Debbie," Ben said as he kissed her lips lightly. "No one's ever said anything like that to me before. Now, what was it that the princess did to change her frog into a prince?" He framed her face with his hands and brought their lips together in a searing kiss.

Debbie gasped and opened her mouth to his sensual embrace. Touching, tasting, they let their mouths meet and mingle as Ben pulled Debbie close to him in the warm water of the river. The water glided over them like fine silk, caressing them gently as they clung together. Debbie's fingers found and stroked the hard skin of Ben's back and shoulders, and her legs intwined with his under the surface of the water. She could feel the evidence of his desire for her as their bodies melted together. She could feel Ben's hands as they touched her shoulders, her breasts, the sensitive skin of her back and sides. Desire raging within her, she stroked Ben's hard body feverishly, greedily, wanting him, needing him.

It was Debbie who finally pulled back. "Don't you ever doubt your appeal again, Ben. You are the most sensually appealing man I have ever known. Promise?"

"I promise," Ben agreed as he held her close to him. She couldn't help but feel a little sorry for Ben, since all of his other relationships must have been so shallow that no woman had ever told him just how compelling, how sensual he was. He waded to the bank, where he picked up a bar of soap. "Come over here where it's a little more shallow," he said. "We can soap down."

Debbie waded to where the water lapped at her knees. Ben dipped his soap in the water and lovingly soaped every inch of Debbie's body, starting with her face and working down to her neck and shoulders. Her breasts received special attention, as did her arms and her waist. Debbie trembled in the warm summer air as Ben's fingers drifted lower, becoming more intimate as he caressed her hips and thighs. "Here, hold up your leg," he said. "Let me get your feet."

Debbie held up one foot at a time and Ben scrubbed the dirt from each one. She took the soap from Ben and dipped it in the water, sensually soaping his body as he had hers, her fingers gliding over the strength of his chest and shoulders, the leanness of his waist, the velvet hardness of his back. Ben moaned when she reached the center of his masculinity and caressed it lovingly before drifting downward. Her touch was sensual, provocative, deliberately tormenting, as his had been. She sought to give him the same pleasure he had given her, to bring him the delight that she knew they would both revel in.

Ben groaned as he took the soap from her and laid it on the bank. "Here, let's go back out and rinse off," he said as he took her by the shoulders and pushed her into the deeper water. Debbie stopped where the water just reached her breasts and dipped her shoulders and neck in the water, scooping water with her hands and wiping the soap off her face.

Ben splashed the soap off himself and drew Debbie to him. "You're the most beautiful woman I've ever known," he murmured as he drew her body to his. He caressed her under the surface of the water, touching her breasts, her hips, her waist. "I've got to have you, Debbie," he murmured as he held her bottom in his hands and pulled her to him. "Wrap your legs around me. Let me take you."

"Here?" Debbie asked, startled, but her sense of rightness took over, and she wrapped her legs around Ben as he possessed her with a single quick thrust. She clung to him, her arms around his neck and her legs around his waist, as he anchored his hands on her waist and with gentle, passionate motions set the pace of their lovemaking. Debbie let Ben take over and let herself go to the intimacy, the passion, of their embrace. Together they swirled higher and higher, the silky caress of the water adding to the passion of their touch. Debbie gasped when the moment of pure pleasure came, shuddering in Ben's embrace as they shivered together in the warmth of the night.

Debbie sat crosslegged on the sleeping bag, naked but for the mosquito net wrapped around her from the neck down, and tilted her head so that Ben could work a wide-toothed plastic comb through her tangled hair. "I guess I ought to cut it," she mused as Ben's gentle fingers worked out a particularly fierce snarl.

"Oh, please, no," Ben said as he eased the comb through the tangles, smoothing them down her hair and into oblivion. "Your hair is one of the nicest things about you." He ran the comb over the surface of her scalp and down the back of her hair. "It was one of the first things I noticed about you."

"One of the first things?" Debbie mused. "And what else did you notice?"

"Your breasts," Ben said as he smoothed a lock of hair that had fallen down the side of her face.

"My breasts?" Debbie asked, blushing. "But they're not big!"

"No, but they're perfectly proportioned to the rest of you," Ben said as he bent his head and kissed one of them through the mosquito netting. "I imagined what they would look like under your clothes, and I must admit I wasn't disappointed."

"Notice anything else?" she asked.

Ben thought a minute. "You reminded me of your father," he said. "Oh, not your looks, but the way you wouldn't take no for an answer."

"Neither would you," Debbie reminded him. Ben removed the last tangle from Debbie's hair, and put the comb back into her backpack.

"What are you thinking about?" Ben asked as he sat down beside Debbie and pulled a section of mosquito net over his bare legs. Debbie's expression indicated that her thoughts were far away, probably on her friend again. "Is something bothering you?"

"Ben, is it true that Oriental women . . . um . . . know things to do in bed?"

Ben's mouth flew open as he stared at Debbie, and tried not to laugh out loud. "You're Oriental, Debbie. You should know."

"I'm not Oriental like that, Ben," Debbie said. "And I've always heard all these stories about them—that they knew different things that men liked. I know you've spent a lot of time in this part of the world and . . . well . . ." She blushed and turned embarrassed eyes on him. "I don't know all that much," she admitted. "There was never anyone else besides Kevin. I just don't want you to get bored."

Ben threw his head back and let loose with a whoop of laughter. "Debbie, I have to agree that you don't know

173

much, if you can come out with something like that after what we've shared. Can't you tell that I'm enchanted with you?" he asked as he cradled her in his arms. "Can't you tell that I'm obsessed with the perfection of your body? That I crave those little cries you make in the back of your throat when I bring you pleasure? That I can hardly wait to touch you and have you again? Couldn't you tell, when I dragged you halfway across the world to be with me? Bored? Debbie, I have yet to spend a boring moment with you, in the sleeping bag or out of it."

"I'm glad, Ben," she said as she pushed him down on the sleeping bag and arranged the mosquito net over the both of them. "I'm glad, because I feel the same way about you. I just can't get enough of you, Ben." She trailed light kisses over his face and his neck. "I want you. I want all of you." Her lips traveled down his chest, paying special attention to his hard nipples, and on down his smooth, hard chest to his stomach, where she teased and tantalized the inside of his navel. Ben gasped as her mouth drifted lower, finding and caressing him until he was nearly to the breaking point. When Debbie sensed that release was near, she moved over him and made them one, their union swift and breathtakingly sweet as waves of pleasure broke over the both of them.

"And you were worried that the Oriental women had something on you," Ben teased as Debbie rolled off his spent body. "Debbie, that was the most, the finest . . ." He shrugged helplessly at his inability to articulate his feelings. Murmuring tender words to her, Ben cradled Debbie to his side and soon was asleep in her arms, his head pillowed on her chest, between the breasts he thought so beautiful. Debbie stared out at the sparkling waters of the Perfume River. She had not meant to, she even had tried not to, but she had fallen in love with Ben

Sako. She loved him deeply, dearly, more fiercely than she had ever loved Kevin. She had fallen in love with a man who didn't even believe in the emotion. What on earth had she done?

But did Ben have it in him to change his mind about love? She had seen another side to him since they had come to Vietnam. He had shown her kindness and patience in the jungle when she found it slow going, and as a lover his passion and tenderness were beyond anything she had ever known. He had it in him to love. But would he? Would he ever break down the barriers he had placed around himself and let himself care about her?

Debbie blinked her eyes, holding back her tears. Somehow, she believed that it all hinged on Li. If Li still loved Jim, if she had stayed loyal to him, then Debbie had a case, a powerful case, to present to Ben. Look here, she could say. It *is* real, it *does* exist, it *is* powerful. But if Li had forgotten Jim . . . ? If Li had fallen in love with someone else . . . ? Debbie shivered in the darkness. If that had happened, she would never be able to convince Ben that he was wrong about love.

# CHAPTER TEN

"You know, I wish that woman hadn't given us a ride yesterday," Debbie complained as she trudged down the road beside Ben. "It's going to be late in the afternoon before we get back to the farm."

"Gripe, gripe, gripe," Ben teased. "If my memory serves me correctly, you and I were both pretty quick to get on her cart and take a load off our feet."

Debbie did not respond to Ben's teasing. She clenched her fingers into tight fists of tension. "I know Li's still at Phu Bai, I just know it!"

Ben reached out and took one of Debbie's tightly clenched fists in his hand. "Then why so tense?" he asked. "If you're sure she's there?"

Debbie shrugged, unwilling to admit that she was afraid that Li didn't want to come out of the country. She had awakened this morning with a feeling of dread at what she was going to learn on this visit to Phu Bai. After weeks of defending Li to Ben, she was terrified that she was about to find out that Ben was right about Li—that Li preferred to stay in Vietnam with her new love, Hung. She tried to pull her hand away from Ben's, but he held it tightly. "Come on, Debbie, why so tense?" he asked. He looked over at her pinched face and her tight lips. "You're afraid she doesn't want to come out, aren't you?"

"Yes, I *am* afraid she doesn't want to come out!" Debbie snapped. "I'm afraid she's involved with that Hung idiot and doesn't want to go to Jim. There, does that make you happy?"

Ben's eyes widened at the unexpected attack and his face hardened. "Well, getting yourself worked up over it isn't going to make a difference one way or another, is it?" he asked. "If she wants to come she will, and if she doesn't she won't. It isn't that big a deal."

*Sure it isn't, not to Ben,* Debbie thought angrily. But to Debbie it was crucially important. It was the only way she was ever going to convince Ben of the reality of enduring love between a man and a woman. If Li still loved Jim, if she wanted to join him in San Francisco, Debbie would be able to use Li and Jim as a powerful example to Ben. She had hoped from the beginning to be able to demonstrate the reality of love to Ben. At first her desire to prove that true love did exist had been purely academic, for the sake of argument, but now her desire to show Ben that love was real had become very personal. She had come to love this man who was convinced that love wasn't possible, and Li and Jim were about the only means at her disposal to help her change his mind.

As Debbie had predicted, it was late in the afternoon by the time they returned to the farm. Concealing themselves in a small grove of trees, they watched the farm for a few minutes. Except for the guard, the cluster of buildings appeared to be deserted, the workers all working the outlying fields. "Should I try to find her now or wait until night?" Debbie asked.

"Let's go poke around a little now," Ben said. "Just to

find out where the women stay. You can go back to the women's hut after dark."

Careful not to let the guard see them, Debbie and Ben skirted the fence that surrounded the front part of the farm and sneaked into the back part of the farm, staying close to the buildings and out of the guard's sight. Ben pointed to three buildings on the left for Debbie to look over, and peered into a window of one of the huts on the right. Fighting back fear, Debbie peered in the window of the first hut. The little building was deserted, the straw mat beds neatly made and the inhabitants' meager possessions put away. Debbie stepped inside and looked around for a minute, but could see nothing that would identify one of the occupants as Li.

Debbie checked outside the door before she left the hut. She scurried across a dusty path and looked in the window of the second hut. It was furnished similarly to the first one, but the beds were not made as neatly, and random items of men's peasant clothing and straw shoes were scattered around the room. Debbie didn't even bother to step into this one. Men in all cultures were alike!

Glancing around, Debbie walked to the third hut. She peered into the window and noted the same neatness she had seen in the first hut. She stepped inside and glanced around, freezing when she saw a woman lying on a cot in the back of the hut, well away from the other cots. The woman's back was turned and she appeared to be asleep, but Debbie was terrified that the woman had heard her come in.

As Debbie started to back out the door, the woman turned over and opened sleepy eyes. "Hung, is that you?" she called out weakly.

Debbie gasped and stared into the woman's face,

searching every feature. After over ten years she was afraid to trust her memory, but she could have sworn the woman's voice was Li's. The woman's eyes were sunk back into her head and her skin was pasty; and, the lower part of her face was covered by the thin sheet she lay huddled under. Debbie would have to step closer if she wanted to know for sure. She took a couple of steps further into the hut. "No, I'm not Hung," she said in Vietnamese.

The woman tensed for a moment before she lay down on her back. "Did Hung send you to give me my medicine?" she asked. "I told him I was strong enough to get up and take it myself." She let the sheet slip down to her chin and shut her eyes.

Debbie took another couple of steps into the hut. She had to be sure, very sure, that this was Li before she gave herself away. She searched the woman's thin, sallow face for a moment. The shape of the woman's nose was very much like Li's had been, and her mouth had a similar bow across the top. Debbie took another step closer. "Li?" she asked softly.

The woman's eyes flickered open and she stared at Debbie for a moment. "No, I'm just getting sick again," she muttered to herself. "Seeing faces from the past. Hearing voices from the past. You're not Debbie. You just look and sound like her."

"No, you're not hallucinating, Li," Debbie said as she pulled off the straw hat and knelt down beside the cot. She took one of Li's hands and held it to her face. "Open your eyes and look at me, Li," she said as tears welled up in her eyes. "It's me. Debbie Cheong."

Li's eyes opened curiously. She reached out and with pitifully thin hands touched Debbie's face and her hands, and fear gave way to astonishment as she looked into the face of her friend from the past. "Debbie?" she breathed. "What? How?" She struggled to sit up, but Debbie pushed her shoulders back down. "What on earth are you doing in the middle of Vietnam?"

Debbie's eyes overflowed, and with impatient movements she wiped her tears away. "It's a long story, Li," she said. "Jim sent me to find you."

"Jim?" Li asked, her pale face lighting up. "Oh, Debbie, did Jim send you here for me?"

"Yes, I came with a mercenary soldier who can get you out, if you want to come," Debbie said.

Again Li struggled to sit up, and this time Debbie helped her up and kept a supporting grip on her shoulders. "If I want to come?" Li asked incredulously. "Debbie, of course I want to come! I want to be with Jim." She turned tearful eyes on Debbie. "Tell me, how is he? What is he doing? Where is he now?"

"He's fine. He's been working as an interpreter for the last three years, and he's waiting for us in Hong Kong," Debbie said.

"I would have been with him by now if I hadn't gotten sick," Li said. "When I got his money last year, I was so happy! I could bribe my way south and buy passage to Indonesia. But I got this far and I got some kind of fever, the doctor here couldn't tell what, and I've been sick like this for months. I would have been well sooner, except that there isn't that much food and I'm still so weak! The only thing that kept me alive was the thought that when I got well I could go to Jim."

"Nobody took the money while you were sick?" Debbie asked.

Li reached inside her dress and withdrew a leather pouch from between her breasts. "No one here knows of the money but a man named Hung," she said. "He has befriended me in my illness."

Debbie thought of Ben's comments. "Have you become fond of Hung?" she asked. "The man who brought me thought you might prefer to stay here with him."

"Oh, Debbie, *no*," Li assured her in a barely audible whisper. "Hung's been a friend, but I love Jim, Debbie. I want to be with him." Tears spilled out of Li's eyes and down onto her cheeks.

"Li, you will be with him," Debbie murmured reassuringly. "Now, don't use up all your energy crying! We'll have to get you out of here tonight, and you have to be able to help us."

Li's tears dried instantly. "I share this hut with five other women," she said. "They will be asleep a couple of hours after dark, but the girl nearest the door wakes easily."

"All right, we'll take you out that window," Debbie said, pointing to the window just above Li. "Have your shoes on under the covers and your hat where you can reach it. Ben has a sleeping bag for you in his backpack. Do you have any other possessions you want to bring?"

"Just this," Li said as she touched the bag of gold hidden under her blouse. She hugged Debbie as tightly as her weak arms could. "I'll be waiting."

"Good. Now sleep for the rest of the afternoon," Debbie said. "We'll come as soon as Ben thinks it's safe."

Li lay back on the cot. "Ben?"

"The mercenary. Ben Sako."

"He is—"

"I've got to go, Li," Debbie said as she pushed her hat back on her head. "I'll tell you all about Ben tomorrow." She raised her hand in salute to Li and backed to the door. She glanced around before she left the hut and ran back to the grove of trees where Ben was waiting impatiently for her.

"Took you long enough," he said as Debbie ducked behind a banana tree. "I was beginning to think you were in trouble."

Debbie put her arms around Ben's neck and danced a little jig around him. "Ben, I found her! I talked to her!" Debbie's face was beaming and her eyes were wet with happy tears. "Oh, Ben, you were wrong about her! She wants to come with us! She's still as crazy about Jim as she ever was!" She gave his neck one final hug and let him go. Her eyes were gleaming as she looked at Ben almost smugly. "She does still love him, Ben. Just as much as she ever did."

Ben sat down on a fallen log, his face impassive. "No, she doesn't," he scoffed. "She just wants to get out of Vietnam."

"Ben, that's not true," Debbie said firmly. "You wait until you see how her face lights up when you mention his name. Sure, maybe she wants out of here—who wouldn't?—but she's going to be with Jim, not to be away from here."

"If she loves him all that much, why is she still here? Why hasn't she left by now?"

Debbie's face sobered and she sat down beside Ben. "She's been sick, Ben. In fact, she's still sick and weak. She picked up one of those fevers, and the doctor at the farm wasn't sure what kind, and she's been months getting over it. She said the only thing that kept her alive was the thought that when she got well, she could go to Jim. She's been sick a long time, Ben. She hasn't had enough to eat and she couldn't regain her strength." She paused a minute. "Will we even be able to travel with her?"

"I don't know. Is she as heavy as you are?"

Debbie winced. "Oh, Ben, she's a good twenty pounds lighter, maybe closer to thirty. She's skin and bones."

"Hop up," Ben said as he turned his back and knelt down a little.

Debbie hopped up on Ben's back and wrapped her arms around his neck. "Piece of cake," Ben said. Debbie let go of Ben's neck and slid to the ground.

"I can take her and your pack, and you can take mine," Ben said as they sat down on the log together. "At least until she regains enough strength to do a little hiking. It's going to be slow going for a while, Lotus."

"That's all right," Debbie said. "Do you want me to fix anything to eat?"

"Not this close to the farm," Ben said. "We'll get her out of here, and we'll get a couple of miles away before we camp. There's an old base a couple miles that way we can stay in tonight." He jerked his thumb toward the west. "Besides, from what you've said, we need to feed Li up a little. I sure hope the money lasts until we get to Thailand."

"Well, if yours runs out, Li has plenty," Debbie said. "She still has most of what Jim sent her. I guess they can use it as a down payment on a house."

"That is, if she marries him when we get out of here," Ben muttered.

Debbie made an exasperated motion with her hand. "You just don't want to believe, do you?" she demanded impatiently. "You just can't stand being wrong! Well, Ben, you were wrong. You've been wrong all this time about her. She does still love him, and she can hardly wait to see him again."

Ben turned to Debbie, a grudging smile on his face. "And you're enjoying the hell out of this, aren't you?"

Debbie tried and failed to curb the superior, satisfied smile that crept across her face. "Yes, as a matter-of-fact I am, Ben. I'm enjoying this very much!"

"You would," Ben muttered disgustedly.

The light of the moon was not quite as bright as it had been last night, but it still cast quite a bit of light on the farm and surrounding fields. Debbie and Ben had watched as the workers trudged back from the fields at dusk. They had eaten together in a communal dining hall, and Debbie had seen a figure that looked like Hung carrying a bowl into the hut where Li waited. The workers had drifted toward the huts after the evening meal, and slowly the candles and the oil lamps had winked out, leaving the farm buildings in darkness. A lone guard stood in front of the fenced area, yards from where Debbie and Ben would be helping Li to escape.

"Do you think it's safe to go now?" Debbie asked as she peered through the foliage at the dark buildings of the farm.

"No, let's give it just a few minutes to be sure," Ben said as he gazed up at the shining moon. Debbie fidgeted impatiently until Ben finally tapped her on the arm. "Ready?" he asked. "I think they've all gone to sleep."

Debbie nodded, her mouth suddenly dry with fear. "I'm scared, Ben," she whispered.

Ben squeezed her hand. "Piece of cake," he reassured her.

They left their backpacks under the banana tree and made their way across the clearing into the back of the compound, walking as swiftly as they could but still moving quietly. They made their way through the quiet cluster of buildings to the window that Debbie had told Li they would use. Debbie's heart pounded in her throat, but Ben seemed cool and relaxed as they pushed open the window. Li was laying on her mat, and Debbie thought she must have gone to sleep until she saw Li's eyes fly open. Putting her finger to her lips, Li threw her sheet off her and sat up slowly, swaying a little with weakness.

Ben saw Li's extreme weakness, and before Debbie knew what he was planning, he picked Debbie up and thrust her feet first through the high window. Trying not to make a sound, Debbie groped for a minute, then she quickly moved to Li's cot and helped her friend to her feet, supporting most of Li's weight while Li shuffled the two steps to the window. Ben reached in the chest-high window and picked Li up under the arms while Debbie grasped her around her pitifully thin thighs, and the two of them lifted Li's emaciated body through the window. Debbie flinched when one of the sleeping women sighed in her sleep and turned over, and she grasped the edge of the windowsill and as quietly as she could scrambled up the wall of the hut and out the window, breaking her fall to the ground with her palms and scratching them up. Debbie watched Ben in the moonlight as he hoisted Li onto his back. She scrambled to her feet, and she and Ben picked their way back across the compound, neither of them noticing the door of the men's hut opening ever so slowly.

They hurried to the clearing, and Ben sat Li down on the log where he and Debbie had spent most of the evening. "Well, we did it, Lotus," he said as Debbie hugged Li's neck. "We got her out." He put out his hand to Li. "Li, I'm Ben Sako. I'm pleased to meet you."

"My pleasure, Ben Sako," Li said, her English lightly accented. "Thank you for coming in for me."

"You're more than welcome," Ben said as he picked up

the heavier backpack. "Come, put this on, Debbie. We need to get moving."

At that moment they heard the sound of footsteps running into the grove. Debbie and Li froze as Hung came crashing into the clearing, a long, slender knife in his hand. "You can't have her, you foreign devils," he said as his wild eyes looked at Ben and Debbie. "I'll save you, Li."

"No, Hung," Li said sharply. "I want to go with them." Her face softened. "Jim sent them, Hung."

Hung shook his head back and forth. "I knew they were up to no good when they came to the compound yesterday looking for you. You don't belong with them, Li." He turned his eyes from Debbie and Ben and looked pleadingly at Li. "You don't belong with that Imperialist who wants you to live with him in a strange land with strange people and strange customs. You are a daughter of Vietnam, you belong here." He moved closer to Li, close enough so that Ben dared not try to disarm him where he stood.

"No, Hung," Li protested. "I love Vietnam and will miss it, but my place in this life is with Jim, wherever he is."

"But I *love* you, Li!" Hung cried. "I've loved you ever since you came to this camp." Ben looked at the knife in Hung's hand and over at Debbie, raising his eyebrows at her. If she would distract Hung, he would take away that knife before the fool used it on one of them. Debbie nodded slightly and Ben stepped into the shadows.

"Hung, I'm sorry," Li said gently, her voice soft in the night. Debbie and Ben both paused. It would be better if Li could talk Hung into letting her go. "But I told you all along that I loved Jim and that I was going to join him as soon as I could. This woman is a friend of mine from the old days. She came to find me."

"A friend from the old days?" Hung sneered. "Li, that part of your life is over. Your friends are here in Vietnam, not Imperialists from a foreign land. With the money you have, we could live here in comfort for the rest of our lives."

"Do you love Li or just her money?" Debbie asked suddenly, sharply.

"How dare you!" Hung said as he whirled around and advanced toward Debbie, the knife poised in front of him. Ben lunged forward, catching Hung in the throat with a well-placed karate kick. The knife flew out of Hung's hand and Debbie bent down and snatched it up, backing away as Hung sat up and lunged toward Ben, catching Ben around the knees and pulling him to the ground. Debbie and Li watched as Hung wrestled with Ben for a moment in the clearing. Hung was a big man, bigger than Ben, and Debbie clutched the knife in her hand in case she had to go to Ben's rescue.

In less than ten seconds it was all over. Ben smashed one fist into Hung's nose, and while Hung was still trying to get his bearings from that, Ben gave him a hard chop with the side of his hand in the jaw, knocking the back of Hung's head into the dirt and knocking him out cold. "What did you do to him?" Debbie whispered, her relief overcoming the revulsion at what Ben had to do. "Where did you learn to do that? Did you kill him?"

"In the service and, no, Debbie, I did not kill him," Ben said as he grabbed up the backpack and shoved it on her shoulders. "He'll be out for a half hour or so, and he'll have a few bruises by which to remember me." He adjusted the lighter of the two backpacks around his neck and knelt down so that Li could climb on his back, securing her weak arms and legs with his strong arms. "Now, ladies, let's get just as far from Li's admirer here as we can before he wakes up and decides to follow us."

Li trembled in the darkness as Ben and Debbie made their way out of the grove of trees. Relieved that the danger was over and that Li was out, Debbie felt a little giddy. "Tell me, Li," Debbie whispered as they made their way back to the road into Phu Bai. "How is it that you can inspire such undying love in not only Jim but Hung here? Do you have a perfume that I don't?"

Ben could feel Li's body shaking with amusement. But the shaking stopped as she peered over at the grove of trees. "The sad part is, he really thought he loved me, I guess. I told him about Jim, but he just never would believe me."

"I think that tonight he got the hint," Ben said harshly.

Debbie followed Ben down the dusty road, past Phu Bai and down a rutted road that led in a northwest direction. It was slower going with Li on Ben's back and Debbie carrying the heavier pack, and it took them a couple of hours to reach the old American base where Ben had mentioned camping. Debbie spread the extra sleeping bag down in one of the shelters and Ben laid Li down on it. The exhausted woman shut her eyes and rested while Debbie and Ben built a fire in one of the old pits that lined the base, so that their campfire could not be seen from a distance. Debbie thought Li had gone to sleep, but when she brought Li a bowl of rice and snow peas, Li opened her eyes and struggled to sit up. "Here, let me," Ben said as he supported Li so that she could eat. Debbie knew it was ridiculous, but a stab of jealousy shot through her at the sight of another woman in Ben's arms, and she shuddered to think how she would feel someday if she ever saw Ben with another woman.

Li picked up the chopsticks and bowl and ate hungrily. "That's the most food I've had at one time in the last ten years," she said as Ben helped her lay back down.

Debbie stared down at Li, horrified. "You mean you're not just thin from the illness?"

Li shook her head. "I was this thin before I got sick," she said. "Didn't you notice how thin Hung and the others were?"

"We've had plenty to eat on the trip!" Debbie said.

"But, Debbie, we had the money to buy it," Ben reminded her.

"A couple of times I bought food with Jim's money, but I tried to hang on to as much of it as I could, so I would be sure to have enough to get away," Li said. "Debbie, tell me about him! What has he been doing for the last ten years? Where does he live? Does he like his new job?"

"Tomorrow, Li," Ben said firmly, shaking his head at Debbie. "You and Debbie will have plenty of time to talk about Jim in the next couple of months. You need to rest."

Li nodded. "You're right. But how are we going to get out of the country? I still have most of Jim's money if you think it will help."

"It's not enough to get the three of us out by boat," Ben said. "We'll have to walk out through Cambodia. We'll take the high-speed trail through the Ashaw Valley to Cambodia and go to Thailand from there."

"What's the high-speed trail?" Debbie asked.

"They used to send North Vietnamese troops down it into South Vietnam during the war," Ben said.

"I saw it on my way to Phu Bai," Li volunteered. "It's

overgrown but still passable. I know my way around Cambodia, Ben, if that's any help. We used to travel there when I was a teen-ager."

"Sure it will be a help. Debbie, how's your Cambodian?"

"I can get us by," she said. She cleaned up the wok and bowls while Li and Ben spoke in low tones, planning the best route to take to get them through Cambodia and into Thailand. Li and Ben quickly worked out a tentative route, and Li lay half asleep as Ben took their sleeping bags and placed the one on top of the other, just as he had every night for the last two weeks. He positioned them a few discreet feet away from Li, although they were close enough to hear her if she needed them.

Li's eyes widened and she looked at Debbie with surprise. Debbie blushed furiously as she nodded slightly, hoping that Li wasn't too horrified by the fact that she was sleeping with Ben. Li blushed a little herself before her eyes fluttered shut and she went to sleep.

Ben covered Li with a mosquito net and looked down into her sleeping face. "She's exhausted," he said. "Sick and half-starved and exhausted. I wish to hell their leaders would wake up and take a good look at their precious system!" He put his arms around Debbie. "Are you ready to go to bed?" Seeing the strained look on her face, he continued. "I just want to sleep beside you. But if it bothers you, we can sleep apart for the rest of the trip."

"No, I don't want that," Debbie said quietly in the darkness. "I want to sleep beside you, and to make love with you when we can. We can work out some way that we can have some privacy. Li will understand that we want to be alone."

"Thank you, Lotus," Ben said as he pulled the mosquito net over them both.

Debbie lay still in Ben's arms. She had been embarrassed when Ben had spread the sleeping bags together, but she loved him too much to move her bag away. She blinked at the moon-dappled darkness. They had finally found Li, and now Ben had seen with his own eyes that Li did love Jim after all this time, that Li's and Jim's love had lasted the long separation. Would that love make an impression on Ben? Would the evidence of Jim and Li's love, coupled with her own deep love for him, convince Ben that he was wrong about love? Debbie sighed and snuggled closer to Ben. It had to. It just had to.

Ben tightened his arms around Debbie and held her as her breathing slowed and took on the regular rhythm of slumber. He glanced over at the sleeping figure on the other bag several feet away. So she wanted to come out of Vietnam after all. Jim Anderson hadn't wasted his money. He had paid dearly, but he would have Li by his side in America.

Ben stared out into the darkness, listening to Debbie's soft breathing beside him. Was Li really coming with them to be with Jim, or just to get out of a Communist country? He tried to convince himself that she just wanted to live in America, but her words to Hung kept coming back to mock him. Li didn't particularly want to leave Vietnam, nor did she particularly want to stay. She just wanted to be wherever Jim Anderson was. Or was there some other motivation that escaped him? He wracked his brain, trying to come up with some other reason that Li would want to go with them, but could find none. It all boiled down to the fact that Li wanted to be with Jim.

Ben shrugged inwardly. Li's reasons for coming with them were her own concern. What was beginning to concern him, and concern him badly, was his increasing obsession with the woman who lay sleeping in his arms. Usually, after he had made a woman his lover, his fascination with her would start to fade, sometimes slowly, sometimes quickly, but it would sooner or later fade away and die. But with Debbie it was different. The longer he was with her, the longer he wanted to be with her. And the more often he made love to her, the more often he wanted to. And this irritated Ben. He didn't like the power this woman seemed to have over him—he would have preferred to be in control of the relationship, and he knew that he wasn't in control, though neither was she. Ben didn't know who or what was in control, or why he was increasingly drawn to Debbie Cheong, but he also realized that there wasn't much he could do about it. And that fact irritated him just that much more.

## CHAPTER ELEVEN

"I thought this was supposed to be a high-speed trail," Debbie complained good-naturedly as she shifted Ben's heavy backpack to her other shoulder and trudged behind Ben and Li. "The only thing high speed around here are the mosquitoes." She slapped one of the hungry insects that had landed on her arm.

Li turned her head and smiled sympathetically. "I'll be able to walk in a few days," she told Debbie. "We'll make faster progress then." She turned around and peered over Ben's shoulder. "Are the San Francisco freeways still impossible at rush hour?" she asked.

"No, now they're impossible all the time," Debbie said. "I don't even try to drive to work. I take the bus in the morning and the ferry in the afternoon."

"And Jim? Does he drive to work?"

"Yes, Li, Jim drives in every morning," Debbie said patiently.

"What kind of car does he drive?" Li asked eagerly.

"A 1976 Monte Carlo. That's a Chevrolet, maroon with a white vinyl top and white upholstery and a taped-up rip in the back seat," Debbie replied dryly, knowing she may as well give Li every detail. If she didn't, Li would drag them from her question at a time.

"Does he still drive too fast?" Li asked. Debbie giggled as Ben rolled his eyes in exasperation.

"Usually," Debbie admitted. "Say, do you remember that little singer, Michael Jackson? The one who sang with his brothers in the Jackson Five?" Li nodded. "Well, you wouldn't believe what he's doing now!" She launched into the Michael Jackson phenomenon, complete with descriptions of his costumes and hair style, and when she had finished with Michael Jackson, Ben gave Li a run-down of the video music boom in general. Anything to get off the subject of Jim Anderson!

Since they had rescued Li a week ago, Jim had been the subject of nearly every one of Li's conversations. Hungry for knowledge of her lost lover, she plied Debbie with question after question. Where did Jim live? What did he do for the State Department? What was his favorite food? Did he still drink wine? Did he have a lot of friends? What did he do for fun? Debbie had answered the questions good-naturedly, knowing that Li was like a starving woman at a banquet table, but Ben soon became heartily sick of the subject of Jim Anderson, and even Debbie was tired of talking about him by now! Li had left one question unvoiced, however, carefully avoiding the topic of other women in Jim's life over the last ten years, and Debbie longed to reassure Li on the subject of Jim's fidelity to her. But she hated to go into the subject around Ben, who earlier had expressed his doubts about Jim's fidelity. She didn't want Li to pick up on Ben's cynicism and think that Debbie was lying.

They spent several days on the high-speed trail in the Ashaw Valley, making their way to the border of Cambodia. Although the trail was overgrown now, it was still clearly delineated, and it made their passage through the rain forest much easier than it would have been otherwise. Although Ben was still carrying Li, Debbie could see her friend becoming stronger by the day, and it would not be too many more days before Li would be able to walk with them. Debbie looked forward to that day, as much for her own sake as for Li and Ben's. By the end of the day Ben's heavy backpack bouncing against her gave her a fierce backache, and she longed to relinquish the heavier pack to Ben and return to her own light one.

They broke and set up camp about dusk, building their fire in the shadow of an abandoned, rusted-out bulldozer left behind by the American troops. Li ate hungrily the rice and the game birds Ben roasted, managing to think up some more questions for Debbie about Jim, these regarding the furniture in his apartment. Debbie answered her patiently, promising herself that once she got home she was never going to answer another question about Jim as long as she lived. Ben got up and wandered off for a few minutes, probably just to get away from the topic of Jim Anderson.

Debbie waited until she was sure Ben was out of earshot before she turned to Li, who had fallen silent and was staring wistfully out into the night. "It won't be long now, Li," she said. "A couple of months at the most, and you'll be with Jim again."

Li smiled into the night. "I know, and the thought makes me very happy. It's been a long ten years for me."

Debbie patted Li on the shoulder. "It's been a long ten years for him too, Li. He's aged a lot from worry. He looks a lot older than he is."

"I don't care," Li said as she fingered her thin face. "I'm no beauty anymore either. Was he really lonely, Debbie?"

"Yes, Li, he was really lonely," Debbie said, waiting

for the question that never came. "Aren't you going to ask if he found comfort in his loneliness?"

"No, I'm not," Li said, her voice curiously resigned. "I don't want to know about that. It's enough that he found me and he sent for me. I don't need to know about the years in between."

"But it bothers you, doesn't it?" Debbie pried gently.

"A little," Li admitted. "I was faithful to him, of course, but things were different on the work farm. He was in a free society, and he is a very attractive man."

"Yes, he is, but he may as well have been a homely hunchback for all the advantage he took of that attractiveness," Debbie said. "Jim and I have been friends, Li, for the last ten years. We've worked together and we've been close, as close as two friends can be. We celebrated together the day he found you, and he shed tears with me the day my divorce became final. I would have known if there had been anyone else in his life. And there hasn't been, Li. He's been true to you."

Li smiled, even though her eyes were misty. "Thank you for telling me, Debbie," she said. "I'm sorry he spent so many years alone, but I'm glad he waited for me." She wiped her eyes. "I've been so busy asking you about Jim, Debbie, that I've asked you nothing about yourself. I didn't realize you'd been married."

"I've been divorced for two years," Debbie said. She told Li about her marriage to Kevin and how his family had eventually torn them apart. "I guess we just didn't have the kind of love you and Jim have," Debbie said. "But I want that kind of love, Li. I want it a lot."

"And what of the man you love now, Debbie?" Li asked.

"Ben?" Debbie shrugged. "He doesn't believe in love, Li. He thinks it doesn't exist, or at least he didn't before he met you and Jim. He may still believe it's all physical attraction."

"But you do love him," Li said.

"Yes, I do love him. I love him a lot. But whether he will ever believe in that love or return it, I just don't know."

"I hope so, Debbie," Li said as she squeezed Debbie's hand. "Goodness knows, you have it coming." They sat quietly for a minute. "Does Jim really look that old? Does he look as old as I do?"

Debbie laughed as she hugged Li's neck. "Oh, Li, Jim doesn't look ancient," she said. "And neither do you, now that you're getting enough to eat. By the time we get you back to San Francisco and raid the cosmetics counters and hit the beauty salon, you're going to be a raving beauty! Now, you better get some rest if you think you're going to try to hike part of the day tomorrow."

Debbie spread Li's sleeping bag down in an old bomb shelter, and took hers and Ben's and spread them a few yards away. Li laid down and was asleep immediately, as she usually was, and Debbie sat crosslegged on the bag, staring out at the stars. In just a few minutes she heard a rustle from the forest, and Ben sat down beside her and pulled off his shirt. "Well, did you two thoroughly exhaust the topic of Jim Anderson tonight?" he asked. "If I hear one more word about that man, I think I'm going to scream."

"Yes, we talked about Jim," Debbie said absently.

"Well, what did you cover tonight? His brand of toothpaste?"

"No, I told her that there hadn't been any other women in his life for the last ten years. And we talked about Kevin."

"Does it really matter now?" Ben asked harshly.

197

Debbie turned to him in surprise. "Jim's faithfulness? Or Kevin?"

Ben shrugged. "Both, I guess."

"She had made up her mind that it didn't matter if there had been others, but she was glad to hear that there hadn't," Debbie said honestly.

"You don't know that," Ben said.

Debbie sighed. "Ben, I would have known if there had been anyone."

"And why is it so important, anyway, Debbie?" Ben challenged her. "If he cared enough to send for her, what difference would it make if there had been others in between?"

"On one level it wouldn't matter. His sending for her proves he still loves her. But there's an element there I can't explain, Ben," Debbie said quietly. "You either understand why something like that is important or you don't."

"And the other?" Ben prompted.

"Kevin? She wanted to know about my marriage, of course. So I told her about Kevin and what happened to us." Debbie lay down on her back and stared up into the night sky.

Ben lay down and pulled the mosquito net over the two of them. "Is he still important to you?" he asked.

"Kevin?" Debbie thought a minute. "No, he's not important to me anymore." *Only you,* she added to herself as Ben took her into his arms and covered her lips in a scorching kiss. Kevin was out of her life, a part of the past that no longer mattered. The only man that mattered to her now was the man she held in her arms.

Ben stroked her face with gentle hands. "I'm glad he isn't important to you anymore," he said as he trailed loving kisses down Debbie's face. Debbie waited to hear more, to hear perhaps that Ben wanted to be the important man in her life, but no further declarations were forthcoming as he took her into his arms and made sweet, sweet love to her. His touch was gentle, his lovemaking was caring as well as passionate, but when it was all over Debbie stared out into the night, not falling to sleep as she usually did after Ben's tender lovemaking. Ben would go only so far and no further. He was glad that Kevin was no longer important to her, but he would not commit himself to being the important man in her life. Debbie didn't know what else to do to convince Ben that love was real. She had talked until she was blue in the face, and Ben had seen how Li and Jim still felt after all these years. Ben would have to come to his own conclusions about love, and she would just have to give him the time to do this.

The next day Li managed to hike for two hours in the morning, and every day she walked a little bit longer. Debbie commented once or twice on how well Li was doing, and Li admitted that it was the first time in ten years that she had been able to get enough food to eat, one of the reasons she had never fully recovered from her illness. To Debbie's delight, by the time they had reached the Cambodian border Li was close to being well, although she was still too thin. Ben ditched the stolen Vietnamese uniforms, which they hadn't used since Phu Bai, at the border, in case they were stopped and searched in Cambodia. They sneaked across the Cambodian border without incident, trooping through the forest to avoid the inevitable guards at the dirt roads leading into the country.

They wandered through the mountainous forests of teak, and seeing the undamaged countryside, Debbie could appreciate what the war, with its extensive shelling and defoliation, had done to the mountains and forests of Vietnam. Conditions in Cambodia were not too different from conditions in Vietnam—the country was poor and it was also under Communist domination. Debbie and Li both knew some Cambodian, and since Debbie's accent was less foreign than Li's, they practiced the local dialect every night after they ate, Li teaching Debbie additional words that she might need in the markets where they continued to buy food. Their diet was much the same as it had been in Vietnam, but the extra food and Ben's vitamins continued to work their magic on Li. Her face and figure filled out some, and her pasty complexion cleared and took on a healthy glow. She still looked tired, they all did, but she was slowly becoming the beautiful woman nature had intended her to be.

But by the middle of the second month in Cambodia, Debbie was starting to feel tired, more tired than she had felt even in the beginning of the mission, or when she had been carrying Ben's backpack. She hated getting up in the mornings, and she was really tired by the time Ben called a halt to the day's hiking. With Li's help, she would make supper and go to sleep soon afterward, sometimes even before Li. She didn't mention her tiredness to Li or Ben, since they would have insisted on slowing down, and Debbie was as eager to get to Thailand as they were. Very little escaped Ben, however, and after several days, he lay down beside Debbie after supper and put his arm around her. "You're really tired, aren't you?" he asked.

Debbie turned her face into his shoulder. "Yes, but so are the two of you," she said. "How much longer before we get to the border?"

"Just a couple of days," Ben assured her. "Look, Debbie, I'm a little worried about you. You're exhausted. Are you sure you're all right?"

"Of course I'm all right," Debbie said as she put her head on his chest. "I'm just not used to traipsing through the jungle for months at a time like you are."

Ben smiled tenderly as he stroked her hair. "Debbie, Li's down at the river washing her clothes. She said she wouldn't be back for a couple of hours." He waited for Debbie to raise her head and kiss him passionately, as she always did when Li tactfully disappeared for an hour or two. "Debbie? Did you hear me?"

In response Debbie snored softly against his chest. Ben stroked her hair as he gazed down at the sleeping woman. He would have her out of here in a couple of days, and when they got to Bangkok she could sleep for a week like he always did after a mission. And once they were back to California, she could spend the weekends at his vineyard and rest some more there. Ben had never taken a woman to his cabin in the mountains, and he was surprised at wanting Debbie to come there. He was surprised at how natural it felt for him to want Debbie to stay there with him, for as long as he wanted her to be a part of his life.

Debbie, Ben, and Li stood at the crest of the hill, staring over at the jungle-covered hills of Thailand. "It's just a few more miles away," Ben said with satisfaction.

"Freedom," Debbie murmured. "I'd swear the air smells better in a free country."

"It does," Li assured her. "And in just a few more days I'll be with Jim."

"I'll send word to him in Hong Kong to meet us at the camp," Ben said. "He'll have to bring Debbie's and my passports."

"Yes, George, he sure will," Debbie teased. "Are you going to use your alias in Thailand?"

"I guess I better not," Ben said. "My real passport's in the lining of my suitcase. I'll resurrect George another time. Li, do you have any kind of document proving your identity?"

Li nodded. "In the pouch with my money."

"How long will we have to wait at the camp?" Debbie asked.

Ben shrugged. "A week at the most. It may take several days for Jim to get the message, but he'll get there pretty quickly. Come on, we still have to get across the border, and this one's heavily guarded."

Debbie cringed at Ben's warning. "How are we going to get across?" she asked as she and Li followed Ben down the side of the hill through the forest. They had not traveled on a road for the last three days.

"I'm not sure yet," Ben admitted. "I've never gone from Cambodia to Thailand before, but there are refugees doing it every day, so it's not impossible."

They hiked to within a mile of the border. Ben told Debbie and Li to go ahead and prepare a meal before dark, so that their fire would be less visible, and left them while he made his way nearly to the border through the thick forest. The border was bounded by a tall barbed-wire fence and patroled every hundred yards or so by a soldier. But the dense foliage that would not stay cut back from the fence obscured patches of the fence here and there from the guard's gaze, and it would be possible to cut a wire and go through at one of the overgrown points.

Debbie and Li boiled a little rice and waited for Ben to return. Li was excited and happy, chattering happily about all the things she and Jim were going to do in San

Francisco, but Debbie grew increasingly nervous as they waited for Ben. Were they going to be able to get across the border all right? This was not going to be like going from Vietnam to Cambodia.

Ben returned over an hour later and sat down beside Debbie. "The border's fenced and guarded, but not impossible to get across," he said as he took a bowl of rice from her. "They haven't kept the trees and plants trimmed back too well, and those will hide us from the guard long enough for me to get the wires cut and us under the fence. We'll wait until after dark."

"I bet that fence leaks refugees like a sieve once the sun goes down," Li said.

"And it's about to leak three more," Ben said as he got out the .38 and loaded it.

Debbie and Li cleaned up their dishes, and they waited quietly until the sun sank behind the hills in a glowing ball of red and orange. Even Li had stopped her usual chatter about Jim and sat silent as dusk fell over the land. A tiny sliver of moon cast a little light on the landscape, but for the most part the night was dark, which would make their trek through the forest harder but add to their safety at the border.

With Ben in the lead, they made their way through the forest, their hands in front of them as they groped through the dimly lighted grove of trees. Debbie stumbled a couple of times, and Li caught her foot on a vine and fell down. Finally, when it seemed like they had been groping through a dark maze forever, Ben halted and pointed to a clearing to their left. Even in the dim light of the moon, Debbie could see the tall posts of the fence that separated Cambodia and Thailand. "The guard's down there." He pointed to the right, where the trees and shrubs grew all the way to the fence. "We go under there."

As silently as they could, they groped their way for the last seventy-five yards through the dense foliage, reaching a point where the fence was only about ten yards away. Ben peered up and down the fence but could see no sign of the guard. He withdrew his wire cutters from his shirt pocket and nodded at the women. Together the three of them made a run for it, Ben reaching the fence first and clipping the lower two wires and holding them back. Li rolled under the fence first, followed closely by Debbie, who bounced up and grasped the ends of the wires through the fence, piercing her finger on one of the sharp barbs. She bit her lip to keep from crying out as Ben rolled under the wire. As he came up and grabbed her hand, they heard the sound of a rifle shot aimed in their direction.

"Over there!" Ben said as he pointed to a grove of trees about twenty yards away. He grabbed Debbie and Li each by the hand and ran with them toward the trees as bullets whizzed over their heads. They reached the trees and ran further into the grove, dodging tree trunks in the dark as they ran farther and farther away from the rifle shots of the guard. When the shots died down, they slowed their flight to a walk.

Debbie pulled her punctured hand away from Ben's and cradled it in her other one. "I guess it beats a bullet hole, but it hurts!" she complained.

Ben stopped and got the medicine kit out of the backpack. "I can patch you up for now," he said as he cleaned the wound with alcohol and squeezed on the last of their antibiotic. "They can handle it better once we get to the camp." He looked back over his shoulder at the border of Cambodia. "You know, either that guard didn't really want to stop us, or he sure is a lousy shot!"

It was late in the afternoon by the time they made it to the refugee camp. They had walked a half mile or so in the forest of Thailand before Ben had called a halt and they had slept for a few hours. The next morning they made their way to a road, where they learned from a sign that the nearest refugee camp was five miles east. Debbie stared with mingled relief and dismay at the huge, crowded refugee camp, acres and acres of primitive tents and makeshift shelters housing hundreds of refugees who had also fled Vietnam or Cambodia. It was a welcome sight after the months they had spent alone, yet Debbie dreaded the noise and the crowding and the smells that would accompany such a place. They wandered through the outskirts of the camp, and Debbie asked where the offices were and who was in charge. A thin woman with a missing front tooth pointed out a large green tent in the middle of the melee, but said she didn't know who was in charge of the camp.

Debbie thanked her and they made their way to the large green tent, dodging scruffy-looking dogs and half-dressed children playing between the assorted shelters. The tent was an American surplus like the ones used by MASH units, and the first face to greet them at the door was an American one. A green-eyed nun with soft brown hair came to the door. "I'm Sister Mary. May I help you?" she asked in halting Vietmanese.

"I'm Ben Sako, and this is Debbie Cheong and Nguyen Li Ha," Ben said in English. "Debbie and I are American citizens, although at the moment we don't have our passports, and Li is a Vietnamese citizen. Is there a way for me to get a letter or a telegram out of here today to someone in Hong Kong?"

205

Sister Mary's face broke into a smile. "We've been expecting you." She turned around to a teen-ager sitting on the desk behind her. "Go get Mr. Anderson, Kai."

Debbie's mouth dropped open and even Ben looked surprised. "You mean he's *here?*" Li cried. "Jim's *here?*"

"Yes, he's been waiting here for the last month," the nun replied. "Apparently he got word through the underground that your boat was blown up but that you two had gotten off safely and were in the country. He said you didn't have enough money to buy passage to Indonesia, so he took a chance that you would come out here, near this camp."

"Oh, Debbie, I'm really going to see him!" Li said as her eyes filled with tears. "He's *here!*"

Debbie bit her lip to keep from crying with joy along with Li. "Here, let me comb your hair," she said as she whipped out her comb and made a few swipes at Li's mussed hair, smoothing it back behind her ears. She dried Li's tearstained face with the hem of her dress. "You're ready," she whispered as a blond man dressed in mud-spattered blue jeans ran through the camp, dodging the tents and stumbling over children.

Jim ran to the clearing around the tent and skidded to a halt. He and Li stood frozen for a moment, staring at one another, drinking in the sight of each other after ten long years apart. Li was thin, exhausted, and dusty, and the remnants of her illness still showed in her face. Jim was old-looking, his blond hair almost silver from the gray in it, and tired. His face was lined and his jeans were muddy. But none of it mattered. To each other they were the most beautiful sight in the world. A lone tear ran down Jim's cheek as he opened his arms to his beloved. "Li," he whispered.

Li ran across the clearing and threw herself into Jim's arms. "Oh, Jim, I love you!" she said, sobbing as she wrapped her arms around his waist. "I've missed you so much!"

## CHAPTER TWELVE

Debbie watched as Jim wrapped his arms around Li and held her to him. "Oh, Li, I've missed you too." He cried openly, not caring who saw him. Li's body was shaking, gasps of joy tearing through her as Jim cradled her in his arms. "Oh, Li, I've—I—" Jim gave up trying to speak and just held her tightly, tears running down his face as he finally cradled the woman he loved in his arms.

They clung together for long minutes, oblivious to the circle of people who stood in the clearing with them. Debbie wiped the tears from her cheeks with the sleeve of her dress, and Sister Mary's eyes were damp. Only Ben remained impassive, his face carved out of stone. Debbie nudged Ben with her elbow. "This makes the whole thing worth it," she said as she sniffed back tears. "Seeing them so happy. It's worth everything we went through to get her out." She gave up and let the tears run down her cheeks.

Finally, Jim bent his head and kissed Li tenderly before he let her go, but he grasped her hand tightly in his as he turned to Debbie and Ben. "Ben, Debbie, what can I say? What can I do to thank you?"

"You can let George Hirohito go about his business," Ben said dryly.

Jim had the grace to turn a deep shade of red. "I

wouldn't have done it, you know," he said. "I told—" He broke off and blushed even redder.

"I knew you had withdrawn your threat when I went in, Jim," Ben said. "I went in of my own free will." He extended his hand to Jim.

Jim shook it, then enveloped Ben in a strong embrace before he turned to Debbie. "And what can I say to you? Oh, Debbie, thank you!" he said as he hugged her tightly for a moment. "Now I owe you a lot more than just money."

At the mention of money, Li reached into her blouse and pulled out the leather pouch. "Maybe this will help," she said softly. "It's almost all of what you sent me, Jim." She put the leather pouch into his hand. "It's a long story," she said when Jim started to question her. "And I'll have plenty of time to tell it to you."

"Yes, now you will," Jim said as he put his arm around her shoulder. He hesitated for a moment. "Do you still want to marry me?"

"Yes, oh, yes," Li said. "You shouldn't have even had to ask."

Jim glanced in Ben's direction. "It's just that I've had it brought to my attention recently that you might not want to, after all this time. Are you sure, Li? Are you very sure?"

"I've been sure for the last ten years," Li said. "I don't want to wait any longer."

"All right, then," Jim said. "We can either be married here by Father Reilly, or we can wait until we get back to Bangkok and marry there. I'd wait until we got back to San Francisco and marry you in my parish church, but we have to be married for you to get your visa."

"Here. Tonight," Li said. "I've waited ten years. I don't want to wait another day."

"Are you sure?" Jim asked. "Won't you miss getting married in a white dress and having flowers?"

Li shook her head. "No, Jim, this dress will be fine."

"Jim, did you bring my luggage with you?" Debbie asked. "I have a dress in there that would be a perfect wedding dress."

"Yes, I brought all of yours and Ben's things with me. If I go find the Father now, he can marry us tonight. We want you two to stand with us, of course."

Ben nodded his consent. "Of course," Debbie replied. "If you don't mind the maid of honor crying a few happy tears."

"Along with everyone else's," Sister Mary said. "Come with me, ladies. Debbie, I've kept your luggage and Mr. Sako's in my office. I'm sure you would like to wash up and rest a little before the wedding."

Li shook her head. "You go ahead, Debbie. I want to spend a few minutes with Jim before I get ready." She clutched Jim's hand tightly in hers.

Sister Mary left them at the door of the tent and Ben followed Debbie into Sister Mary's office. "This is the first time I've been in a wedding," he whispered as he picked up his suitcases. "What do I do?"

"Hold Jim up in case he gets drunk beforehand," Debbie whispered. "Or gets scared and starts to faint. Or push him to the altar if he starts to change his mind. Just whatever."

"Woman, you are something else," Ben said. "I drag you around the jungles for three solid months, trying to teach you some respect, and your mouth's just as big as it ever was!" He leaned over and enveloped her mouth in a long, lingering kiss. "You were a real trooper, Lotus. Thank you."

"Don't thank me, Ben. I got my reward just a few

minutes ago. I've never seen Jim so happy in the ten years that I've known him." She threw her arms around Ben, almost knocking the suitcases out of his hands. "Oh, Ben, weren't you happy for them? Weren't you just thrilled?"

"Yes, I'm glad they're happy," Ben said seriously. He kissed Debbie once and pulled away from her. "You better go ahead and get ready. It won't be too long until the wedding. Oh, and do something about that barbed-wire cut."

Sister Mary passed Ben in the door and handed him a clean towel. "We have an outdoor shower in the back of the tent," she said as she handed Debbie another towel. "It's not much but it's better than nothing."

"A shower, even a cold one, sounds like the epitome of luxury," Debbie said. She opened her suitcase and unearthed a bathrobe, and found a bar of soap and a bottle of shampoo in her makeup kit. "Oh, yes, Sister Mary, this is luxury."

Debbie followed Sister Mary to the shower, a crude portable but well-screened from prying eyes. Debbie took off the peasant clothing, intending to keep them as a souvenir, but decided to give them to Sister Mary instead in case someone needed them. She spent a long time under the shower, washing and shampooing away the dirt and dust she was covered with, and washing out the cut on her hand. Wrapped in a bathrobe, she went back into Sister Mary's tent, doctored her cut, and put on a green linen wraparound. She propped her makeup case open and was just putting the finishing touches to her makeup when Jim stepped through the door of the office and sat down on a folding chair. "Jim, hadn't you better be getting ready for the wedding?" Debbie asked. Jim was still dressed in his mud-spattered jeans.

"I have plenty of time. Father Reilly has set the ceremony for eight." Jim hunched forward and leaned his elbows on his knees. "Li said that you and Ben are lovers."

"Oh, no, I hope she wasn't horribly shocked," Debbie said as she shut the makeup case. "I forget how different the Vietnamese mores are."

"Oh, no, Li wasn't shocked. She thinks he's some kind of swashbuckling hero, put here on this earth to sweep you off your feet," Jim replied dryly. "But, Debbie, I'm concerned. I thought you didn't like him."

"I didn't," Debbie admitted. "Not at first. I thought he was totally cold and ruthless."

"Isn't he?" Jim asked.

Debbie shrugged. "I saw a different side of him over there. He can be kind, Jim, and tender, and not just when we're making love. He's really a pretty decent human being underneath it all."

"I always got the feeling he thought the love Li and I feel for one another was a lot of nonsense."

"His exact words were 'hogwash' and 'garbage,'" Debbie said. "And worse. Jim, he did feel that way in the beginning, and we've had some terrific arguments on the subject." She sat on the edge of the desk and fiddled with a lock of damp hair.

Jim got up and paced the floor. "Debbie, I'm not trying to play the heavy uncle or anything like that, but you were hurt so badly by Kevin, and this man has the potential to hurt you even worse if you fall in love with him." Jim glanced at the expression on Debbie's face. "You're already in love with him, aren't you?"

"I probably wouldn't have become his lover if I hadn't been in love with him," Debbie admitted.

"And how does he feel about you?"

"I don't know, Jim. His actions tell me that he cares, that he cares a lot. But he's still never come out and said that he's changed his mind about love. I'm hoping that seeing you and Li and the way you love each other has changed his mind."

"You think seeing me and Li has convinced him?" Jim asked.

"I sure hope it has," Debbie said. "Now, you quit worrying about me and get Li over here so I can turn her into a beautiful bride!" She ran her hand down the side of Jim's face. "But thank you for caring, Jim." Debbie's eyes filled with tears and she wiped them away impatiently. "I don't know what's the matter with me! I have to stop being so emotional over things."

"Debbie, don't you know that women in love are emotional about everything?" Jim said as he wiped tears out of his own eyes.

"And men in love aren't?" Debbie asked softly.

"Yeah. Yeah, they are," he admitted as he walked out of the office.

Li came in the door a few moments later and Debbie pointed her toward the shower. When she returned, she put on some of Debbie's underwear, blushing a little at the lacy confections, and slipped on the white linen dress that Debbie had laid out for her, the loosely cut lines disguising her still thin body. Since Li was out of practice, Debbie helped her choose the makeup that would best enhance her still sallow skin, and while Li put on her makeup, Debbie picked out some of her prettiest underwear and nightgowns and put them into a fold-out bag she had stored in her suitcase. She added several of her nicest dresses, and she put the makeup Li had just finished applying into a separate plastic sack. "Here, let me do your hair," she said as Li fumbled with a bobby pin.

She pinned Li's hair up on top of her head in a loose topknot, letting just a few tendrils escape, and gasped as Li turned around to face her. "Oh, Li, you're as beautiful as you ever were!" she said to the transformed woman sitting in front of her. Li looked a little older than she was, but she was still a lovely woman.

"You became a beautiful woman, too," Li said. "If you had walked into the hut with braces on your teeth, I would have known you immediately."

Debbie laughed. "Here are some of my things to tide you over until you can go shopping," she said as she pushed the fold-out bag into Li's hands. "Wear the white gown tonight."

"Debbie, how can I thank you?" Li asked as she peeked into the bag. "You've done so much for me and you still keep doing."

"A year's worth of your spring rolls? Come on, your groom's waiting, along with a best man who doesn't know what to do."

Jim, Ben, and the priest were waiting for them in the makeshift outdoor chapel at the edge of the camp, along with some of the refugees, who were curious about what these strange foreigners were doing. Jim looked self-assured and handsome in his three-piece suit, and Ben looked unexpectedly handsome in an expensive business suit. Ben stared at the transformation in Li and Jim kissed her cheek gently. "I said that I wouldn't have cared how you looked, Li, as long as you came to me. But I was wrong. I'm glad you're still beautiful." Li shook her head and started to protest, but Jim silenced her protest with a kiss.

Li and Jim signed some papers that would make their marriage a legal one in Thailand, a requirement if Li was to be issued a visa; and, since Li and Jim were both Catholic, the priest had consented to conducting a full mass in the fading light of dusk.

Debbie watched as Jim and Li stepped up to the makeshift altar. They were both calm, their faces serene as their strong, sure voices made their vows before God and man. Debbie did not find herself moved to cry, but rather to marvel at these two people, who had waited so long and had overcome so many obstacles to be together. Li's face was wreathed in a smile as she made her vows to Jim, and his face glowed with happy assurance as he declared his love for Li. They were now making public the vows they had made in their hearts so many years ago.

Father Reilly came to the part of the ceremony where rings were exchanged. He glanced at Jim, and Jim nodded as he pulled the little dragon ring off his finger and, after the priest's blessing, put it on Li's finger. It was then that Debbie's eyes filled with tears, for she had never seen Jim without that ring on his finger. Debbie glanced over at Ben and saw that he was watching Jim and Li intently. What was he thinking? Had Jim and Li's devotion proven to him that love was real? He hadn't said so, of course, but Debbie couldn't help but hope that it had.

Ben watched Jim as he placed the dragon ring on Li's finger. So those two had finally managed to tie the knot. Well, good for them—they had been through enough, and if being together mattered that much to them, then more power to them. He glanced over at Debbie. She was standing there taking it all in. This wedding had her more convinced than ever that this love she kept talking about was real. But he still doubted it, although he admitted to himself that something other than physical attraction was responsible for the wedding tonight. It would be interesting to see how this relationship fared in the future, after the Romeo-and-Juliet syndrome wore off, and Jim and Li were living together on a day-to-day basis.

The priest pronounced Jim and Li man and wife and offered communion. Not being Catholic, Debbie declined, and she was surprised when Ben partook of the wafer after Jim and Li. Several of the women who had come to the ceremony partook also, and the priest said the blessing for Jim and Li. Jim kissed Li gently and shook hands with Ben and the priest.

There was hugging and kissing all around, and Sister Mary invited them back to her tent for a wedding supper. Debbie and Ben laughed out loud when the wedding supper turned out to be rice, but this rice was delicately flavored with chunks of vegetables and chicken and was so delicious that Debbie, who had vowed never to eat another grain of rice as long as she lived, had a second helping. Jim had brought several bottles of champagne with him from Bangkok just in case, and his and Li's future was toasted all around.

It was quite late when the party broke up. Jim and Li planned to spend their wedding night in Jim's tent, and Sister Mary had offered to let Debbie and Ben stay in her office. Debbie watched Jim and Li stroll away together into the soft, starry night, making their way through the crowded camp to where Jim's tent was pitched on the edge. "I wish Li had a better place to spend her wedding night," Debbie said and sighed as Li and Jim disappeared into the night.

Ben snickered. "Oh, I don't think she'll find it so bad after camping out for the last two and a half months." He pushed Sister Mary's desk aside and unrolled their sleeping bags, laying one on top of the other as he always did.

"Yes, but every bride deserves a nice wedding night," Debbie said as she unzipped her dress and let it slide off her shoulders. "You know, champagne, satin sheets, that kind of thing. All she's got is a dumb old sleeping bag."

"Want to bet?" Ben said as he laughed out loud. "Your friend Jim came well-prepared, just in case."

"What did he bring?" Debbie asked, mystified.

"Would you believe he brought satin sheets and a queen-sized air mattress?"

"WHAT?"

"Yes, he really did. It takes up the whole floor of his tent. I helped him fix it before the wedding."

Debbie sat down on the sleeping bag and laughed out loud. "You're kidding! I can imagine what Li thinks."

"She probably thinks he intends to make up for lost time," Ben said as he untied his tie and shucked off his jacket and shirt. He stripped to his underwear and sat down beside Debbie on the sleeping bags. "I know this isn't exactly satin sheets like they have, but we can endure the sleeping bags one more time. You know, for old times sake. The next time we make love it will be in a bed."

Debbie pretended to think about it while Ben unhooked her bra. "On the sleeping bags, huh?" He caressed her bare breast while he nibbled her nape. "Well, I guess I could," she said as she put her arms around Ben and pulled him down on top of her, their bodies melting together as they always did. "For old times sake."

Debbie sighed and snuggled down into the sleeping bag. She was tired, so tired, and she didn't want to face another day of hiking. Loathe to shut her eyes, she groped for the mosquito netting and snuggled closer to Ben. But something wasn't quite right. The mosquito netting felt wonderfully soft to her hands. The sleeping bag felt soft, too soft. And Ben was too far away.

Debbie's eyes flew open and she looked around the luxurious Bangkok hotel room. No more sleeping bags and mosquito netting for her. Now it was satin sheets all the way! Well, maybe percale. She turned her head on the pillow and gazed across at Ben's dark, tousled hair against the white pillow case, and her heart swelled with love for this brave, hard man. She loved Ben Sako, she loved him with all her heart, and she could only hope that he had found, or would find it in himself to return her love.

Raising herself on her elbow, Debbie leaned down and planted a soft kiss on his cheek. His eyes fluttered open and his lips curved into a smile. "Good morning, sleepyhead," Ben said as he raised his hands and buried them in the thickness of her hair. He pulled her head down to his and explored her mouth in a long, tender kiss. "This is the first time in ages you've been awake before me."

"The first time ever, I think," Debbie admitted. "I'm surprised you didn't wake up earlier this morning."

Ben put his arms around Debbie and snuggled her down beside him. "I'm tired, Lotus. I'm always tired after a mission."

Debbie turned surprised eyes on Ben. "You never seemed tired over there," she said as she planted a tender kiss on his jaw. "You always seemed so, oh, not exactly energetic, but you never seemed to slow down or get tired."

"Discipline," Ben said as he feathered light kisses on Debbie's temple. "I impose a sort of discipline on myself when I'm working, so I really don't feel tired, even though I am. And then after it's all over, I crash."

"Is that what happened last night?" Debbie asked innocently. "I thought I had lost all my sex appeal." She ran her hand down Ben's taut stomach.

Ben reddened slightly. "You weren't much better," he said. "You were dead on your feet and you know it." His hand caressed her shoulder and ran down her arm.

"Yes, but you went to sleep while I was in the shower," she reminded him. "I put on this sexy gown so you could see me looking pretty for a change, and when I came back out here, you were snoring."

Ben's chest shook with laughter. "I'm sorry, Lotus. But it's funny too. I can just see you, standing there looking beautiful for me, and I'm asleep!" Without warning he flung the covers off them both. "Well, it's not too late to see you beautiful for me," he said as he surveyed Debbie's body, her slender curves outlined by the sheer peach gown that she wore.

"Oh, I'm not beautiful in the morning," Debbie protested as Ben's eager gaze enveloped her tousled hair and sleepy face before drifting lower. "You saw me dozens of times in the morning in Vietnam."

"And every time I thought you were the loveliest woman I'd ever seen," Ben said as he dipped his head and covered her mouth with a sweet, sweet kiss. "But the gown is beautiful, Lotus. And you're beautiful in it."

He kissed her again and sat up. "Ben?" Debbie asked.

He grinned wickedly at her as he ran his hand down the length of her body, paying special attention to her breasts. "I'm not putting an end to the delightful beginning," he told her. "But I better call the airline and make reservations to fly back. Day after tomorrow all right with you? That will give us a little time to go sightseeing and sleep before we have to fly back."

"Sounds wonderful," Debbie said as Ben sat up and dialed the operator. Debbie scooted over so that she was lying beside Ben on the king-sized bed. Absently her fingers trailed around his waist and played down the back of his spine as she thought about Li and Jim's wedding two nights ago. It had been beautiful, so beautiful, and Li had been blushing but radiant the next morning when the rickety old bus came to take the four of them into Bangkok. The bus ride had taken most of the day, and Li and Jim had parted from Debbie and Ben at the bus station, so they could check into their hotel and get to the embassy before it closed. They would have to stay in Bangkok for a couple of weeks, while Li had a medical examination and the paperwork was completed for her visa, and they were planning to combine the wait with a honeymoon in Thailand. Ben and Debbie had checked into their hotel, and Debbie had insisted that they take a brief look around the old city with so many temples. Ben swore before the afternoon was out that Debbie intended to see all of the twenty-three thousand temples in the city before she flew back to California. They had dined at one of the city's finest restaurants, but exhaustion coupled with a bottle of wine had taken its toll, and they both had fallen asleep on the romantic evening they had planned.

So why not make it a romantic morning? The motion of Debbie's hands grew less absent and more purposeful as she teased and tormented the skin at the base of Ben's spine. He squirmed and moved farther away from her teasing fingers, but Debbie inched closer to him and drew circles on his back with her fingertips. "Debbie, stop that!" Ben whispered. "Oh, yes, operator, what was that?" He wiggled away from Debbie's pursuing fingers. "Yes, could you put me through to the ticket office in the lobby?" He turned around to Debbie. "Debbie, please! Uh, oh, yes, this is Ben Sako in Room 414. Could you arrange for two flights out of here day after tomorrow?"

Debbie giggled as she continued her sensual assault on Ben. She sat up and pushed her gown off her shoulders, letting her breasts rub lightly against Ben's back. Ben swore and inched forward on the bed, until he was sitting on the edge of the mattress. Debbie placed quick, little kisses on his back and his nape, her partial nudity visible in the mirror of the dresser. Ben groaned at the vision of loveliness she made, her nightgown down around her waist and her tender breasts hard with desire for him. "Debbie, please—yes, the two o'clock flight will be fine. Thank you." He hung up the telephone and with a swift motion whirled around and grabbed Debbie's wrists, and pushed her down into the mattress, pinning her to the bed as he plundered her mouth in a long, hard kiss. Debbie moaned and opened her mouth to his, tasting the warm sweetness of his mouth as he sampled the warmth of hers. "You little witch," he said when he finally released her lips. "You were driving me crazy. Do you know that? I only hope we don't end up in New York City or something."

Debbie grinned impudently up at him. "Then you shouldn't have been so tempting," she said as she drew circles on his shoulder with her tongue. "Sitting there, not a stitch covering up your attributes, and you expect me to leave you alone. What do you think I'm made of, stone?"

Ben released Debbie's wrists and pulled the gown from her body. "Anything but that," he whispered as he touched her body eagerly. "You're anything but stone, Debbie Cheong." He touched one breast, then the other with the tip of his tongue, watching as the tips grew hard with desire for him.

Debbie's freed hands found their way to Ben's body and touched his sides and his chest. "You're not stone either," she said as his hard, warm flesh trembled under her touch. "You're warm and you're so very good to touch. Let me touch you, Ben," she said as her fingers found and caressed his waist, his stomach, the hardness of his hips.

They touched and caressed one another for long moments, each one murmuring their delight and appreciation. Their pace slow and unhurried, they made up for all the times they had come to a quick fulfillment, knowing that Li would be back soon. Debbie's hands found the warm curve of his bottom and caressed it lovingly. Her fingers found and touched the strong muscles of his upper thighs, and she delighted when he tensed beneath her touch. "Do you like that?" she asked as she stroked the tender skin of his inner thighs.

"Yes, I like that," he said as his lips grazed the undersides of her breasts. Nibbling and kissing, he inched down her body, past her ribcage to her waist, where he paid special attention to her narrow waist. "But you shouldn't even have to ask if I like it. You know I like it, Lotus. I like it a lot. Just like I know you like this." He dipped his tongue into the gentle indentation of her navel.

"Yes, I like that," Debbie said as Ben touched and caressed her stomach with his lips.

"And this," he said as he kissed the lower part of her stomach, below last year's faint bikini line.

"Yes," she whispered.

"And this," he said as his lips traveled even lower, finding and touching the softness of her femininity.

"Yes, Ben, this," she moaned as Ben touched and caressed her intimately. He had discovered just how much she liked this on a hot night in Vietnam, and he delighted in bringing her pleasure this way, secretly proud of his ability to do so. He touched her and caressed her until her body tightened in waves of delight. "Oh, Ben, oh . . ." she whispered as she felt an explosion inside of her.

Moving swiftly, Ben parted her legs and made them one, knowing her body was ready for his. He moved over her, quickly bringing her back to the point of feverish desire for him. Debbie arched and moaned beneath him, twisting and turning so that they would each receive the maximum pleasure. Ben groaned as he felt the shooting stars behind his eyes. No, no, he wanted to give her pleasure first. Valiantly holding off the tide of passion that threatened to tear from him, he waited until he felt Debbie arch and gasp beneath him before he joined her on the crest of the wave. Trembling in each other's arms, they floated with the tide, as it bounced them up on the shore and left them spent.

Ben lay quietly for a moment in Debbie's arms before he rolled away from her and cradled her to his side. "Does that make up for last night?" he asked.

Debbie chuckled. "Well, I wasn't going to fall asleep on you." She propped her head on her hand. "How often do you think you'll be able to see me in San Francisco?"

Ben covered her lips with a long, slow kiss. "At least every weekend. Sometimes during the week, too. As often as we can manage it. We have a good thing going, Lotus."

"I know," Debbie said as she kissed him. She sat up and ran her fingers through her hair. "Now, let's get a shower and put some clothes on. I believe you promised me a few more temples." Ben groaned and turned over as Debbie hopped out of bed and took a cotton sundress from her suitcase.

Debbie showered quickly and put on her underwear. Ben, dressed in a thick robe, had just closed the door and was wheeling a cart with coffee and rolls into the room.

His eyes widened at the sight of Debbie, dressed in her lacy bra and panties. "If you don't get something over that sexy body of yours, we're liable to spend the day right here, and you'll never get to see those temples."

Debbie grinned as she pulled the sundress over her head. "The coffee and rolls were a good idea. Thanks."

She sat down on the side of the bed and poured herself a cup of coffee as Ben disappeared into the bathroom for a shower. He returned a few minutes later, his hair damp from the shower, and dressed in a pair of cotton slacks and a knit shirt. "Joe Tourist at your service," he said as he poured himself a cup of coffee.

Debbie sipped her coffee and nibbled her roll. "I hope Jim and Li have a little time to see the sights," she said. "I hope they don't have to spend all their time at the embassy getting her visa."

"Oh, I imagine they'll have plenty of time to see the country," Ben said. "At least they'll see what they want to take time to see. Remember, they're on their honeymoon."

Debbie's face softened. "Wasn't it the most beautiful thing you ever saw? They were so happy to be together again." She took another bite of her roll. "Seeing them together makes me feel so happy inside, to know that there is such a thing as lasting love between a man and a woman." She wiped her lips with a napkin. "I was beginning to wonder."

"What makes you so sure that they're going to last, now that they're together?" Ben asked as he took a bite of his roll.

Debbie's mouth dropped open. "What makes you think they're not? After all they've been through, how can you even ask if that marriage is going to make it?

Ben, those people *love* each other! Isn't what they've gone through to be together proof enough of that?"

Ben crossed his legs and looked at her steadily. "Or is what they've gone through the only thing holding them together?"

Debbie stared across the room at Ben. "Maybe you better explain just what you mean by that," she said, her voice curiously emotionless.

"Just that. Look, Debbie, what happened to them was very tragic, but it was also very romantic. Two lovers torn apart by a war, they take years to find one another and the man arranges for the woman to be rescued and spirited to freedom and into his arms. All very romantic, right? But what's going to happen once they get back to San Francisco and settle into suburbia? Money problems, in-law problems, a plugged-up kitchen sink, diaper rash. All very unromantic, all very mundane. And Li and Jim are very romantic people. How long do you think their love's going to last in the real world?"

"You just don't *want* to believe that love's real!" Debbie said as she threw down her napkin and stood up. "You look for the worst in a relationship! You try to find holes to pick, to support your belief that love doesn't exist."

"That's because, Debbie, it doesn't exist!" Ben said as he gulped his coffee, burning his mouth on the hot liquid and cursing softly. "You just want to believe in it. You're not willing to look at reality. You're looking at one couple who has just had a dramatic reunion, and you're trying to say it's possible for all of us. Well, it ain't, babe. Look around some more. Look at your parents. Look at my parents. Look at your own marriage, for crying out loud. Did any of them last? Did any of those so-called love matches last?"

"No, but I can point out those that did. Look at Jim's parents. Forty-five years, Ben, and he still brings her flowers. Li's parents were devoted to one another until her mother died. My grandparents, Ben. They were married over fifty years. So how can you explain those relationships, if love isn't real?"

"I don't know, Debbie," Ben said heavily. "But I'll tell you this. I've sure as hell never felt the emotion. And I really don't think I'm ever going to."

Debbie recoiled as though she had been slapped. "I'm sorry, Debbie," Ben continued. "I know you had hoped that I would declare my undying love for you, but I can't do that. I don't believe in love. I've never felt the emotion in my life. And I'm too honest to pretend otherwise. Besides, what's the matter with what we have? We have a good relationship, we have fun, we're good together in bed. Why do we have to drag love into it?"

"If I have to explain it to you, Ben, then it's hopeless," Debbie said as she raised tear-filled eyes to meet Ben's cynical ones. "But I want to explain something to you. This 'good relationship,' this 'fun' that you spoke of has another name, at least it does on my part. I call it 'love,' Ben. I love you. I've loved you for a long time. I loved you for a long time before I even realized it. I'm not ashamed of the love I feel for you, and I'm not afraid to acknowledge that love to you. What I feel for you is stronger than anything I ever felt for Kevin."

She paused as she paced across the room. "But I can't continue as your lover, Ben. I had intended to stay with you for as long as you wanted me to, but now I know I can't. I can't stay in a one-sided relationship, giving love but receiving none in return. I have to be loved in return, or it's going to destroy me."

"Oh, Debbie, for God's sake, grow up!" Ben ground

out as he stood up. "What do you want me to do? Lie to you? Say the right words?"

"No, I don't want you to say the right words!" Debbie said as she choked back her tears. "I wouldn't care if you never spoke, as long as you felt some love, some caring for me. Damn it, I want you to love me! Is that so hard to do? I don't have any trouble loving you, Ben." She grabbed her nightgown off the floor and shoved it in her suitcase.

"What are you doing?" Ben demanded as Debbie marched into the bathroom and started putting her make up in her makeup case.

"I'm going home. Today." She turned tear-streaked eyes on Ben. "Ben, I've had it with you and your pig-headedness. You've seen the same evidence I've seen. You've seen Jim and Li, you've heard him and you've heard her. And you've heard me tell you that I love you. You've soaked up the love I've given you the last two months. And you still refuse to believe, because it would rattle your notion of the way things are just a little too much. Fine. You can stay in your loveless life, motivated by hatred, ambition, and what was it? Oh, yes, greed. But count me out, Ben. I want some love in my life." She locked her makeup kit and stepped past him.

"Debbie, you're being ridiculous," Ben sputtered. "Throwing away a good thing like we have!"

"It might be a good thing for you, Ben, but for me it has the potential of turning into a living hell." Debbie shut her suitcase and picked up the telephone. She asked to have a bellboy sent up, and made a second call to the airline ticket office. Sniffing, she hung up and sat on the edge of the bed. "I got a flight out of here at one this afternoon," she told Ben.

"Are you sure this is what you want?" Ben demanded.

"Because if you walk out of here, that's going to be it for us."

Debbie shook her head slowly as a knock sounded on the door. She answered it and told the bellboy to take her bags to the lobby before she turned back to Ben. "No, Ben," she said, "this isn't what I want. This isn't what I want at all. But it's what I have to do. I need something you can't give me." She squared her shoulders and walked out of his life.

Debbie walked blindly to the lobby and got into a cab that would take her to the airport. She fought back tears, unwilling to cry in front of the cab driver even though her heart was breaking. She had given her love to a man who was incapable of loving her in return. He refused to believe in it because he had never felt it. Or perhaps he had never felt it because he didn't believe in it. Either way, Ben was incapable of giving her the love she needed so badly in her life, and she had to get away from him before he destroyed her completely.

Ben walked blindly through the red-light district of old Bangkok, staring at the women who offered themselves for his pleasure. Some of them were young and quite lovely, but Ben felt the old familiar numbness coming over him, the sexual numbness and apathy he had felt before Debbie Cheong had marched into his life. He would have paid his money and taken his pleasure tonight if he thought it would do any good. But Ben was more honest with himself than that. He felt no desire for these women of the streets, and his money would probably be wasted in a fruitless attempt to lose himself for a few minutes, to forget the deep loneliness he had felt since Debbie had walked out of his life a week ago.

Ben grimaced as he lit a cigarette with his expensive

new lighter. He hadn't thought it possible to miss a woman like he missed her. He had never missed one before. And he didn't understand why. There were plenty of other women in the world, and a lot of them were younger and prettier and more knowledgeable in the art of sex than Debbie. But at the moment none of them would do. Only Debbie, and she had left him because he didn't believe in the love she thought she needed.

Ben stood on the corner and watched a well-dressed businessman solicit one of the women on the street. He tried to tell himself that was what it was all about, but he no longer believed that. He was beginning to think there must be something more for some people. Maybe love did exist for people like Jim and Li Anderson, and for Debbie. Maybe it was possible for them, he still wasn't sure. But he did know one thing. He had never in his life felt the emotion. Love certainly didn't exist for him.

## CHAPTER THIRTEEN

Debbie stood beside Mr. and Mrs. Anderson at the San Francisco airport as they peered out the windows, trying to pick out the jumbo jet on which Jim and Li would be arriving. "Do you think that's it?" Mr. Anderson asked as a large jet circled overhead.

"It might be," Debbie said. "But remember, we came early and their plane isn't due for another fifteen minutes."

"Oh, I hope you don't mind us dragging you out here so early," Mrs. Anderson said as she patted her hair nervously. "It's just that we're so anxious to see Jim and meet Li. We've waited so long for this day. Debbie, do I look all right?" She patted her freshly set hair and straightened her collar for the fifth or sixth time.

"Mrs. Anderson, you look just fine," Debbie reassured her. "Believe me, you look a lot better than Jim and Li did when they saw each other for the first time in ten years!" Debbie glanced down at her freshly manicured nails and thought of how ragged they had been that day. "We were all a mess."

"You still look tired, Debbie," Mrs. Anderson said. "That trip through the jungle wore you out." She put her arm around Debbie and hugged her. "But I have to admit that I'm grateful to you for going, although I'm glad

Jim was smart enough not to let any of us know you'd gone in until you were out safely. I'd have worried myself sick—it was bad enough worrying about Mr. Sako getting Li out. What on earth did your father say when he found out what you did?"

Debbie grinned. "Well, let's just say that I couldn't have quoted him directly in the newspaper or on television. He nearly came apart at the seams, but later after he had calmed down, he gave me the third degree about what I saw over there. He always loved that country, even though he went over there to fight a war." Debbie covered her mouth to stifle a yawn.

"You're still worn out from all that hiking," Mrs. Anderson said, taking in the deep shadows under Debbie's eyes. "Are you getting enough rest?"

Debbie nodded. After her break with Ben, she had expected to lie awake half the night thinking about him, but to her surprise she found herself falling asleep the minute her head hit the pillow, and sleeping through to her alarm. Yet she couldn't shake her fatigue. She barely made it through the day, and collapsed every evening in front of a TV dinner, except on the nights she ate with Gordon and Nyen-Nyen. She had expected the tiredness to improve in the two weeks since she had left Bangkok, but she still felt as tired as she had when she left the Orient.

Or was her depression over her break with Ben making her tired? She had not heard from him since she had walked out of their Bangkok hotel room, nor had she expected to. They had both recognized that their split was final. She desperately wanted to be loved, and he simply couldn't do that. There was no way they could compromise, there was no way they could "work it out." Debbie was lonely, and she missed Ben terribly, but she knew that there was no way she could continue to give her love to a man who didn't return it and didn't even believe in it. She had heard that one of the manifestations of depression was fatigue, and thought that perhaps she was just grieving her breakup with Ben.

Beside her, the Andersons were starting to fidget. "Do you think she'll like us?" Mrs. Anderson asked anxiously. "Do you think she'll mind living in the apartment over the garage?"

"I hope she can get used to our ways," Mr. Anderson fretted. "We're bound to seem strange to her."

"Hey, relax, you two," Debbie said. "She's probably just as worried about you two liking her. Hey look, that jet was theirs!" The big jet they had spotted moments ago was pulling up to the terminal.

They watched as the passengers spilled from the doors of the tunnel. Debbie spotted a familiar blond head and waved her hand. "Over here, Jim!" she called.

Jim saw her and pointed Li in their direction. Mr. and Mrs. Anderson watched as Jim escorted his tiny, nervous bride across the terminal. "Mom, Dad, this is Li," Jim said as Li extended a slightly trembling hand to her new mother-in-law.

Tears glistened in Mrs. Anderson's eyes as she took Li into her arms and embraced her tenderly. "Oh, Li, welcome to our family," she said. "We've waited so long for this day."

Mrs. Anderson released Li and Mr. Anderson hugged her. "We're so glad to have you with us."

Li smiled, her eyes misty but her earlier nervousness gone. "Thank you both so much," she said as she gripped their hands. "Jim has told me how you helped him save the money to send for me, and how you've stood by him all these years. He's lucky to have parents like you." She turned to Debbie and hugged her. "Ben didn't come with you today?"

Debbie shook her head, her face grim. "No, and I won't be seeing him again. I'll tell you and Jim about it later," she added in a whisper.

The five of them retrieved Jim's and Li's luggage and piled into the Andersons' station wagon. Li and Jim were both exhausted, so Debbie left them at Jim's garage apartment, promising to pick Li up in the morning for a shopping expedition. She went home and fixed another TV dinner, but her stomach felt a little queasy, and she threw it out after eating only half of it. She showered and went to bed early, dreaming of a dark-eyed man making love to her in the light of a bright yellow moon.

Debbie picked Li up promptly at ten. Jim offered to go along with them, but both women declined, knowing Jim's aversion to shopping for clothes. Li shivered as she stepped from the apartment and pulled one of Mrs. Anderson's sweaters around her. "This cool weather is going to take some getting used to," she said.

"It's a little cool, even for September," Debbie admitted. "But it won't get a whole lot worse. You could have found yourself married to a midwesterner and buried in snow for seven months out of the year."

They got into Debbie's car and sped toward her favorite shopping center. Li peered out the windows for a while, commenting on various changes in San Francisco, before she turned to Debbie. "Want to tell me what happened between you and Ben, or is it too private?"

Debbie shrugged as her lower lip trembled. "I thought he would change his mind after he saw you and Jim, but he didn't. He made love to me like I've never been made love to before and then looked me in the eye and told me that there was no such thing as love, that he had never felt the emotion in his life." Impatiently, Debbie wiped a tear off her cheek, trying not to smear her eye makeup.

"He's wrong, Debbie," Li said.

"I know. I spent three months trying to change his mind and I couldn't," Debbie said. "I couldn't convince him that love's real."

"No, I didn't mean that," Li said. "The man does love you. I could see it in his eyes when he looked at you. He loves you. He just doesn't realize it."

"Sure," Debbie said bitterly.

"No, really, he does care for you, Debbie," Li said. "He may not recognize it in himself, but I saw it in him, and I think you felt it from him. Are you sure that breaking up with him was the best thing to do?"

Debbie shrugged. "I don't know, but what's done is done. Until he changes his mind about love, it's hopeless for us anyway." They pulled into the parking lot of the mall. "Now, let's go in and fix you up."

They spent most of the day at the mall. The picked out lacy underwear and frilly nightgowns, too many, really, but Debbie could understand Li's desire to have fine, feminine things after having none for so long. Li tried on several kinds of designer jeans before she found a brand that looked good on her, and she picked out several dresses and one wool suit. Debbie laughed when Li turned her nose up at the high-fashion punk look. They found Li a few blouses and visited the cosmetics counters, and wound up the afternoon buying shoes and a couple of purses. Except for the punk look, Li loved the changes that American fashion had undergone, and she eagerly showed Jim all of her purchases as she and Debbie carried the bags and boxes to the apartment.

Li and Jim invited Debbie to have dinner with them, but she declined, thinking the newlyweds needed to be alone. Besides, her stomach felt a little queasy again to-night, and she doubted that she could do justice to Li's dinner anyway. She went home and ate a bowl of cereal and pushed a nagging worry to the back of her mind.

But the nausea did not go away over the next two weeks, nor did the nagging worry. Debbie knew the facts of life as well as anyone. She had taken no precautions in the forests of Vietnam and Cambodia, and she knew that tiredness and nausea were two of the earliest symptoms of pregnancy. Her cycle had never been regular, but as she stared at the calendar on her refrigerator, she had to acknowledge that she had never gone this long before. She spent several days trying to convince herself that she was just weary from the trip and that she had picked up a stomach virus, but the day she had to run to the ladies room to keep from throwing up her lunch at her desk, she knew she couldn't keep putting off the inevitable. She called her gynecologist's office and asked if she could trust a home pregnancy test. The receptionist advised her to come on in for a test that afternoon, and they could have the results in an hour or so.

She picked up her purse and stepped into Jim's office. "Jim, I have to go to the doctor's office for a little while," she said. "Can you cover for me if the boss asks where I am?"

Jim looked up from a Chinese newspaper and nodded, frowning when he saw how miserable Debbie looked. "Are you all right? God, what a stupid question. Of course you're not, if you're going to the doctor. And you have been looking tired lately. Did you pick up some-thing over there in the jungle?"

"I'm afraid so," Debbie said, trying not to sound sar-castic.

"Well, you let me know the minute you get back," Jim said. "I'm worried about you, Debbie."

Debbie thanked Jim for his concern and took a streetcar to the doctor's office. She gave the receptionist her name, and a lab technician called her to the back and took a specimen, instructing her to remain in the waiting room until the doctor could see her. Debbie sat down on a couch and leaned her head back, closing her eyes as she waited to hear her name called again. Her mind whirled as she wondered what on earth she was going to do if she was indeed pregnant.

A different nurse called her name this time, and Debbie followed her into an examination room. She took off her clothes and put on the hospital gown, tying it in front as she had been instructed to, and sat on the examining table with a sheet over her. She swallowed nervously as Dr. Osgood stepped into the room. "Well, am I pregnant?" she asked as the nurse stepped in behind him.

Dr. Osgood nodded. "I gather it's not exactly welcome news?" he asked.

"Not exactly," Debbie admitted.

"Well, let's get you examined and then we'll discuss your options."

Dr. Osgood's examination was swift but thorough. "I'd estimate that you're about two and a half months along," he said. "Although if you're still as irregular as you were when you were trying to conceive before, we can't tell for sure without a sonogram."

Vietnam. Her child had been conceived somewhere in the forests of Vietnam. Debbie knew she was being foolish, but she couldn't help but feel that it had happened that beautiful night on the Perfume River. "When is it due?" she asked.

"Oh, sometime in April," Dr. Osgood said. "I'll know

236

more after a sonogram, if that's what you want. Now, you get dressed and wait for me in my office. I have a patient in the next office who may be in the early stages of labor and I need to check on her."

Debbie put her clothes back on and waited in Dr. Osgood's office. A baby. She was carrying a child. Her child —hers and Ben's. She bit her lip to keep from crying. She loved Ben, and under other circumstances would have loved to have had his child.

Dr. Osgood came in and sat down behind his desk. He noticed the tears in Debbie's eyes and handed her a tissue. "You don't have to have it, you know," he said gently. "I gather this wasn't planned?"

"Well, out in the middle of Vietnam there wasn't much I could do about preventing it," Debbie admitted. She gave Dr. Osgood a rundown of her summer, omitting the fact that she had fallen in love with Ben and had fought bitterly with him, merely saying that they had parted when the mission was over.

"Debbie, as I see it you have several options," Dr. Osgood said. "If you like we can terminate the pregnancy. Or you can have the baby and give it up for adoption. There are hundreds of Oriental couples who have waited for years to adopt an Oriental infant. Or you can have it and keep it. Tell me, do you intend to contact the father?"

"No." Debbie's voice was firm.

"You don't have to make your decision today," Dr. Osgood said. "But you need to make up your mind fairly quickly. If you intend to go through with the pregnancy, you need to be taking some vitamins. You're a little anemic. And I can give you something for the nausea if you need it."

"Go ahead and prescribe the vitamins," Debbie said

slowly. "And the nausea pills. I doubt that I'll be having an abortion."

Dr. Osgood wrote her out a prescription for a multivitamin and the nausea pills, and told her to contact him if she changed her mind about carrying the baby full-term. She thanked him and left his office, stopping by a pharmacy before she returned to her office. She reached down and gently touched the lower part of her stomach. Ben's child. Her child. Their child together. Debbie had no particular moral qualms about abortions in general, and if circumstances had been different, she would not have hesitated to have one herself. But she could no more terminate this pregnancy than she could stop breathing. She loved Ben, and she already loved the child they had created together. She would have to see this pregnancy through, and she would not be giving up the child for adoption. She would raise Ben's child herself.

Debbie paid for the medicine, then took the streetcar back to the office. It was already late, but she had promised her boss that she would translate a Chinese communiqué. She sat down at her desk and tried to work on the communiqué, but her mind wandered as she tried to imagine what it was going to be like, raising a child alone. It wasn't going to be easy, that was for sure, working and trying to be both mother and father to the baby. Her father would have a fit when he found out about the baby. And what was her beloved Nyen-Nyen going to think? The tears in her eyes caused the print to blur so that she couldn't read the figures. She tried to fight back the tears for a while, but finally gave up and put her head down on her desk and sobbed.

Debbie raised her head when she felt a gentle hand on her shoulder. "Debbie, what on earth did you find out at the doctor?" Jim asked. "Or is it something else?"

Debbie sat up and tried to stem the flow of tears, but they simply would not stop. "Oh, Jim, I'm pregnant!" she said, sobbing. "I'm pregnant with Ben's baby."

Jim utttered a curse word under his breath as he knelt down and cradled Debbie against his shoulder. "It isn't the end of the world," he said soothingly as he patted her shoulder.

Debbie raised her head and sniffed. "Jim, what am I going to do?"

"You're going to calm down, first thing," he said as he wiped her eyes with a handkerchief. "And then you're going to come home with Li and me."

"No, I couldn't intrude on you and Li tonight," Debbie protested. "I'll be fine."

"Don't be silly," Jim said as he picked up her telephone and punched in a number. "Li, Debbie's coming home with me for dinner, so would you fix a little extra?" He paused a minute. "No, love, everything's not all right. We'll tell you about it when we get there."

Li was waiting for Debbie and Jim at the door. She took one look at Debbie's tearstained face and handed her a glass of wine. Debbie started to drink it but shook her head and handed it to Jim. "I can't have it in my condition."

"Are you sick?" Li asked.

"Not exactly. In the last ten years doctors have found out that pregnant women shouldn't drink."

"Oh." Debbie and Li sat down on the couch. "You're sure?" Li asked.

Debbie nodded. "I spent most of the afternoon at the doctor's office."

Jim sat down across from Debbie. "Do you want to eat now or after we talk?"

"I don't think I could eat right now if I had to," Debbie admitted. "The nausea pill hasn't worked yet."

"I haven't fried the spring rolls yet, so don't worry about dinner," Li said. She turned anxious eyes on Jim. "This is all our fault, Jim," she said. "If we hadn't—"

"If *I* hadn't, you mean," Jim said heavily. "Debbie, I'm sorry. This is my fault. I should never have insisted that you go in Jerry's place. God, I feel like a heel."

Debbie laughed in spite of the misery she was in. "I don't quite know how to say this, but I think Ben and I had a little to do with the conception of this child. *I* should have known better. Even my father warned me about Ben. I knew exactly what he was like when I became his lover. I went into it with my eyes open, Jim. You and Li had nothing to do with it."

"Yes, but if I hadn't sent you off with that bastard, you wouldn't have become his lover and none of this would have happened." Jim stood up and put his hands in his pocket. "Debbie, you don't have to have the baby, you know."

"Jim!" Li cried, horrified.

"No, Li, abortions are pretty common here now," Jim assured her.

Debbie shook her head. "No, I couldn't possibly do that. I love Ben, God help me, and I love this child—his child—and I'll raise it. I'm just worried sick about how I'm going to manage it alone. And Gordon and Nyen-Nyen are going to be so upset!" Tears welled in her eyes and she sniffed them back. "They're going to be so hurt."

"No, they won't," Li said. "They'll love your baby."

"And you're not alone," Jim said. "You're far from that. You have us, you have them, and you have something else." He disappeared into the bedroom for a minute and handed her two checks totaling nearly twenty

240

thousand dollars. "I meant to bring these to you today and forgot. Jerry Chan refunded his part of the fee, and we sold the gold coins that Li still had with her. This is what was left after I paid Sako the rest of what I owed him."

"But this is your money, Jim!" Debbie cried. "I can't take it."

"Debbie, it's what I borrowed from you," Jim said.

"But you and Li could make a down payment on a house," Debbie protested.

"You need the house more than we do," Li reminded her.

"Take it, Debbie," Jim pleaded. "Please. You risked your life for us. Now let us at least pay back what we owe you."

Debbie took the checks reluctantly. "Now, are you going to tell Sako about the baby?" Jim asked her.

"No," Debbie replied instantly.

"Don't you think he ought to be told?" Li asked her gently.

"Why? So he cannot love it the way he doesn't love me? No, thanks. This baby's going to know what it is to be loved," Debbie said.

"We'll help you, Debbie," Li promised. "You're not alone in this, any more than we were alone with our problem."

Debbie thought a minute of all the support she and others had given Jim and Li over the years. "I'm not alone, am I?" she asked.

"No, Debbie, you're not," Jim assured her. "Li and I will stand by you, and you know your father and your grandmother will, too, once they get used to the idea. Now, you look a little thin. Think you can eat?"

Debbie nodded. The nausea was fading, at least a little,

and Li's dinner smelled tempting. She managed to relax with Jim and Li, and was able to eat a decent meal and keep it down.

The days drifted together for Debbie as September became October. The nausea pills helped her some, but she was still tired a lot of the time and didn't feel like eating. Jim made it a point to take her home with him several nights a week so that Li could cook her dinner, and after Jim took her back to Sausalito, she would fall into bed and sleep until she had to get up the next morning. Gordon and Nyen-Nyen had both noticed that Debbie looked tired, but Debbie assured them it was the aftereffects of the hard months in the Orient. Debbie dreaded facing her father with the news of her pregnancy, so she kept putting off telling him. She didn't know how he was going to react, but she was certain that he would have a few choice words for her for getting involved with Ben, especially after he had warned her about the man.

And she hated telling Nyen-Nyen. Her grandmother wouldn't yell at her, but she was going to be hurt and disappointed. As the weeks drifted by, Debbie realized that she was only postponing the inevitable. She had to talk to both Gordon and Nyen-Nyen and tell them about the baby, and only hope that they weren't too terribly disappointed in her. She decided to talk to Nyen-Nyen first, and tell her father after she had seen how her grandmother reacted.

Debbie drove her Corvette across the bridge and into Chinatown late on Saturday afternoon. She had called Nyen-Nyen to make sure she was home and her grandmother, as always, insisted that Debbie stay for dinner. Debbie had agreed, since she knew she would be hungry for her grandmother's cooking. She had not lost any weight since she had found out that she was pregnant, but she hadn't gained any either, even though her waist was getting thicker and her slacks and skirts were getting tight. She didn't know if she was supposed to be gaining yet, but she wanted to eat enough so that the baby would have plenty of vitamins.

She knocked on Nyen-Nyen's door and her grandmother greeted her warmly. Since it was a little early for dinner, she sat down on the couch and Nyen-Nyen brought her a cup of tea. "When are you going to bring your friend, Li, to see me?" Nyen-Nyen asked as Debbie sipped the hot tea. "I've so looked forward to seeing her again."

"I'm sorry I haven't brought her sooner. I've been meaning to, Nyen-Nyen," Debbie said. "Maybe we can drive over next weekend. I've been taking her out for driving lessons in the Corvette, and we could drive over here."

"And how are the newlyweds doing?" Nyen-Nyen asked.

Debbie smiled. "Super. Just super. They couldn't be any happier."

"I'm glad they're happy, Debbie. I only wish you were." Nyen-Nyen's eyes were sad as she looked at her granddaughter. "You think I can't see the sadness, the hurt in your eyes, every time I look at you? What is it, Debbie? Does seeing them together remind you of the husband you lost?"

"Kevin? Oh, no, Nyen-Nyen, I've been over Kevin for a long time. It's something else." She stopped and bit her lip. "I'm pregnant, Nyen-Nyen."

Nyen-Nyen's eyes widened. "How far along are you?"

"Three and a half months at least. Dr. Osgood's not sure."

"It happened while you were in Vietnam then. And the father is the mercenary soldier you went with?"

Debbie nodded. "I feel like a fool, Nyen-Nyen. Father told me not to get mixed up with him, that he was a user and wasn't capable of loving another human being, and I fell for him anyway."

"Are you going to have the baby, Debbie?" Nyen-Nyen asked gently.

"Yes, Nyen-Nyen, I have to. I guess I'm the fool that I feel like I am, but I love the child's father and I can't bring myself to get rid of it, or to give it up for adoption." She lowered her eyes. "Are you horribly disappointed in me, Nyen-Nyen?"

Nyen-Nyen scooted over on the couch and hugged Debbie tightly. "Don't you ever think that I'm disappointed in you, child. I love you and I'm proud that you have the courage to raise the child you conceived in love. You do love the father, don't you?"

"Yes, Nyen-Nyen, I love him very much," Debbie admitted.

"Then have your baby and apologize to no one, Debbie," Nyen-Nyen said firmly. "Don't regret the love you felt for this man, and be proud of the fact that you're bringing his child into the world."

Debbie stared at her grandmother in amazement. "Do you mean that?"

"I certainly do, child. You be proud of your baby, and you be proud of the love you felt for its father."

"Oh, Nyen-Nyen, thank you," Debbie said as her eyes filled with tears. "I had no idea you would feel this way. I was so afraid you would be hurt and disappointed."

"Never. What did Gordon say when you told him?"

"I haven't," Debbie admitted. "I know he's going to give me hell for getting involved with Ben in the first place. I'm on the verge of tears most of the time anyway, and I know I'll start crying when he starts yelling."

"I doubt that he'll give you hell," Nyen-Nyen said slowly. "And I think he'll be hurt worse the longer you put off telling him."

"I know," Debbie said miserably. "But I just don't have the strength to face that kind of scene right now. Maybe in a week or two."

Nyen-Nyen poured them each another cup of tea and asked Debbie if she was going to stay in her tiny apartment. They ate dinner and made plans for the baby, Debbie finding out that her grandmother had a wealth of practical knowledge about babies and their needs.

It was late when Nyen-Nyen finally showed Debbie to the door, and her worried gaze followed Debbie down the stairs and across the street. Debbie was trying so hard to be brave, and she had been so hurt by this man she had fallen in love with. Nyen-Nyen picked up the telephone and dialed Gordon's number.

"Gordon, this is your mother," she said. "I need to see you either tonight or early in the morning. No, no, son, I'm fine, it isn't my heart again. This is about Debbie. No, she hasn't been hurt, but I'd rather not talk to you about it over the telephone. Yes, if you want to come over tonight, I'll be up. I won't be able to sleep anyway. Thirty minutes? Thank you, Gordon." Nyen-Nyen hung up the telephone and sank down on the couch, deep in thought.

## CHAPTER FOURTEEN

Debbie flinched in her sleep at the sound of a loud knock on her front door. Who in the world could that be? She looked at her alarm clock and swore at the late hour. It was after eleven, and she had planned to clean up her apartment a little and go see a movie this afternoon. Now she would have time to do one or the other but not both. She dragged herself out of bed and wrapped a robe around her as she ran for the door. "Father!" she said as she opened the door. "Uh, come in, Father." Gordon came in and sat down on the couch. "Would you like me to make you a cup of coffee?"

Gordon shook his head. "You go get dressed, and I'll make some coffee, if it won't make you sick to smell it. It bothered your mother when she was carrying you."

"So you know," Debbie said dully. "I guess Nyen-Nyen told you."

"Yes, and your grandmother threatened to remove my head from my body if I said anything to make you cry, so you can stop worrying about World War Three coming up," Gordon said dryly. "Now, can you take the smell of coffee or not? If you can, I could sure use a cup." Gordon's face looked tired and his eyes were shadowed, and Debbie was afraid that he had gotten very little sleep last night.

"No, it doesn't bother me," Debbie said. "In fact, I could use a cup myself. Dr. Osgood isn't a fanatic about avoiding caffeine altogether, just about not overdoing it."

Debbie pulled on a pair of jeans, which she could only zip halfway up, and an oversized shirt, and brushed her teeth and her hair. She returned to the living room and took the plate of toast Gordon gave her. "The coffee will be ready in a minute. You need some food in your stomach."

"I've eaten a lot of this in the last month," Debbie admitted as she nibbled the dry toast.

Gordon waited until she had finished her toast and the coffee was ready. He poured them each a cup of coffee and sat down across from Debbie. "I'm not trying to fuss at you, Lotus, but what happened? I warned you about the man."

"I know, Father," Debbie said. "And I could have resisted him if Jerry had been able to make the trip with him to Vietnam instead of me. But we got over there and, uh, well . . ."

"He took advantage of you," Gordon finished dryly.

"No, Father, I can't really say that." Debbie stopped and thought a moment. "I saw another side to Ben over there. He's hard and ruthless, and all the other things you said about him. But he can also be kind, and gentle, and very, very tender, and not just when he's being intimate."

"But he stopped seeing you after the mission was over."

"Yes, we had one hell of a fight in Bangkok," Debbie admitted. "He doesn't believe in love, Father, and after all we'd shared he looked me in the eye and told me that he had never felt the emotion in his life. I couldn't continue in a relationship with a man who feels like that."

"Ben *wanted* to continue the relationship?" Gordon asked in surprise. "In the old days he was always the one to break it off."

"Yes, and he was furious that I was walking out on him," Debbie said. "He said that I was walking out on a good thing."

Gordon sat and thought a minute. "I gather he doesn't know about the baby."

"No, and he's not going to, either," Debbie said. "I'm not having the father of my child tell that child that he doesn't love it. My child's going to be surrounded by love. It's not going to have a parent that doesn't love it."

"Like you had?" Gordon asked gently.

Debbie looked at Gordon. "I always knew you loved me. You just couldn't show it very well."

"I do love you, Lotus. I was talking about your mother. I don't think that woman was capable of loving anyone."

Debbie thought a minute. "I guess that's exactly what I'm trying to avoid," she admitted. "I don't want that for my child."

"But you don't know for sure that Sako would be that way with a child," Gordon said slowly. "He might love it with all his heart."

"That would be a cold day in hell," Debbie said. "I'll raise the child without him."

"Debbie, that isn't fair to you or to the baby," Gordon argued. "Your child needs two parents, and your child deserves to be born legitimate. I don't care if the public's opinion has relaxed on the subject, that still matters."

"Love matters more," Debbie argued stubbornly.

Gordon sighed. "I know you think love's important, but so is responsibility. This man's responsible for the baby you're carrying, and he has a duty to do right by you. Debbie, I'll see that he marries you."

"Father, *no!*" Debbie cried, horrified. "That's the last thing this baby and I need. Please, Father, don't interfere in this! Ben Sako marrying me out of responsibility is the last thing I need!"

"Why?" Gordon asked, totally baffled. "Wouldn't it make it easier to have some help with this?"

"Don't you understand, Father?" Debbie pleaded, her eyes filling with tears. "I *love* him, and he just doesn't love me. It would tear me apart to live with him day in and day out, loving him and receiving no love in return. And that wouldn't be any kind of atmosphere in which to raise a child."

Gordon moved to the couch and put his arm around Debbie. "Don't cry, Lotus, please," he said gently. "I promised your grandmother I wouldn't make you cry. But I just don't understand."

"I don't expect you to," she said.

Gordon handed her a handkerchief and stood, staring out the window. "Have you started looking for another place to live? These steps are going to become a burden before long."

"They already are," Debbie admitted. "I was thinking about buying a small house in this neighborhood. I have the money for a down payment."

"That would be a good idea," Gordon agreed as he checked his watch. "It's nearly lunchtime. What do you say we go out to eat and feed that grandchild of mine? She's probably hungry."

"She?" Debbie asked.

"I hope so," Gordon said, his eyes suspiciously moist. "I hope it's a little girl, just like you."

Debbie's eyes swam with happy tears as she stood up.

"Thank you, Father," she said softly. "Let me change my clothes and you can feed me some of that broiled shrimp at the cafe down the hill." She disappeared into the bedroom and Gordon sat down on the couch to wait for her. She had her mind made up that she wasn't going to tell Sako about the baby. And that wasn't right. Even if the bastard didn't care anything about her or the child, Sako had a right to know of its existence, and his hardheaded daughter wasn't going to tell the man. Debbie wasn't going to thank him for his interference, but there were times when a father could see things more clearly than his child could, and this was one of them.

Ben narrowed his eyes and stared out at the Buick that was coming through his gate. Was this the man who was supposed to contact him about the job in China? Ben had received a telephone call three days ago about another mission, this one involving a prison breakout in Northern Manchuria, and he had agreed to go whenever he received word that the arrangements had been made. He had not planned on going on any more missions this year, and if things had gone differently with Debbie, he would have refused the job. But she had left him, and there was no reason for him to refuse the mission. The money would come in handy next year when he planted vines and bottled his first wine.

Ben watched as the man shut the gate and drove up to the house. Somehow he didn't think this was his Chinese contact. He stood on the porch as the man approached him, his mouth set in a grim line. "Colonel Cheong," Ben said, surprised, as his old commanding officer climbed the steps. The visit was not about the Chinese mission. Was this about Debbie, or did the colonel have another mission to offer him?

Ben extended his hand and Gordon shook it. "Sergeant Sako," he said as they both looked at the changes the years had made in the other. "You're doing well, I see."

"So are you, sir, according to Debbie."

Gordon released Ben's hand. "May I come inside?" he asked. "I need to talk to you about my daughter."

Debbie. Almost against his will, Ben thought of the gentle face and smiling eyes of this man's daughter. He had missed Debbie Cheong, he had missed her more than he had thought it possible to miss a woman. In fact, he had been downright lonely since she had left him, and he had almost called her more than once. Mystified, Ben followed Gordon into his cabin and perched on the edge of the bed; Gordon sat on the chair. Gordon said nothing, but stared at him for long moments. "Uh, you said you wanted to talk about Debbie," Ben said finally. "Is she all right?"

"No, she's not all right!" Gordon said coldly. "She's as sick as a dog most of the time, unless she takes nausea pills. And she's worn out and can hardly make it through the work day, according to Jim Anderson."

"She's pregnant," Ben said tonelessly as his mind spun. Gordon nodded. This was his child. Debbie was pregnant with his child. "When is she due? Why on earth didn't she tell me?" he asked angrily. "If she's pregnant with my child, I have a right to know it."

"She's due in April." Gordon got out a pack of cigarettes and offered Ben one. He lit both cigarettes and sat back in the chair. "Debbie's a very sensitive, very caring woman, Sako. And she's a romantic. She wants her child to be surrounded by love, the kind of love that Debbie never got from her own mother." He looked Ben in the eye. "She has this idea that you wouldn't care anything about the child."

Ben's face reddened a little. "I'll admit that I think that love, romantic love, between men and women is a pile of horse manure, but I would care about my own child, sir." He stood up and smoked his cigarette. "I'm sorry I got her pregnant. I'm used to women who take care of that, and I never even gave it a thought."

"Debbie isn't stupid," Gordon said thoughtfully. "Perhaps her emotions got in the way of her common sense."

*I love you, Ben.* She had murmured it many times as they had made love, and she had finally yelled it at him in that hotel room in Bangkok. She had loved him, cared for him, and she had taken her chances because she cared. Ben turned to Gordon. "It isn't fair for her to have to go through this alone," he said slowly. "I do care about what's happened, sir, and I want my child to bear my name. I'll marry her."

"I thought you might feel like that," Gordon replied. "And even if you didn't, you had a right to know about the child. Debbie couldn't understand that."

"I wish to hell I'd known sooner," Ben said. "Why didn't you come to me before now?"

"I've known about it for less than a day," Gordon admitted. "She's known for a month, but she was afraid to tell me, afraid I'd give her hell about getting involved with you." He looked Ben straight in the eye. "I told her before she left that you were the last man on earth she had any business getting involved with—that you'd only hurt her. And you've done a good job of that." He looked at Ben and his eyes were bitter. "Why couldn't you have left her alone, Sako? Why did you have to have Debbie? Why did you have to hurt *her,* for God's sake?"

Ben swallowed. For the first time in his entire life, he felt the miserable pangs of conscience. "I'm sorry, sir," he mumbled. "I'm sorry I hurt her and I'm sorry I got her pregnant. I'll do right by her."

Gordon stood up. "I thank you," he said as he walked out the door.

Ben watched him drive off, then sat down and buried his face in his hands. He had gotten Debbie pregnant, and she thought he was so cold and hard that she wouldn't even tell him about his own baby. How could she think he wouldn't care about his own child? The child they had created together? Good lord, didn't she realize that he had a responsibility to the two of them? He went to the closet and pulled out a shirt, and a few minutes later he was driving to Sausalito.

Debbie nibbled her sandwich and stared at the movie on the cable channel. She hadn't made it to the movies today after all, but she had taken an hour and cleaned her apartment after Gordon had brought her home from lunch. She wasn't really hungry after the big lunch she had eaten, so after a few bites of the cheese sandwich, she pushed it aside and managed to get mildly interested in a fast-paced police thriller. When it was over, she stood up and was flipping through the channels when she heard a knock on her door. She threw open the door and froze when she met Ben's eyes.

Debbie stared into the face of her former lover. He no longer looked tired, as he had when they had escaped to Thailand, but his face was bleak and his eyes were cold. "May I come in?" he asked as his glance raked down her figure, taking in her slightly swollen breasts and thickening stomach. His penetrating gaze did not miss the paleness of her face or the deep circles under her eyes.

"Father told you," Debbie said bitterly. "*Damn* him!"

Ben took her by the shoulders and gently moved her

aside so that he could enter. He pushed his hands in his pockets and turned to face Debbie, his mouth set in a grim line. "How could you think I wouldn't care about my own child?" he accused her.

"It was easy." Debbie slammed the front door shut and flopped down on the chair. "You looked me in the eye and told me that you had never felt love in your life, and that you doubted that you ever would."

"You're twisting what I said that day!" Ben snapped as he paced the floor. "I said that I hadn't ever experienced this weird romantic condition that you and Jim and Li call 'love.' But damn it, I care about the child, Debbie." He sat down across from her. "I came to ask you to marry me."

"Why?" Debbie challenged, raising her eyebrow.

Ben looked at her changing body. "I think that should be fairly obvious. You're pregnant with my child. I have a duty, a responsibility to you. And to the baby."

Debbie's eyes narrowed in anger. "You can take your duty and your responsibility and shove it!" she snapped. "I don't want a damned duty marriage, and I especially don't want to be your responsibility."

"Damn it, Debbie, you *are* my responsibility!" Ben thundered. "You and my baby."

"This is *my* baby, Ben!" Debbie said bitterly. "I'm not sharing my child with a parent who can't love it. I know how it feels to have a mother who doesn't love you."

"So do I!" Ben said. "And a father too. Maybe that's why I want our kid to have two parents."

"And what good will you be as a parent, Ben?" Debbie taunted. "You've said that you're incapable of love. A parent like that is worse than no parent at all." She lowered her voice. "And what about me, Ben? My needs haven't changed in the last two months. I still need what you can't give me."

Ben sat down on the edge of the couch. "What are you planning to do about the baby if you won't marry me?" His face was pinched, his eyes bleak.

Debbie bit her lip. Ben seemed to care about the child she was carrying, even if nothing in his manner indicated that he cared about her. Should she test the waters? She swallowed and linked her fingers together. "I'm thinking about having an abortion."

*"Like hell you will!"* Ben roared as he came up off the couch and grasped her shoulders, hauling her out of the chair to face him. "There is no way, *no way,* that you're going to do that."

"Why, Ben?" Debbie asked softly. "Why are you so opposed to doing that?"

Ben released her shoulders and paced the floor. "Two reasons," he said. "First off, you would be killing the child we created together. And there is no way you're going to do that. I care about that child, Debbie, even if you don't.

"And the second reason that you're not going to do a thing like that is because it could hurt you. You've waited too long to have an aspiration abortion, if you're due in April; and if you had one now, it would have to be a saline injection. And those things are dangerous to the mother. You could end up sick or injured and unable to have more children. I just won't permit it, Debbie. You're going to go through with this pregnancy. Do you understand? You're not going to take the life of my child, and do God knows what to yourself in the process."

Ben looked over at Debbie, expecting to see anger or rebellion on her face. He was not expecting the look of genuine surprise he saw there. "You do love the baby and you love me," Debbie said. She looked strangely satisfied. "You do love me, after all."

"I—I never said that," Ben stammered.

"Yes, you did. You said it just now," Debbie said. "I said I was going to get an abortion and you nearly came apart at the seams. There's only one reason why you would react like that, and it would be that you loved me and the baby we made together. Ben, I would no more have an abortion than I would take a gun and put it to your head and shoot. Because I love you, and I love the child we made together, just as much as you do."

Ben's shoulders sagged. "Well, that's a relief. So why won't you marry me?"

"Because I don't want to be married to a man who isn't being honest with himself or with me. When you walked in here tonight I thought you didn't love me, that you weren't capable of love, and that you were here out of a sense of responsibility. But you are capable of loving, Ben, even if you won't admit that to yourself or to me. But you're going to have to admit it to me, Ben, if you want me to marry you. Just once. Just once you're going to have to let go of that macho facade and tell me that you love me."

"Debbie, you're being ridiculous," Ben said. "You need me, and I have a responsibility to you. You're letting this mythical 'love' get in the way again."

Debbie shook her head back and forth. "It's not mythical, Ben. It's real and you're bound to know it, because you feel it for me and for our child. But you're chicken, Ben."

"Chicken?" Ben asked.

"Yes, you're chicken. You're scared to be honest with me, and with yourself, and admit that you love me." Debbie threw open the front door. "And my child doesn't need a coward for a father. Go home, Ben. And think about it. When you're willing to be honest with yourself, and with me, and admit that love is real and that you love me, come back and see me. And we'll plan a wedding."

Ben shrugged as he walked toward the door. He stopped in front of Debbie and lowered his lips to hers, very gently, kissing her almost reverently before he walked out the door and pulled it shut behind him. Debbie stood in the middle of the floor, her fingers touching the spot that Ben had kissed. She had just taken the biggest gamble of her life. Ben might never come back again. He might not love her after all—his reaction to the thought of an abortion might just have been possessiveness, or pride in the pregnancy he had helped cause. Or he might never come to the point that he could acknowledge his feelings for her and for their baby. But she had to hope that he did and that he could. Because Gordon and Ben were both right. She needed Ben in her life. And so did her child.

Ben sat at his kitchen table and stared down at the Scotch and soda he had mixed for himself. It had been three days since he had seen Debbie, and he had thought about her almost constantly since then. She swore that he loved her, and that he loved the child she was carrying. He had carefully examined his feelings for her and the baby since he had left her Sunday night, and he was still no closer to knowing whether he "loved" her than he had been when she had so triumphantly informed him of the state of his emotions.

What was love, anyway? He had always desired her, of course, from the first time he had laid eyes on her. He liked to talk to her, to hear her opinions, to make her laugh. He had admired her courage and her spunk in the forests of Vietnam and Cambodia. And he had felt a tremendous need to care for her and protect her, both on the mission and on Sunday, when he had seen how pale and tired she looked. But Ben just wasn't sure that this was the love she kept talking about.

And the child. Already he had opened a savings account for the child's education. And he was going to be a part of his child's life, whether or not Debbie agreed to marry him. That child was going to know who its father was. Ben smiled a little in the dimly lit kitchen. A father. He was going to be a father.

He finished his drink and put the glass in the sink. He needed to talk to Debbie again, to explore his feelings with her. She was so sure that love existed, maybe she could tell him just what it was he was supposed to feel for her if he loved her. He would call her tomorrow and take her out to dinner, and they would talk more then.

But Debbie never got that telephone call. Late that night, the message that Ben had been expecting about the Chinese mission finally arrived. He was to be at the San Francisco airport by three that morning to catch a private jet to Korea and be smuggled across the border into North Korea and then into China the day after. Ben swore viciously when he got the message. He wished his sense of responsibility wasn't so strong—he would have loved to have told the leaders of the mission to forget it. But he knew he had to make the trip—he had committed himself weeks ago, and the commander of the mission was counting on his expertise.

Ben threw a few things into a duffel bag and made the long drive to the airport. He longed for a few minutes to find a pay phone, but the commander of the mission was waiting for him in the parking lot to take him to the airplane. He considered writing Debbie and mailing it from the Seoul airport, but he was traveling under an alias again and was afraid of being traced if he did. Because the mission was of a very sensitive nature, Ben was afraid for his own safety and the safety of his fellow mercenaries, if their presence in the country were known.

Rubbing his hand across his tired eyes, he followed the commander to the waiting jet. He could only hope that Debbie didn't give up on him during the long weeks he expected the mission to take.

# CHAPTER FIFTEEN

"Debbie, where do you want me to put these boxes?" Jim asked as he staggered through the door of Debbie's new house, balancing a couple of boxes piled high with linens. A brisk salty gust of January wind followed him in the door.

Debbie peeked in the boxes. "Bathroom," she said. "Li, you aren't supposed to be picking up heavy boxes," she fussed as Li walked in carrying a box. "You're nearly as pregnant as I am."

Li looked down at her only slightly bulging figure and over at Debbie's much larger one. "Debbie, that is not entirely true," she said. "Besides, this box just has a few knickknacks in it. Where do you want it to go?"

"Uh, back in the baby's room for now," Debbie said. "I'll put them out later." She put her hand behind her and rubbed her aching back.

"Lotus, the movers just pulled up," Gordon said as he carried the last of the boxes from the trunk of his Buick. "It took them most of the morning to get that stuff down all those stairs, and you can be sure that they had a few choice words for your former place of residence."

"I'll bet," Debbie said and laughed. She stood in the middle of her small living room and directed the movers as they brought in her living room and bedroom furniture and placed it around her freshly painted rooms. In the last two weeks, since she had closed on the house, Gordon and Jim had repainted every room for her, so that the inside of the house sparkled. Debbie had paid a little more for the small house in Sausalito than she would have had to pay for a similar house across the bridge, but she wanted to stay in the Sausalito area and take advantage of the better schools.

The movers unloaded her furniture quickly, and Jim and Li spent the afternoon helping her unload boxes of dishes and pots and pans. Gordon had returned to his shop after moving several carloads of boxes to the new house, but he promised Debbie that he would come back around suppertime and bring her a meal. They worked hard but laughed and talked a lot about the babies that were coming. Jim was very careful to see that neither Debbie nor Li, who was expecting a baby in June, overdid it or climbed ladders. Debbie and Li finished in the kitchen and started unloading Debbie's clothes into the bedroom closet. Debbie held a particularly pretty maternity dress up to Li and sighed. "It's a shame you didn't wait just a few more months to get pregnant, then you could have inherited all my stuff!"

"Oh, but we figured we better have a family just as soon as we could," Li said. "Jim will be forty-three this summer, and I'm over thirty." She hung a handful of Debbie's dresses in the closet. "I just hope we won't be too old to enjoy the baby."

Debbie laughed. "That's ridiculous, Li. Besides, I'm counting on Jim to be something of a father figure to mine too, and if he isn't too old to serve as father to mine, he sure isn't too old to be a father to his!" She hung up a handful of maternity blouses.

Li sat down on the floor and pulled over a box of

261

shoes. "What about Ben, Debbie? He never has contacted you since that time in October, has he?"

Debbie shook her head. "No, just that once. I gambled and I lost that night."

Li laid out Debbie's shoes in a neat row on the floor of the closet. "Debbie, I could have sworn that man loved you, especially after he reacted the way you said he did when you told him you wanted an abortion. I just can't believe he could seem to care so much and then not even call you back."

"Father was right about him, and I was wrong, that's all. He doesn't care anything about me and the baby. The only reason he came over here that day was because he felt responsible." She stacked her purses neatly on the shelf above the clothes bar. "And when I informed him that he didn't have to feel responsible, he took the easy way out." She wiped away the annoying tears that clouded her eyes.

"You still love him, don't you?" Li asked.

Debbie nodded. "And I'll be a long time getting over him, I'm afraid." She touched her swollen body. "But I have his child, and I'm going to do my best to see that this baby doesn't turn out like its father."

Jim and Li stayed until late in the afternoon, helping Debbie unpack and get settled into her new house. They had been a tower of strength to Debbie, as had Gordon and Nyen-Nyen. All of them had showered her with love and support, trying to make up for the fact that Ben had apparently decided not to contact Debbie. Gordon had offered to drive out to the vineyard and see him again, but Debbie adamantly refused the offer. If Ben couldn't tell her that he loved her, if he didn't love her and the child that she carried, then she and the child were better off without him.

Debbie thanked Jim and Li as they left, and set the table for the take-out dinner that Gordon had promised. He was a little late, and Debbie, who had gotten over her bouts with nausea by Thanksgiving, was ravenous by the time his car pulled into the driveway. She eagerly took the box of fried chicken and fries and opened it in the middle of the dining room table. "Oh, Father, this smells delicious!" Debbie said as she loaded her plate with chicken and fries.

"Glad it appeals, Lotus," he said as he took a more modest portion than she did. "You should be putting on a little more weight, shouldn't you?"

Debbie shrugged as she ate a bit of fried chicken. "Dr. Osgood says I'm right on target," she said. She looked down at her stomach. "It's just that I'm so big there, the rest of me looks smaller!"

Gordon eyed her figure thoughtfully. "I wouldn't have thought your baby would be that large," he said. "Sako's not that large a man."

"The sonogram showed a normal-sized baby for my being six months along," Debbie said. She ate a bite of chicken. "I don't think the size of the parents has that much bearing at this stage."

"You still love him, don't you?" Gordon asked, shaking his head.

"Yeah, I still do," Debbie said. "And I guess I did the wrong thing, telling him what I did." She sipped her iced tea. "I should have taken what he was offering that day instead of holding out for love. I lost my chance with him."

Gordon wiped his greasy fingers on a napkin. "I'm sure that you're better off without a man like that," he said. "I think you did the right thing."

Debbie's piece of chicken froze halfway to her mouth.

"But I thought you wanted him to marry me!" she said. "What made you change your mind?"

"Remembering what my marriage was like," Gordon said. "That day I found out about the baby, I was so incensed on your behalf I think I would have put a shotgun to Sako's head if he had said he wouldn't marry you. But then I started thinking about my marriage to your mother. She didn't love me, and she didn't love you. And, you know, that hurt me. I wanted her to love me, Debbie. And I wanted her to love you, even more than I wanted her to love me. It used to tear me apart when she would ignore you. And I don't want that for my grandchild. I would rather see you raise it alone than have that little child feel the rejection you did when you were little."

"I told Ben that," Debbie said slowly. "I told him that unless he could love me and the child, and tell me so, that he would be no good as a parent."

"He wouldn't, Debbie. And living with a man who doesn't love you would tear you apart as well. I think you did the right thing. And Jim and I will try to take the role of a father to your child, although I think I'll let Jim play all the touch football. And speaking of that baby, I have a little something in my trunk I picked up this afternoon," Gordon said. "I'll be back in a minute."

Debbie cleared the table while she waited for Gordon to return. He came back inside balancing a large, flat box. "I'll put this in the nursery," he said as he half-pulled the heavy box across the carpet.

"A baby bed!" Debbie cried. She looked at the picture of the fancy crib that was unassembled inside the box, and waited until Gordon had put the box in the nursery, where she threw her arms around his neck. "Oh, it's beautiful! Thank you!"

"You and that baby are more than welcome," Gordon said as he hugged his daughter. "If you'll forgive me, Lotus, I've got to go now. I have a party at which I have to make an appearance tonight."

"Of course, I understand," Debbie said.

"I'll come back over here next weekend and put the bed together," Gordon promised her as he left.

Debbie loaded the dishes into the dishwasher and worked late into the evening, unloading records and books into the stereo case and bookcases in the living room. She pampered herself with a long, leisurely bath before bed, and was just pulling a flowered cotton nightgown over her head when the doorbell rang. She wrapped her robe around her and peeked out the window, unwilling to open the door this late at night. "Who is it?"

"It's me, Lotus," Gordon said. "Me and Ben."

Ben? What was Ben doing here? Hurriedly, she threw open the door. Ben passed Debbie in the door and sat down on the couch. He had on no overcoat, and his clothing hung loose on his gaunt frame. "I had to see you tonight, Debbie. I have to talk to you. I think I love you." He ran his fingers through his hair, looking toward the door leading to the hallway. "Which way's the bathroom?"

Debbie was simply too astonished to speak. She pointed the way toward the bathroom and stared at Ben's retreating back until Gordon turned her around and placed a huge teddy bear in her arms. "He was waiting with this on my front step when I got home," he said as he dropped Ben's duffel bag on the floor. "He went to your apartment this afternoon and couldn't find you, so he waited there for me. I tried to get him to wait until morning to come and see you, but he insisted that I bring him over here right now."

"What happened to him?" Debbie asked, her voice anguished. "He looks like he's lost twenty-five or thirty pounds, and he really didn't have it to lose."

"I don't know anything, except that he's suffering from the symptoms of semistarvation, like Li was in Vietnam. He said the mission had been rough."

A mission! That was the one thing Debbie had never considered. She had assumed that he was spending the winter at the vineyard. "He must have been away on a mission," Debbie said slowly. "I guess it was a hard one, to leave him in that shape."

"I'm going on home. I think you and Sako have some talking to do this evening." Gordon kissed her forehead. "Call me if you need me."

"I will, Father," Debbie said as Gordon left. She waited impatiently for long moments, trying to make sense of what Ben had said to her. He had to see her. He had to talk to her. He thought he loved her. But what did he mean, he *thought* he loved her? How could he not know whether or not he loved her? And if he did, could she forgive him for leaving her all these months?

Ben's voice called out to her from the bathroom door. "Debbie, there aren't any towels in here. Could you scrounge around and find me one?"

"Sure, Ben," Debbie said as she put the teddy bear down on the couch. She found a stack of towels in the spare bedroom and took several to the bathroom door.

Ben answered her knock and took the pile from her. "Thanks, Lotus," he said. "Did you like the bear?"

"Yes, I did." Debbie stared at Ben gravely.

"I bought that damned thing in the Seoul airport," Ben said. "I've been on planes for the last two days trying to get back here. We need to talk, Debbie."

Debbie nodded as she looked into Ben's painfully thin

face. "I know, but let me feed you first," she suggested. "You've lost so much weight."

"I know. Two weeks without food does wonders for the old figure. Would you make me something while I shower?"

"Sure thing," Debbie promised. Ben disappeared back into the bathroom and Debbie hurried to the kitchen. She cooked up a huge plate of scrambled eggs, more than she thought he could eat, and made a pile of toast. When he was finished, Ben came into the kitchen, clad only in a pair of loose jeans. Debbie winced at the hollowness of his chest and his prominent ribs. She filled a plate with food and put it in front of Ben. "Eat up," she said. "You probably weigh less than we do."

"Unfortunately, you're probably right," Ben observed as he waded into the eggs and toast she put in front of him.

Debbie took a small portion of eggs for herself, mostly to be sociable. "Was the mission a long one?" she asked.

"I left three days after I saw you last, and I got in today at two in the afternoon," Ben said. "I would have seen you sooner, but I had no idea where you had moved, and Jim and Li weren't home. I had to wait for your father." He sipped his coffee. "I meant to call you the day I had to leave. I would have called you anyway, but it was one in the morning and I had to be to the airport two hours later."

"I thought you weren't ever coming back to us," Debbie admitted in a low voice.

"I knew that's what you probably thought," Ben said. "I thought about you every damned day I was over there. At first, when it only looked like a month-long mission, I thought that maybe you wouldn't give up on me, but by the end of the third month I knew you had. You would have had to."

"I honestly never thought that you might be on another mission," Debbie said. "Where was this one?"

"Interior of Manchuria. I was supposed to go in and break out a couple of Chinese political prisoners. But we were seen and reported and had to disappear into the mountains for a month, and then the snow blocked our escape for a while."

"But did you get your prisoners out?" Debbie asked.

"Yes, we did," Ben said. "Although I doubt that I'm going to accept any more winter missions in Northern China."

Debbie watched as Ben ate ravenously. She wanted to take his shoulders and shake him, and yell into his ear the question that had haunted her since he had walked in the door. What did he mean, he thought he loved her? Had he found it within himself to love her? She nearly screamed in frustration when Ben asked her to scramble a few more eggs, but she could hardly look at his gaunt frame and say no. He devoured the second plate of eggs and drank another cup of coffee. "Thanks, Lotus," he said as he picked up the palm of her hand and kissed it. "It's more than I deserve after what I put you through."

"Yes, it is," Debbie agreed as she took their dirty plates and put them into the sink. "I should have made you eat some more rice."

"After this last mission even rice would taste good," Ben said as he grasped Debbie by the hand and led her into the living room. "I want to talk to you, Debbie. I know it's a little late, but I want to continue that conversation we were having in October."

They sat down together on the couch. "I had planned

268

to call you the day that I had to leave," Ben said as he held her hand.

"I thought you had decided that you didn't love me, after all," Debbie admitted. "I knew I was taking a gamble that night when I said those things to you—I didn't really know whether you loved me or not, even though I thought you might when you had a fit about an abortion."

"I didn't know what I was feeling that night," Ben admitted. "I didn't know whether or not I loved you, Debbie. What is love, anyway? Or what do you think it is? I was going to ask you that night I was called away."

Debbie thought a minute, then spoke. "It's a lot of things, Ben. Part of it's physical desire, and goodness knows we have enough of that." She glanced down at her swollen figure. "Or at least we had it."

Ben ran his free hand down her side and grinned wickedly. "Have, Lotus, have."

"All right, have. But it's other things, too. It's wanting to talk to each other, caring what the other one thinks. It's wanting to take care of that other person, make sure they're all right, but not stifle them. It's being lonely when you're not together. It's caring about the child you've created together."

Ben got up and put his hands in his pockets. "What I feel for you *is* love, then," he said slowly. He turned to her, tears running down his cheeks. "I'm sorry, Debbie. I've loved you for a long time, I just wasn't sure I loved you."

Debbie's heart went out to Ben. She had never dreamed that she would see tears on this hard, tough man's face. "But how could you not know?" she asked, bewildered. She reached out her arms and Ben sat down beside her and let her hold him, putting his arms around her. "How could you not know that you loved me?"

Ben moved away from her and cleared his throat. "Because I didn't know what love was," he said. "I felt all those things for you that day we fought in Bangkok. I felt that way about you when we conceived that baby somewhere in Vietnam, but I didn't know it was love. I thought you and Jim and Li were talking about something that would come and hit me over the head. You know, lightning and thunder like in those old movies. And nothing ever did. It kind of grew slowly, you know?"

Debbie brushed the tears off Ben's cheeks. "We should have had this talk months ago," she admitted. "I had no idea you didn't know what we were talking about. Where did you pick up that kind of concept of love, anyway?"

Ben shrugged. "From the movies, I guess." He stood up and put his hands in his pockets. "Debbie, how much do you know about my childhood? How much did Gordon tell you?"

"He told me that your father abandoned you and your mother, that your mother turned you over to the state, and that you were raised in a series of foster homes. No details, just the bare facts."

"The bare facts are enough," Ben said. "I don't dwell on the past, but I want you to understand so that maybe, maybe you can forgive me for the hell I've put you through these last months. Debbie, you're the first person, and as far as I know, the *only* person, on the face of this earth who has ever loved me. My parents, all those foster parents, the women in my life—" He made an impatient motion with his hand. "Most people learn to love as children, Debbie, but I didn't. Nobody ever came along who cared enough about me to teach me how to love another human being. Until you, Debbie. You taught me to love, and then I was too hardheaded and blind to see love for what it was. I wasn't sure of my feelings, and what feelings I had I kept resisting."

"When did you start thinking you might really love me?" Debbie asked slowly. "When did you start to recognize that love for what it was?"

"In China, on the mission. Oh, Debbie, please don't look so hurt! I wish I could say that it was when you took me to task, but I walked out of here that night still not knowing whether or not I loved you, and not particularly wanting to. Then I got to China, and our mission in Vietnam was a piece of cake compared to this last one. I thought I was going to die, Debbie. I really thought a couple of times that I had bought it. Before, the thought of dying never bothered me much, but this time I was terrified."

"Why?" Debbie asked, almost holding her breath.

"Because I would never see you again," Ben admitted. "Because I would never see your face or hear you laugh or hold the child we made together. I wanted to come home to you."

"That night we argued, I accused you of being afraid to tell me you loved me," Debbie said. "Are you still afraid?"

"Not of loving you, and not of telling you that I love you," Ben said. "I love you, and I'll say it every five minutes for the rest of my life." He slid to the carpet and knelt in front of her, her chin clasped lightly in his hand. "But I am afraid I've destroyed all your love for me. You gave me your love and I threw it in your face, Debbie. Can you ever forgive me for that?"

Debbie sat frozen for a moment. Yes, she still loved him, but could she ever forgive him the hurt he had caused her? She looked into Ben's eyes and saw, not the tough, hard man he was today, but the vulnerable child that he had been so many years ago, the child that nobody could find their way to love. Yes, she could love him and forgive him, but could this man fulfill her deep desire to be loved? "I'm afraid, too, Ben," Debbie said slowly. "I still love you and I can forgive you, knowing about your past, but do you really love me? Can you really love me the way I need to be loved? I lacked my mother's love too, and while it made you tough and hard so that you don't need to be loved, it made me just the opposite. I need to be loved, Ben. I need it badly. Can you love me like that?"

Ben stared deep into her eyes. "You're wrong about me not needing your love. I do need it, I need it desperately. But can I love you the way you need to be loved? I don't know, but I swear to God if you'll marry me I'll spend every day of the rest of my life trying. I'll make love to you and cherish you and talk to you and bring you whatever I can afford to buy you. Will you give me a chance to try to love you the way you need to be loved, Lotus? Or is it too late for us?"

Debbie reached up and brushed happy tears off her cheeks. "No, it's not too late," she said. "Oh, Ben, love me, just love me, please. I've missed you for so long." She could not stop the sobs of joy that racked her body.

Ben sat down beside Debbie and took her into his arms. "Oh, Debbie, I will. I swear I will," he said as he cradled her sobbing body next to his. "I'll love you so much you won't know what to do with all that love. And I'll love our baby, Debbie." He ran gentle hands up and down her swollen body. "I love it already. I even started a savings account for our child's education."

272

Debbie raised her head and looked at him in surprise. "When did you have time to do that?"

"I did it back in October," Ben admitted. "The account is in the name of Baby Sako." He reached out and brushed the tears from Debbie's cheeks. "It will be Baby Sako, won't it? You will marry me, won't you?"

"Yes, Ben, I will," Debbie said as she clasped her arms around his neck. "I'll marry you tomorrow, if you can arrange it."

"Well, maybe not tomorrow, but pretty soon from the looks of you," Ben teased. He held Debbie's face between his hands as he captured her lips in a long, lingering kiss. "I wish I could make love to you today," he said as he rained gentle kisses on her lips and her cheeks.

"Why can't you? Oh, Ben, did you get hurt over there?"

Ben shook his head. "No, I'm fine, but you can't very well make love in your condition."

"Where did you get an idea like that?" Debbie asked. "Dr. Osgood told Li it was all right until she was eight months or so."

"Li's pregnant too?" Ben asked.

"Yes, they've nicknamed it Bangkok," Debbie told him, laughing.

"I think it was those satin sheets," Ben teased. "But that doesn't have anything to do with you. You might be different."

"Ben, I'm fine," Debbie assured him as she wound her hands around his neck, showering warm, moist kisses on his face. "Honestly."

"You wanton seductress, you're trying to rob me of my innocence," Ben teased as he tried to push her away.

"Or am I not attractive to you like this?" Debbie asked

as she unwound her arms and started to move away from him, hurt in her eyes.

Ben pulled her back into his arms. "Debbie, you're the most sensually appealing woman I've ever known, do you know that? I haven't even felt desire since you walked out of that Bangkok hotel room. The pregnancy just makes you that much more appealing, that's all." He shared a gentle kiss with her. "Tell you what. Call Dr. Osgood and make sure it's all right. I just don't want to hurt you or the baby."

"Ben!" Debbie cried, but Ben was insistent, so she called the doctor and explained the problem, blushing at every other sentence. She put down the telephone and sighed. "He says we can't make love for the next five years."

"You little devil!" Ben laughed. He stood beside her and cradled her in his arms. "Is it really all right, Lotus? Can I make love to the woman I love?"

"Yes, we can make love, Ben," Debbie assured him. "I don't think you better try to carry me to bed, though. I probably weigh as much as you do."

"I know," Ben said. "You've gained what?—fifteen?— and I've lost almost thirty. And I would never take a chance of dropping you right now." She took him by the hand and led him to the bedroom, stopping to kiss him three times on the way, and Ben made a ceremony of shutting the door behind them. He drew Debbie into his arms and buried his lips in her hair. "Oh, Debbie, I missed you so much," he said as he rocked back and forth with her. "I missed you every day I was gone, and every day since you left me last summer."

"I should have stayed around," Debbie said as her hands found the hair at his nape and buried themselves in it. "I should have given you a chance."

"No, you did the only thing you could do," Ben said as he stroked her back. "If you had stayed with me, I would have just kept hurting you over and over. I'm just grateful you could find it within yourself to forgive me." He held her face between his hands and stared into her eyes. "I promise you that you will never have to forgive me for something like that again."

"I know," Debbie whispered. She and Ben shared another long, scorching kiss, his tongue seeking and gaining entrance to her mouth. She moaned and tried to move closer to him, groaning when her swollen body prevented them from moving any closer together. "Do you ever get the feeling that something's coming between us?"

"We'll just have to figure out a way around it." Ben whispered as his fingers untied the sash of her robe.

Debbie froze, suddenly embarrassed by her pregnant body. "What is it, Lotus?" Ben asked.

"I look terrible," Debbie cried. "I don't look like I did last summer. I'm huge and I feel silly."

Ben immediately sensed the aching vulnerability underneath those words. "I wish I had been here to watch you grow," he said. "You wouldn't feel so self-conscious around me now." He put his hand to his zipper and stripped his baggy jeans and underwear from his body. "Look at me, Lotus. Do I look the same as I did last summer?"

Debbie stared at Ben's gaunt body and his hollow-eyed face. Yes, at least thirty pounds was missing from his already lean frame, and the body that was so well-muscled and sleek last summer was frail, almost sick-looking. But he was just as attractive to her as he had ever been, and she wanted him as much as she ever had. "I love you more now than ever," she said.

Ben pushed Debbie's robe off her shoulders. "Lovers

don't have to look like centerfolds, Debbie. I want to see you and make love to you because I love you." He knelt and drew her gown over her head, grazing the tips of her swollen breasts with his thumb.

Debbie stood naked before Ben. "You're beautiful like that, Debbie," he said as he ran his hands down her body. "You're just as beautiful as when you're thin. No, you're more beautiful." He touched Debbie's shoulders, her arms, her breasts, her sides, quickly, feverishly, like a man starved. "I've needed you so much, Debbie. Let me make you mine again." He pushed her down on her bed and followed her down, lying beside her as he touched her body with light, gentle caresses.

Debbie did not realize until then just how much she had missed Ben's loving touch. Like a sponge she soaked up his loving touches, his tender caresses. His fingers left no part of her body untouched—he caressed her shoulders, her breasts, her still narrow hips. His loving fingers loved her where her shape had changed as he murmured his love for her and their unborn child.

Debbie's fingers caressed Ben's shrunken frame, her touch conveying her love for Ben as she stroked his hard, bony chest and caressed where his ribs showed through his skin. Lips following hands, Ben kissed the tender skin of her breasts, his tongue finding and tormenting her nipples until they stiffened into hard knots of desire. His caressing lips traveled lower, past the skin of her waist and even lower than that. "Is this all right for you now?" Ben asked as his touch drifted toward the fullest intimacy.

"Yes, oh yes!" Debbie breathed as he caressed her in the way she loved so much. When she was almost to the brink, Ben pulled back and let her pleasure him with her hands and her lips, unselfishly giving him back the pleasure he had given her and more.

Ben reveled in her touches and caresses for long moments, and when he was moaning beneath her touch, he pushed her back into the pillows. But he looked at her changing body and shook his head. "We're going to have to use our imaginations, Lotus." He continued to touch and caress Debbie as he considered the problem.

"Ben, you're not just going to stop now, are you?" she demanded.

"No way," Ben said as he turned Debbie onto her side and lay down behind her. He nudged her legs open slightly with his knee. "Let me try it this way," he said. They giggled and fumbled a little as Ben joined their two bodies into one.

Debbie gasped at the delight of his possession. It had been so long since they had made love, so long since they had been one together. She reveled in Ben's possession as her body trembled with delight. This was good, this was right, this was what she needed so desperately. Ben's lips found her nape, and he placed gentle, tingling kisses in her most sensitive spots. His hands crept around Debbie and he caressed her breasts, her waist, the softness of her femininity, as he made love to her in a gentle rhythm. He touched her eagerly, greedily. It had been so long since he had known the privilege of possessing her, of making their bodies come alive together.

Debbie's body writhed with the pleasure of his touch, as she moved with the gentle pace of his lovemaking. She was consuming him, being consumed by him. She loved him, he loved her. They were lovers, bound by the cords of love for all time. They climbed higher, swirled faster, and when the tumult came, Ben cried out as well as Debbie, the two of them sharing a shattering fulfillment that left them both breathless and spent.

Debbie lay with the back of her head against Ben's chest. "I like it this way," she said as Ben showered kisses into her hair. "Can we make love like this even after the baby comes?"

Ben's chest rumbled with laughter. "We can do it any way you want to," he said. "Just as long as we do it a lot."

Debbie turned over and kissed his lips lovingly. "I'll take you up on that."

Ben flinched and looked down at where Debbie was pressed close to him. "Was that the baby?" he asked.

"Yes, that was your little one," Debbie said as Ben felt the thump of another foot. "She moves around a lot."

"She? Are you sure?"

"No, of course I'm not sure, although that's what the sonogram looked like. Father thinks it's a girl." She linked her arms around his neck. "But I guess you want a boy."

Ben shook his head as he planted a long, slow kiss on Debbie's lips. "I just want it to be healthy. I'll take whatever." He snuggled as close to Debbie as he could get. "Do you have a nickname for her yet, like Jim and Li do?"

Debbie smiled up at Ben. "Would you believe that this is my Perfume baby? I don't know for sure, but that's when I think she was conceived."

"That was one of the most beautiful nights of my life," Ben said. "Even though we were on a mission and in danger, it was one of the most beautiful experiences I've ever had. Enchanting, almost." He stopped and thought a minute. "I guess those days are over," he said.

"What? Making love in the river? I'll try to manage it

again," Debbie teased. "But it might be a little cold here in California."

"I'll get us a hot tub," Ben said. "No, I mean the missions. I can't very well go on them now, with you and the baby to think of. I'll have to give them up. We ought to be able to live on my income from the vineyard and your salary."

Debbie lay very still for a minute. "Why give them up? You don't want to, do you?"

"Not really," Ben admitted. "I do a lot of good sometimes. But I thought you would insist."

Debbie chose her words carefully. "Maybe you could cut back to just two or three a year, but I hate to see you give them up entirely, Ben. You do so much good on those missions! Look what you did for Jim and Li."

"You won't insist that I quit!"

"No, I wouldn't want to take that away from you. Just as long as you're around enough to be a part of the baby's life."

"I'll be around," Ben promised Debbie. "Thank you for not forcing me to quit the missions." He captured her lips in a loving embrace. "Have you already gotten all of your baby things? Am I too late to be a part of that?"

"Oh, Ben, I've barely started." Debbie laughed. She moved away from him and climbed out of bed, throwing him his jeans before she put on her gown. "Come on, I'll show you what I've gotten so far."

Ben pulled on his pants and followed her to the nursery. "All I have are a few clothes and the crib that Father brought," Debbie said.

Ben squatted down beside the crib. "Fan-cy." He whistled.

"Father said he'd come by and assemble it next week," Debbie said.

279

"Your father's going to be busy next week being the father of the bride," Ben said as he inspected the box. "I'll put it together tomorrow afternoon. Would you mind if I made myself a sandwich? I'm still hungry."

"I'll make it myself," Debbie replied, her eyes shining with love.

## EPILOGUE

Ben roared up to the church in his and Debbie's new Regal. "I hope we're not late," he said as he glanced in the door of the church.

Debbie grinned wickedly at Ben. "And whose idea was it to celebrate the start of Joy's fourth month with a good long nap?" she teased. "A nap for her, that is?"

"You didn't have to say yes," Ben reminded her calmly as Debbie unstrapped their tiny daughter and put her in an infant seat. "You could have told me to stop being a lecherous old daddy."

"No way," Debbie admitted. "I like lecherous old daddies, or at least one that I know of. Come on, Joy, go on back to sleep," she coaxed as Joy moved in her sleep and whimpered a little.

They walked up the steps to the church, the July sun warm on their faces. Jim and Li were standing in the foyer, Jim cradling their howling son. "Are we late?" Debbie asked.

"No, and Father Chan wants us to try to calm him down a little before the ceremony," Li said. "I swear, I don't know what's wrong with him."

Debbie handed Joy to Ben and took the crying baby from Jim's arms. She sat down on a bench and held James Nguyen Anderson in a bent position, rubbing his back until he came out with three good belches. Immediately the baby stopped crying and stuck his fist in the region of his mouth. "You like that as much as Joy does," she crooned as she handed the baby to Li.

"Well, how about that!" Jim said. "Thanks, Debbie."

"You're so good with them," Li added. She was still a little nervous with Jamie, although she and the baby were doing fine.

"Nyen-Nyen taught me that one," Debbie admitted.

Father Chan entered in his robes and the four of them followed him into the sanctuary. Ben handed Joy to Gordon and they stepped up to the altar. Father Chan spoke briefly of the responsibilities of parenthood before he baptized Jamie into the church. As Father Chan spoke, Debbie thought that this was the fourth time in the last year that she, Ben, Jim, and Li had stood together before an altar. There had been the August wedding in Thailand, the January wedding in San Francisco, and Joy Lee Sako's christening just last month in Debbie's church. The year had been rich and full for both couples, and Debbie basked daily in the love that she had once feared she'd never have.

Jim and Li had invited everyone back to their new home for a celebration dinner. While Ben and Jim looked after their offspring, Li fried up her famous spring rolls, and Debbie and Mrs. Anderson put out the delicious dishes, both American and Vietnamese, that Li had worked on late into the night last night, while Jim had walked the floor with his fussy son. Debbie stopped for a minute and looked over Jim's shoulder at Jamie. "He looks like you through here," she said, gesturing to Jamie's jaws and chin. "But he's got Li's eyes."

"He's got her appetite too," Jim teased as Li stuck her tongue out at him from across the room. It was hard for

Debbie to believe, remembering the way Li had looked in that hut in Phu Bai, but Li had actually gained too much weight with her pregnancy and now was trying to take it off. Ben had gained some too, but he still had a few pounds to go before he would be back to his usual weight.

Jim looked over Ben's shoulder at Joy. "She looks just like you, Debbie," he said as he looked down into a perfect replica of Debbie's face. "Thank God," he added to Debbie in a whisper.

"I heard that, Anderson," Ben teased. "The next one's going to be as ugly as sin."

Mrs. Anderson called them all to the table, and they passed around Li's dinner. Jim uncorked a bottle of champagne and poured everyone a glass. "I want to propose a toast," he said. Debbie and Ben, the Andersons, and Gordon listened as Jim raised his glass. "As you know, Li and I were separated for ten years, and if it hadn't been for the courage of two very special people, we would still be separated today. To Debbie and Ben— thank you both for helping us be together again, and for making the birth of our son possible."

The families drank to Debbie and Ben, and Ben raised his glass once again. "We can say the same thing to you," he said. "If you two hadn't wanted to be together so badly, we wouldn't be together today either. To Jim and Li!"

The second toast was drunk, and they began their meal. "I like the way you combined your names for Jamie," Debbie told Li and Jim. "That way he'll carry on both heritages."

"Thank you," Li said. "But I could never understand where you got the name Joy Lee."

"Lee is for my grandmother," Debbie said.

"And the Joy?" Li persisted.

Debbie looked down into her plate. "That's Debbie's favorite perfume," Ben said, his face innocent. "She has this thing about the Perfume River."

"Ohh," said Li, giggling a little. Debbie's face burned, Jim snickered, Andersons looked puzzled, and Gordon choked on his spring roll.

It was late when Debbie and Ben finally left the get-together. They strapped their sleeping daughter into her car seat, and stood together for a moment staring up into the clear night sky, for once not shrouded with fog. "Will you mind staying in the house in Sausalito during the school year?" Debbie asked as Ben took her hand in his. "I really want Joy in those schools."

"Not a bit. Will you mind commuting from the vineyards during the summer?"

"No, I love it there," Debbie admitted as she looked back at Jim and Li's new home. "Ben?"

"Yes, love?"

"Do you think our love would have survived the way theirs did? Would we have made it through that many years apart?"

"We made it through much worse, Debbie," Ben said gently as he drew her close to him.

"How's that?" Debbie asked softly. "They went through so much. They were apart for so long."

"Yes, but they never doubted each other, or the strength of their feelings for each other. My lack of belief in love, my inability to recognize it, and my unwillingness to feel it for you was far worse. Yet we came through that. And, Debbie, if our love could survive that, it could survive anything."

"I love you, Ben," Debbie murmured as she drew her husband close to her. They shared a long, lingering kiss, a kiss of love and of the fulfillment of the promise of their love. Debbie's eyes shone with happy tears as she looked down at her sleeping baby, the child she and Ben had conceived during their season of enchantment, a season that would never be over for them now. "Oh, Ben, I love you so much!" she whispered as she hugged him tightly.

Ben held her to him. "I love you too, Lotus," he said. "Come on. Let's go home."

## All-new Candlelight Newsletter

**An exceptional, *free* offer awaits readers of Dell's incomparable Candlelight Ecstasy and Supreme Romances.**

Subscribe to our all-new CANDLELIGHT NEWSLETTER and you will receive—at absolutely no cost to you—exciting, exclusive information about today's finest romance novels and novelists. You'll be part of a select group to receive sneak previews of upcoming Candlelight Romances, well in advance of publication.

You'll also go behind the scenes to "meet" our Ecstasy and Supreme authors, learning firsthand where they get their ideas and how they made it to the top. News of author appearances and events will be detailed, as well. And contributions from the Candlelight editor will give you the inside scoop on how she makes her decisions about what to publish—and how *you* can try your hand at writing an Ecstasy or Supreme.

You'll find all this and more in Dell's CANDLELIGHT NEWSLETTER. And best of all, *it costs you nothing*. That's right! It's Dell's way of thanking our loyal Candlelight readers and of adding another dimension to your reading enjoyment.

Just fill out the coupon below, return it to us, and look forward to receiving the first of many CANDLELIGHT NEWS-LETTERS—overflowing with the kind of excitement that only enhances our romances!

---

 **DELL READERS SERVICE-Dept. B611A**
**P.O. BOX 1000, PINE BROOK, N.J. 07058**

Name_____

Address_____

City_____

State_____ Zip_____

# CANDLELIGHT
## Ecstasy Supreme

☐ 29 **DIAMONDS IN THE SKY**, Samantha Hughes.................11899-9-28

☐ 30 **EVENTIDE**, Margaret Dobson.................................12388-7-24

☐ 31 **CAUTION: MAN AT WORK**, Linda Randall Wisdom.........11146-3-37

☐ 32 **WHILE THE FIRE RAGES**, Amii Lorin........................19526-8-14

☐ 33 **FATEFUL EMBRACE**, Nell Kincaid.............................12555-3-13

☐ 34 **A DANGEROUS ATTRACTION**, Emily Elliott................11756-9-12

☐ 35 **MAN IN CONTROL**, Alice Morgan.............................15179-1-20

☐ 36 **PLAYING IT SAFE**, Alison Tyler.............................16944-5-30

## $2.50 each

# ON LEAVING CHARLESTON

## ALEXANDRA RIPLEY

Live this
magnificent
family saga
—from the
civilized,
ante-bellum South
through the wreckless,
razzle-dazzle Jazz Age

Southern heiress Garden Tradd sheds the traditions of her native Charleston to marry the rich, restless Yankee, Sky Harris. Deeply in love, the happy young couple crisscross the globe to hobnob with society in Paris, London, and New York. They live a fast-paced, fairy-tale existence, until the lovely Garden discovers that her innocence and wealth are no insulation against the magnitude of unexpected betrayal. In desperation the gentle woman seeks refuge in the city she had once abandoned, her own, her native land—Charleston.

$3.95      16610-1-17

Catch **SPRING FEVER** with Dell

**As advertised on TV**